RAVE REVIEW

THE MAGGODY MYSTERY SERIES

"FUNNY AND FAST MOVING . . .
I ALMOST SPLIT A GUSSET."

—Charlotte MacLeod

"To create living, breathing characters takes talent. To create a whole town inhabited by such characters borders on genius—and this is what Joan Hess has done with Maggody, Arkansas. I love the place and everybody (well, almost everybody) in it."

—Barbara Michaels

"WELL-CRAFTED . . . SHOWS CONSIDERABLE HUMOR AND UNDENIABLE STYLE."

—*Chicago Tribune*

"DOWN HOME FUN . . . Hess' lively wit and well-crafted plot stand up smartly to all the kidding. Check it out."

—*Kansas City Star*

"SUCCESSFULLY COMBINES MURDER AND MAYHEM with the most bizarre goings-on east of the Rockies."

—*Library Journal*

"A GENUINELY WITTY WRITER who applies her wit deftly. The funny lines come naturally to these beautifully drawn people."

—*Drood Review*

MISCHIEF IN MAGGODY

An Arly Hanks Mystery

JOAN HESS

AN ONYX BOOK

ONYX
Published by the Penguin Group
Penguin Books USA Inc., 375 Hudson Street,
New York, New York 10014, U.S.A.
Penguin Books Ltd, 27 Wrights Lane,
London W8 5TZ, England
Penguin Books Australia Ltd, Ringwood,
Victoria, Australia
Penguin Books Canada Ltd, 10 Alcorn Avenue,
Toronto, Ontario, Canada M4V 3B2
Penguin Books (N.Z.) Ltd, 182–190 Wairau Road,
Auckland 10, New Zealand

Penguin Books Ltd, Registered Offices:
Harmondsworth, Middlesex, England

Published by Onyx, an imprint of Dutton Signet,
a division of Penguin Books USA Inc. This is an authorized reprint
of a hardcover edition published by St. Martin's Press.

First Onyx Printing, June, 1991
10 9 8 7

Printed in the United States of America

PUBLISHER'S NOTE
This is a work of fiction. Names, characters, places, and incidents either are the product of the author's imagination or are used fictitiously, and any resemblance to actual persons, living or dead, events, or locales is entirely coincidental.

For my editor, Michael Denneny,
who returns my calls,
and my agent, Cherry Weiner,
who had more faith than I did.

I would like to acknowledge the invaluable assistance given to me by the following professionals, who generously shared their time and expertise (and did not raise their eyebrows at my questions): Washington County Sheriff Bud Dennis, Sebastian County Prosecutor Ron Fields, and Arkansas Game & Fish Commission Officer Randy Johnson.

1

Carol Alice Plummer clutched her teddy bear to her post-pubescent chest. "I don't know what I'm going to do," she moaned, rocking back and forth on the edge of her bed. "It's so damn awful, I may kill myself and save everyone the bother of watching me fade away into nothingness."

Heather Riley put her hands on her hips and glared down at her best friend in the whole world. "Get real, Carol Alice, and stop talking like that. You know perfectly well that you aren't going to kill yourself. I don't even like to hear you say it."

"I might as well. I mean, there's no point in life if Bo Swiggins and I can't get married."

"You can't? I thought you two were almost engaged. You've been going together for more than a year now, and he took you out to dinner on your birthday and gave you a present and everything." Heather bit down on her lip, wishing she hadn't used the word "everything." She wasn't supposed to know that Carol Alice and Bo had engaged in "everything" in the backseat of his uncle's '73 Trans Am, but she knew. Everybody in Maggody knew that sort of thing within fifteen minutes of its happening. Which was the only reason she'd made Billy Dick McNamara keep his hands to hisself the night he'd taken her to the movie in Starley City, and Billy Dick was the best-looking boy at school even with the harelip.

Carol Alice politely overlooked the lack of tact.

"Today after school I found out that we're totally, hopelessly incompatible. There's no way to get around it, even if I change my name—and my pa'd whip me silly if I even said I was thinking about it. But as for Bo and me, it's our vibrations. We can never be harmonious." Carol Alice squeezed her bear hard enough to make his little button eyes bulge. "We could get married, but we'd end up fighting and screaming every night, worse than my oldest sister and her husband what live in Hasty. I might as well tell Bo the truth and break up with him after the game this weekend. See, I already put his letter jacket in that sack to give back to him, along with that chain he gave me for my birthday and that sweet little stuffed dog he won me at the county fair less than a month ago." She began to sniffle. "Then I'm going to commit suicide and kill myself."

Heather sat down next to her. "I don't guess there's any way to get around vibrations," she said solemnly. "After all, it's cosmic fate—yours and Bo's. And Lord knows you don't want to end up like Terri Lee and that jerk she married. Their baby's right cute, but I don't know how she stands him hitting her and getting drunk and everything."

"Bo's such a gentleman; he'd never act like Terri Lee's husband! It's not poor Bo's fault we're so dadburned incompatible and doomed to discord. But there's no closing our eyes to the fact that he's going to be too materialistic for a cosmic mother like me, and we'll grow to hate each other."

"A cosmic mother? That sounds real mysterious. What does it mean?"

Carol Alice flopped back against the daisy-covered pillow sham and sighed. "Well, if I weren't going to kill myself—which I am—I'd make a good nurse or housemother for sweet little mentally retarded children. But if I act all arrogant and ignore my Life Path, I'll end up fat and slouchy . . . like Dahlia

O'Neill. Can you imagine me in one of those tent dresses, stuffing Twinkies down my throat and belching like a sow in heat? That's reason enough right there to kill myself!"

"Why don't you talk to Mr. Wainright about it? Maybe he could tell you what you ought to do." Giggling, Heather poked her best friend in the world. "Besides, it'd give you a reason to talk to him, and he's such an incredible hunk."

"There ain't no point in it, that's why. I've got more guidance than I can stand right now. It's fate. There's nothing anyone can do."

"Oh, Carol Alice, I feel so sorry for you that I could just cry."

Carol Alice handed a tissue to her best friend in the whole world. "How many aspirin tablets do you reckon it'll take to kill myself?"

"Probably a whole bottle," Heather said, blinking. "You ought to get those coated ones that won't give you an upset stomach. I think I've got a coupon in my purse."

Nothing, and I repeat, nothing ever happens in Maggody, Arkansas. The good citizens of Maggody, all 755 of them (counting household pets and a couple of dearly departeds out behind the Baptist church), would agree that the last event of any importance happened well over a year ago, and it wasn't worth talking about within a matter of weeks. Before that, the spiciest topic of conversation involved the night Hiram Buchanon's barn burned down and a cheerleader got caught dashing out in flagrante delicto, smoldering panties in hand. That was a good twelve years ago. Other than that, we're talking five-legged calves, brawls at the pool hall, and shenanigans under the straw of the swine barn at the county fair.

Maggody isn't a quaint, picturesque little village in the Ozark Mountains, and it wouldn't qualify for a Norman Rockwell painting. The grand tour takes about three minutes, presuming you get caught by the one stoplight and have to sit and fume while a stray dog ambles across the highway. If you come in from the west, you'll see a few signs welcoming Rotarians, Kiwanians, and Lions, but the only members of local chapters are out behind the Baptist church I mentioned a while back and not holding the sort of meetings most of us would prefer to attend. The bank branch is on the right and the Voice of the Almighty Lord Assembly Hall on the left, followed by a bunch of boarded-up stores with blind, dusty windows. The pool hall's in there somewhere; you can see a smattering of broken beer bottles in the dust out front, and sometimes on Sunday mornings a drunk out there with them.

After a few clumps of crabgrass and some telephone poles decorated with faded posters, you'll see Roy Stivers' Antiques & Collectibles: Buy, Trade or Sell on the left. I live upstairs in what would politely be called an efficiency flat, were anybody inclined to bother to call it anything. I call it cheap.

Catty-corner to my apartment is the Police Department, a small red-brick building with perky gingham cafe curtains across the window and two parking spaces out front with Reserved signs in front of them. Competition's not real keen for the spaces. It has two rooms, known as the front room and the back room. It also has two doors, known as the front door and the back door. We are accurate in Maggody, if not especially inspired.

Across from the PD is the Suds of Fun Laundromat and the Kwik-Stoppe-Shoppe (or Kwik-Screw, as we locals call it), owned by our illustrious mayor, Jim Bob Buchanon. Hizzoner and I have a history of ill will, but neither of us gives a hoot. Especially during the summer months, when the town's hotter than a sauna turned on full blast, which it had been three months ago when I escaped for a few months. Too hot to hoot, so to speak.

A little bit farther on the right you'll see Ruby Bee's Bar and Grill, a bizarre pink building with a tile roof and a couple of rusty metal signs tacked on the side that still promote Happy Daze Bread and Royal Crown Cola. I never cared for either, myself. In one corner of the parking lot is a sign for the Flamingo Motel, although you won't see said motel since it's out behind the Bar and Grill. Six units, usually rented by the hour. The locals call it the Stork Club, when they bother to call it anything at all. My mother, who happens to be the infamous Ruby Bee, lives in #1. She offered to let me have #2, but I felt obliged to decline her kind gesture. Listening to bedsprings squeal half the night would make me crazier than I already am. Living next door to my mother would qualify me for the butterfly farm, full scholarship.

But moving on, there're a couple of houses on the left, a car dealership on the right, Purtle's Esso Station, which pumped its last drop of gas the decade before I was born, and then not a blessed thing more until you wander north to the Missouri line. Well, cows and trees and potholes and mountains and litter, but nothing worth pulling over to take photographs of. Norman Rockwell wouldn't have slowed down.

So there you have it—a guided tour of Maggody. And, I might add, conducted by the chief of police of same. And the first female to hold the post, due to the fact I was the only candidate for the job and Hizzoner does like Ruby Bee's blueberry pie with ice cream. It's not the most impressive job, but it's safe, and safe was what I wanted. I'd managed to escape Maggody after high school, but I was back for the moment (the going-on-more-than-a-year-and-a-half sort of moment). In the overall scheme of the universe, Maggody is not some sort of cosmic magnet; I came back to lick my wounds after an unsettling divorce. I figured the wounds would scab over before too long, but in the meantime I needed a place that didn't put too many demands on me. Maggody doesn't put any demands on me, because, as I said earlier, nothing ever happens in Maggody.

"Thank the Lord you're back!" Ruby Bee shrieked, coming around the bar to give me a hug. "You will not believe your ears when I tell you all the things that have been going on in Maggody since you left on that so-called vacation of yours in the middle of the summer. I swear, it's been a three-ring circus around here!"

"Why was it a so-called vacation?" I asked mildly.

"Just sit yourself down and let me tell you what's been happening," Ruby Bee continued, ignoring my question with her typical aplomb. She is a master of the delicate art of hearing exactly what she wants to hear, and going stone-deaf when it suits her fancy. "But do you want something to eat first? You're looking a mite scrawny these days."

I sat down on a stool and propped my elbows on the bar. "I couldn't possibly eat until I hear all the big news. Did someone run the red light in my so-called absence?"

"Oh, Arly, you are such a cutup," Estelle Oppers said as she came out the kitchen door behind the bar.

Estelle and Ruby Bee have been friends since the days of the dinosaurs. Ruby Bee is short, stocky, and matronly—although I'd never use that word in her presence; I value my life, boring as it gets. She has blond hair, paid for by the lock, a magnolia-blossom complexion under several inches of powder, and enough eye makeup to do all the girls in the freshman class.

Estelle is tall, thin, and about as jumpy as a tree frog. She owns and operates Estelle's Hair Fantasies in her living room, and had been doing some experimentation lately, if the red curls dangling in her eyes, over her ears, and down her neck weren't an accident of nature. Mother Nature doesn't have that much of a sense of humor. The pair are rather a Mutt and Jeff combination, although they seem to see themselves as the Hardy boys. It has caused a problem or two in the past. If I had a nickel for every time they'd sworn to turn in their junior G-man badges and stop interfering in police investigations, I'd live in Jim Bob's hilltop manor and spend my idle moments harassing the chief of police.

Ruby Bee narrowed her eyes as she wiped her hands on her apron. "If you're going to sit there and act snippety, young lady, you can forget about hearing my news. Maybe it's just not important to someone who's lived in New York City and gone to those plays where the actors get naked and climb all over the audience."

I made the obligatory contrite noises, then said, "So what has been going on, anyway? And could I have a grilled cheese sandwich and a glass of milk while I listen?"

Ruby Bee crossed her arms and gazed at the ceiling. "I don't believe I heard anyone say 'please.' "

"Please may I have a sandwich and milk," I said through clenched teeth. The woman drives me crazy. She was about to drive me to a diet, if not a full-fledged fast.

"I'll fix the sandwich," Estelle said. "You tell Arly all the news."

Ruby Bee rewarded her with a smile that was meant to be a further editorial on certain people's lack of manners. "Thank you kindly, Estelle. Well," she began, settling back against the beer tap, "for one thing, Madam Celeste and her brother have rented that big old house out past Estelle's. You know which one I'm talking about, don't you? It used to belong to old Mrs. Wockermann before her husband died and the bank took it back and sent her to the county old folks' home, where she sat on the porch and rocked herself to death. I can't for the life of me remember what he died of, although Estelle said she heard it was some advanced stage of a nasty disease of the privates."

"Who'd you say rented the house?" I said before I heard a more detailed description of the late Mr. Wockermann's privates. Not on an empty stomach.

"Madam Celeste and her brother. She's a psychic, and she is absolutely fantastic. No one in town can stop talking about how she can see into the future or tell you all your innermost secrets. Gladys Buchanon says that she lost her reading glasses, and Madam Celeste told her exactly where to look for them." Ruby Bee's voice dropped to her version of a dramatic whisper. "And there they were in the top drawer of the dresser under a red scarf. Gladys liked to have swallowed her dentures."

"Oh," I said, trying to look impressed. "And what else has Madam Celeste done?"

"She told Millicent McIlhaney that she was going to take a long journey and it would be a true test of character. About three days later, Millicent and her daughter had to go to her aunt Pearl's funeral in Iowa. They took the station wagon, and the engine caught on fire on the other side of Kansas City. Millicent dashed right out in the middle of the interstate and flagged down a truck driver with a fire extinguisher, not even stopping to consider how she was likely to get herself run down. If that isn't a test of character, I'd like to know what is."

"Oh," I said. I was aware I was repeating myself, but I didn't trust myself not to say something that would cancel lunch.

"I went to visit her last week."

"When did you start believing in that sort of nonsense?"

"You have no call to speak to me in that superior

tone of voice, Ariel Hanks. What I do or don't do is none of your concern. If I choose to spend my money trying to find what all's going to happen in the future—"

"Money? You spent money on this fortune-telling stuff?" I couldn't help it; I really couldn't.

Estelle swept through the door, plate in hand. "Ruby Bee is a grown woman, and she can do whatever she pleases, Miss Big City Girl. Madam Celeste has been very perceptive about a lot of things, and of great assistance. Why, she comes over to the beauty shop and has appointments with my customers while I'm giving perms. She is very popular."

I knew who wasn't. "My apologies," I said meekly, sucking in my cheeks while I stared forlornly at the plate in Estelle's hand. "I'm sure this Madam Celeste is astoundingly perceptive and overflowing with more helpful hints than the sainted Heloise herself."

"She certainly is," Ruby Bee sniffed. "She told me that I was extremely sensitive, and that if I listened to my inner voice, I could hear things no one else could hear and learn all variety of cosmic secrets of the universe. She's going to teach me how to attune myself this week."

Estelle set down the plate in front of me. "And she told me I was going to meet someone who would make a profound impression on the rest of my life." She pushed a coil back and shot me a pinched look. "A man, if you want to know, and with one of those foreign accents. She hasn't been able to tell exactly when I'll meet him, but she's sure it'll be in the near future. I made Ruby Bee go into Farberville with me last Saturday to shop. Madam Celeste says I have to wear aquamarine if I want to meet this fellow."

"Where did this Madam Celeste come from?" I

asked through a mouthful of delightfully gooey cheese.

"She and her brother moved here from Las Vegas, Nevada," Estelle said. "She used to work on the stage in one of those big casinos, reading what was in people's wallets and guessing their birthdays. She was a very big star out there, but she had to leave because it was too exhausting. Her brother's name is Mason Dickerson."

There was a sudden silence. The two exchanged looks that would have been pregnant had menopause not come and gone years ago. I chewed for a minute, then said, "Was he onstage, too?"

"No," Ruby Bee said in a studiously nonchalant voice, "he's Madam Celeste's agent and manager. He takes care of her finances so that she can focus her psychic energy on more important things."

"Such as Gladys Buchanon's glasses? Come on, ladies, why are you acting as if you'd been zapped with psychokinetic kicks to the fanny? Is this Mason Dickerson some sort of crook?"

Ruby Bee raised her eyebrows. "I couldn't say. Do you want to hear what else has been happening? There's a new guidance counselor at the high school."

"Really?" I murmured. "Is there any cherry pie?"

"No, there isn't. He's so handsome that he has all the girls in a dither," Estelle added. "Lottie Estes, the home ec teacher, says every blessed girl in her small-appliances class has gone to his office to pick up college brochures—and she knows darn well not one of them is the least bit interested in college. Most of them aren't even going to graduate."

I tried to peer around Ruby Bee's bulk at the glass-covered pie stands. "Perhaps he'll inspire them. Is that a piece of lemon meringue?"

"Is that all you've got to say about it?" Ruby Bee demanded, moving squarely in front of the pie stand

and sticking out her lower lip at me. "He'll inspire them?"

I blinked at the woman who'd borne me. "What am I supposed to say? There are lots of teachers at the high school, and I'm sure some of them are worthy of girlish attentions and adolescent fantasies. Does that lemon meringue have someone else's name on it?"

Ruby Bee was glaring as she slapped down the piece of pie in front of me. "Your problem is that you don't try, Arly. You're perfectly content to sit in that little brick building all day and your dingy, depressing apartment all night. You don't make any effort to make yourself look attractive. You don't go anywhere or do anything. You're worse than that stagnant pond behind Raz Buchanon's barn."

I refused to take offense, mostly because the pie was divine and I'd spotted another piece that might, with luck and tact, have my name on it. "You're right on the button," I said amiably. "But at this point in my life that's exactly what I prefer to be—a stagnant pond. I need time to think."

"And how much time do you reckon that'll be? You've been back long enough to stop moping around like a motherless calf." Ruby Bee spent several seconds drying her hands on her apron, while I polished off the pie. "That's why I made you an appointment," she said in a voice so low I almost missed it.

"With Estelle? No disrespect intended, but I really prefer my hair as it is. If I ever decide to try a different style, I'll make my own appointment." I said this very calmly.

"With Madam Celeste."

"What?" I said this very excitedly.

"That's right," Estelle said. "Madam Celeste can give you all sorts of advice about what you ought to do with your life. Heaven knows you haven't come up with any good ideas lately. If you want, she can also put you in touch with those who've already gone across."

"Gone across what?" I asked, wishing almost immediately that I hadn't. It was too late, of course, so I decided to blow the whole wad. "The street? The Continental Divide? The fine line between sanity and schizophrenia?"

Estelle put her hands on her hips. "To the unknown. Dead people. Ancestors and folks like that. Madam Celeste conducted a seance for Edwina Spitz and talked to Edwina's grandfather person-to-person. Edwina's grandfather said it was right pretty where he was, and then he forgave Edwina for putting him in a nursing home and never once coming to visit him. Edwina felt mighty relieved afterward."

"Person-to-person and collect?" I said, giving up on a second piece of pie.

Now Ruby Bee put her hands on her hips. "Madam Celeste has expenses just like everybody else, young lady, but you don't have to give her one thin dime. Your visit is a gift from me and Estelle."

"Forget it," I said as I stood up. "I'll visit a psychic about the time I agree to have Sunday dinner with Raz Buchanon. Shall I presume I'm now current on all the significant events of the last six weeks?"

"Not exactly," Ruby Bee said.

She lifted the top of the pie stand so I could get a view of the last slab of lemon meringue, knowing darn well I'd lose a goodly portion of my resolve. Eating is one of my major activities; I'm fortunate to escape without looking like a tub of lard (or Dahlia O'Neill, the local cause of anorexia among the high school girls, who have a reasonable and legitimate terror of ending up like her; although the story that her granny once entered her in the county fair is pure spite—she won that blue ribbon over the mantle for her tomato relish).

"Okay," I said, sitting back down. "Tell me the rest of it."

"You know the Emporium across the county road from the Assembly Hall?" Ruby Bee said as she handed over the payola. "Well, four long-haired crazy hippies bought it from old Merle Hardcock, who was a mite too senile to know what he was doing. In fact, he took the money and bought a big, noisy motorcycle, if you can imagine such a thing. Thinks he's some kind of daredevil and talks all the time about trying to jump Boone Creek."

I winced at the image that came to mind. "I'll see if I can dissuade him. But tell me more about these hippies and the Emporium."

Ruby Bee looked gratified by my attention. "They fixed it up and reopened it last week. They sell hardware, chicken feed, notions, and the regular stuff, but they also sell all sorts of strange-smelling herbs and crystals and little bottles of oil that are supposed to cure headaches and impotency. Right in the store they play weird music that doesn't have any words or melody." She took a deep breath. "What's more, they live together at the end of Finger Road, in that dilapidated old house just past Earl Buchanon's house. One of them told Earl it was a commune. He thought that meant they were communists and was all set to go over with his shotgun, but I told him to wait until you got back from your so-called vacation. Earl's president of the local chapter of the Veterans of Foreign Wars and real touchy about communists."

(Allow me to digress from this fascinating narrative to explain the plethora of Buchanons. There are hundreds of them sprinkled across Stump County, worse than hogweed. Incest and inbreeding are their favorite hobbies, which has resulted in beetlish brows, yellow eyes, and thick lips. They aren't strong on intelligence; the most they can aspire to is animal cunning. An anthropologist from

Farber College once tried to sort out the genealogy, although nobody ever figured out why anybody'd want to do that. Rumor has it she tried to kill herself at the county line, and ranted in the ambulance about third cousins twice removed and fathers who were also uncles and half-brothers. Her family hushed it up with some story about a diesel truck, but everybody in Maggody knew better.)

"I'll see if I can dissuade Earl, too," I said, thinking I never should have left town. "But with the Emporium open again, we won't have to mortgage the homestead to buy nails at the Kwik-Screw, or drive all the way into Starley City for a monkey wrench."

Ruby Bee looked as if she might snatch back the pie. "What about them living in sin and doing all sorts of bizarre things? Why, they sit in the backyard morning and evening—stark naked, I might add—and hold hands and chant all sorts of things nobody can make any sense of. They burn funny-smelling little sticks while they do it, too!"

I curled my arm around the plate, just in case. "How do you know? Have you been out there by invitation? Shall I guess your mantra?"

"I am offended by your saying that," Ruby Bee snapped.

Estelle bobbled her head in support, looking like a hungry guinea hen over a ripe worm. "What they're doing is probably against the law, and you ought to go out there and do something about it before they corrupt all the children in Maggody. Everybody knows they smoke marijuana and engage in group sex like a bunch of farm animals."

"Farm animals don't engage in group sex," I pointed out as I popped the last bite of pie into my mouth. "As long as they do whatever it is they do in the privacy of the backyard, I don't see any reason to stir up problems. They aren't going to corrupt anybody with enough sense to mind his or her own business. For that matter, how does everybody know what they do in the backyard?"

"Kevin Buchanon says he can see their pagan rituals from the top of that old sweet gum tree in his backyard," Estelle said. "His pa caught him and about a dozen other boys in the tree, and whipped Kevin so hard he still can't bend over to tie his shoes. You'd of thought Kevin would have outgrown such foolishness by now."

I started for the door. "Well, I'm not sure who's likely to be corrupting whom. If nothing more exciting turns up, I'll go by the Emporium this afternoon and see if there's any debauchery going on under the notions display. But there are so many exciting things going on in Maggody, and I'm liable to get sidetracked by an armed robbery at the bank or homicide at the Laundromat."

"You are not as clever as you think, young lady," Ruby Bee called to my back.

"And you be at the beauty parlor Tuesday morning at ten o'clock sharp," Estelle added. "I'll take you over to Madam Celeste's and make the introductions."

With my ice skates, since hell would have frozen over about the time I did that.

2

I drove to the PD, reasonably pleased with lunch and already testing excuses for not showing up at Estelle's on Tuesday for my appointment with the psychic, of all fool things. The sheriff's deputy, who'd been minding the store during my "so-called vacation" (I'd forgotten to find out the subtle nuance there), flapped a hand in greeting as I came through the door.

"Welcome back, Arly. Have a good leave?"

"I thought I did until a few minutes ago. I visited some friends on the East Coast, camped on the beach, drank cheap wine, gazed at sunsets, and did everything I could think of to forget this ugly place. Anything happen while I was gone? Did we have a rash of bank robberies, holdups, homicides, Russian spies, and international dope busts?"

"Yeah, I had to beat off the ABC, the CIA, the DEA, the EPA, the KGB, and so forth right down to the V.F.W. Some guy from network television interviewed me, and I received three purple hearts." He gave me a chagrined look as he slapped his chest. "Lordy, I forgot to wear 'em today, just when I had hopes of impressing you."

"I'm sure your wife's impressed enough for the both of us," I said, moving around the desk to my chair, a comfy old cane-bottomed thing that had held my fanny for more than eighteen months without a whimper. Or a splinter. "Anything else?"

"You're going to love this, Arly." He began to

edge toward the door. "Jim Bob Buchanon came by couple of days ago and left a little present for you. It's on the table in the back room."

"A present for little old me? It's not my birthday, and it's nearly two months 'til Christmas. Did Hizzoner the Moron miss me so much that he felt compelled to leave a welcome-back present for his favorite public servant?" Despite my flippancy, I was a tad nervous. "Is there a sentimental, store-bought card along with it?"

The deputy had cleared the door sill and was eyeing his car. "No card, but he had a message for you that'll make your day—ha, ha. He said the town council voted not to hire a deputy for the time being. Budget's awful tight, he said two or three times, but he didn't look all that sad."

"And the present?"

"It's one of those beeper things like doctors and county agents wear so their secretaries can track them down on the golf course. You're on duty twenty-four hours a day, seven days a week."

"You're joking. Please tell me that you're joking."

" 'Fraid not, Arly. But there is some good news—you don't have to clean the PD anymore. Jim Bob said he'd hired a janitor to come in at night and sweep."

I propped my feet on my desk, tilted back in the chair, and closed my eyes. "Somehow, I have a funny feeling about this. I realize I should shoot off some firecrackers and break out in song, but there's something that smells overly ripe about Jim Bob's generosity." I squinted at the deputy. "Since you won't tell me you're joking, tell me why I'm not singing."

He had his car keys in his hand. "Well," he said, easing out of range should anything come flying through the doorway, "your newest employee is Kevin Buchanon. See ya, Arly."

The screen door banged closed, leaving me in

solitude to gripe, growl, and curse Jim Bob Buchanon and the other equally treacherous members of the town council. Twenty-four hours a day, seven days a week seemed extreme, if not unconstitutional, and I didn't fool myself for a minute that I was going to see a pay raise to go along with it. Oh, no, I got a beeper instead, so that I could never hide. Maggody was going to be a one-gun town. Whoopee.

And Kevin Buchanon, who by sheer coincidence was Jim Bob's second or third cousin, was going to invade the PD on a daily basis, which meant I'd feel obliged to be civil to him. He wasn't as objectionable as his more illustrious relative, but he was a pain in the butt. Jim Bob had achieved that level of animal cunning I mentioned, but Kevin couldn't outwit a possum. Kevin couldn't outwit a rock rolling down a hill. I'd have to show him which end of the broom to use. And I'd probably have to show him every day. Worst of all, I'd find myself listening to his personal problems, most of which would center around the love of his life, the apple of his eye, the dumpling in his pot pie, the pork in his pork 'n' beans, a.k.a. Dahlia O'Neill. I was starting to regret that second piece of pie, because I was definitely feeling queasy.

With a shudder, I planted my feet on the floor and picked up the folder of reports the deputy had left on the desk. It wasn't going to be easy to lose myself in them, but I sure was going to give it my best shot. Welcome back, sucker.

Robin Buchanon moved briskly through the thicket, unmindful of the thorns that tried to tear at her arms or poke through the soles of her heavily callused feet. None of that was any bother to her. She carried a hoe and a knife in one hand, a gunnysack in the other. Her eyes were on the ground, darting back and forth as she searched for the telltale crimson berries and five-leaf pattern of the ginseng plant, but she kept one ear cocked for sounds that were not a part of the forest. It took only one ear, since she was more than used to living in the woods and knew every bird and animal sound.

In fact, she liked coons and skunks and snakes and muskrats better than she did most folks, although she didn't mind when once in a blue moon some city slicker from Maggody came to the cabin for a mason jar of hooch and a little romp. Everybody knew she gave as well as she took. She was, however, beginning to be reluctant these days, since she was getting damn tired of all those younguns underfoot. They was worser than field mice. The baby whined if she din't suckle all the time, and the older ones et everything in the root cellar iffen she didn't keep a switch handy. It'd be right nice to pack 'em off to their pappies and have a little peace and quiet—even if their pappies wouldn't jump for joy. As she walked, she tried to think of somebody she could ask if she could make 'em do it anyways. Maybe that woman policeman in Maggody, she decided with a nod. Yeah, she looked right educated and there was most likely some kind of law.

The northern side of Cotter's Ridge was a mite cool this late in October, but it were time to 'seng hunt and she didn't need a damn fool calendar to tell her so. Her worn flannel shirt and tattered jeans held up by a piece of rope didn't help much, but she weren't no city woman what squealed ever' time the wind like to freeze her tits. Hell no.

She curled her lip, exposing a sparse collection of mossy teeth, as she scrabbled up a gully toward the patch. Her patch. It'd been her pappy's afore, and his pappy's afore that. There'd been a worrisome minute when it looked like grandpappy was gonna die right there in his bed without telling anyone where his patch was—grandpappy was about the most ornery sumbitch anybody ever met. But pappy got a bit rough with the old coot and choked it out of him afore he died. It were a good thing, too, because old grandpappy had died right afterward, and 'seng was scarcer than preachers in paradise.

A good 'seng patch was worth a fortune—at least a hunnert dollars every fall, when she sold the dried roots to that oily man what came to Maggody in a big black car. And she'd tended to her secret patch better than she'd tended to her brood of younguns, chickens, pigs, and goat. She always cut the roots real careful, so that there'd be some the next year, and scattered berries every spring. Why, she thought in her ponderously slow way, this patch was at least a hunnert years old by now. And 'seng huntin' was a nice break from making hooch or whuppin' younguns or even lettin' the hound dog get all excited over her like she was a bitch in heat, which was about her favoritest thing.

She was still grinning as she topped the gully. The grin faded as she stared at the half acre that should have been thick with yeller-gold ginseng leaves. "What the goddamn hell . . . ?" she said aloud.

A rage began to bubble deep in her gut. No yeller-gold leaves, no red berries. No ginseng plants—in her goddamn patch that she loved better than most anything in the goddamn world! A growl curled up along her gullet, growing and sparking and burning until it erupted in a cry of primeval fury. A flock of starlings flapped away with squawks of alarm. A squirrel fled across the branches. A polecat lifted his head to consider the wisdom of investigating, then slunk off in the opposite direction. Only a trio of buzzards in a dead tree on the top of the ridge took pleasure in the sound, which hinted of easy pickin's in the future.

Robin stumbled forward, her fingers tightening on her tools of the trade. Some low-down, thievin' sumbitch had been here, that much she could tell. She began to gnaw on her lower lip as she tried real hard to figure out just what the hell was a-goin' on, anyway. Weren't nobody in sight, and she was pretty sure ever'thing had been okay last spring. But why in tarnation would some damn fool dig up her 'seng patch out here on the far side of the ridge? Didn't make a hog's hair of sense.

There was a loggin' road not too far yonder, she remembered. Some sumbitch must have decided to do his farmin' out in the middle of nowhere. But why in her beloved 'seng patch? Her tools fell to the ground as she wrapped her arms around herself and began to wail. It weren't fair. That sumbitch should be tied up agin an oak tree and be learned what a godawful thing he'd done in destroying her patch. Grandpappy's patch.

Below her simian brow, her eyes turned the shade of yeller gold that she should have found. She sure as hell could show him what a sinful thing he'd done, she told herself as she moved toward the tidy rows of plants. She'd just plumb tear up all his plants and throw 'em in the gully to rot. Rip up those plants the way she wished she could rip off his tongue and dick and feed 'em to the hogs. Mebbe have one of the younguns keep watch and run back to the cabin iffen anyone came back. Then she'd bring some barbed wire and—

A click about shoulder height caught her attention. As she turned, wondering what the fuck was a-goin' on now, her face exploded.

"Of course I understand why you're upset," David Allen Wainright said for not the first time in the last half hour. He took a quick peep at his watch, then sighed and leaned back in the chair. "It's admirable that you're showing this deep and obviously genuine concern for your friend. It's important that we share our feelings, especially during our high school years, when it's common for us to be unsure of ourselves."

Heather snuffled into the tightly wadded tissue in her hand. "I feel really awful, Mr. Wainright. I mean, like I shouldn't be telling you any of this because I swore on Carol Alice's Bible that she got when she was baptized last spring at the Voice of the Almighty Lord Assembly Hall that I wouldn't tell a soul. She's my best friend in the whole world."

"Which is why you've shown such maturity by coming to talk to me," David Allen said soothingly. It was almost two-thirty; surely she'd have to leave in a minute in order to catch her bus. Surely. "Sometimes we're so confused by our emotions that we're at a loss to know what to do or where to turn. That's why I'm here." On the other hand, he had no idea why she was here. No one actually believed someone would commit suicide on the basis of some idiotic psychic's dour prediction.

"Then," Heather said through a series of distastefully damp hiccups, "you'll talk some sense into Carol Alice?"

He formed a temple with his fingers and gave her his most professional smile (*Adolescence and Stress*, Chapter Seven). "Well, we may worsen the situation if I confront your friend with the knowledge that I'm aware of her problem. She may be driven to take some sort of drastic action out of fear or embarrassment. We wouldn't want that, would we?" No, we want the buses to be announced on the PA system. We want this drippy little thing to shriek out her gratitude and leave. He realized she was heading for another deluge, and hastily said, "But I do see how serious the problem is, Heather"—was that her name?—"and I won't allow anything to happen to Carol Ann."

"Carol Alice, Mr. Wainright. Thank you so much for letting me talk to you about this. It was so kind of you." Heather picked up her books and purse, and with a hesitant smile stood up. "I feel much better knowing that you'll do something about that awful woman and poor, brokenhearted Carol Alice." She emphasized the last word, just in case he was still confused. Which wasn't hard to understand, considering how many students there were at Maggody High School and him being new and all.

"You may rest assured that we'll deal with this problem. Now, we don't want you to miss your bus, do we? You run along, and I'll spend some time this evening deciding what needs to be done." Over a six-pack and pizza, of course. He was relieved when she left with a coy glance over her shoulder.

Heather, on the other hand, was in love. Why, if she'd seen Billy Dick in the hallway, she wouldn't have slowed down long enough to give him the time of day.

I idled away the weekend in my apartment, dealing with several inches of dust, a smattering of mouse droppings (but no visible perpetrators), and fuzzy things in the refrigerator. For exercise, I periodically dashed across the road to the Suds of Fun to process seventeen loads of dirty laundry through all the appropriate cycles. All in all, it was pleasantly uneventful.

Bright and early on Monday morning I reported (to myself) for duty at the PD. It was dim and smelled of industrial strength disinfectant. The gingham curtains were frayed at the hems. My middle desk drawer was filled with wadded up gum wrappers. The telephone book was missing. The creamer jar was empty. Were I inclined to do so, I could have written my name in the dust on each and every flat surface. Home sweet home.

I finished the reports: one trespassing, two lost dogs, a meager collection of traffic citations, and eight obscene telephone calls—I suspect Elsie McMay relished them more than her caller, since she always insisted on repeating them to me down to the last disgusting syllable and then having me read them back to her. Some of them went on for a couple of pages; I asked her once why she didn't hang up, and she haughtily informed me that that would be rude and she was better reared than that, missy.

I made a pot of coffee, considered opening Jim Bob's present, decided not to, and went out to play with my radar gun on the curve just east of town. After an hour I'd met my quota on Japanese imports (speedy little things), so I drove back through town and parked in front of the Emporium, mostly out of curiosity rather than an urge to arrest the new owners on charges of corrupting the youth of Maggody.

It looked pretty good. The glass glittered, and the windows were piled with merchandise. Someone had painted the name in fat red curlicues outlined with yellow, and done a competent job. Customers were coming and going. I nodded to several folks as I went inside to check out the wild, dope-crazed sex maniacs.

The first wild, dope-crazed sex maniac I spotted was a willowy woman with curly auburn hair, a wide mouth, cinnamon-sugar freckles, and warm, friendly eyes. A cloud of musk drifted behind her. "Hi," she said, taking in my uniform with a wince. "Are you here on official business?"

I introduced myself and told her that I was there out of curiosity. Idle curiosity, I stressed as I looked around. As Ruby Bee and Estelle had told me, there were all the usual things indigenous to hardware and dry goods stores. But alongside them were whole passels of things that were un-Maggodyish, to say the least. Crystals dangling from threads thumbtacked to the ceiling. Cellophane bags of dried herbs. Boxes of incense. Posters of eyes and clouds and butterflies. The music would have been a real challenge to sing along with. Maggody had not yet moved into the New Age. We were still struggling to escape from the Stone Age.

"I'm Rainbow," the woman said. "My friends will be pleased to know you stopped by for a visit. Could I offer you a cup of mint tea and a carob-chip cookie? If you'd prefer something cold, I think there's still some of our homemade apple cider. It's made from organic apples."

"Sounds great," I said, lying through my teeth for the sake of neighborliness. I followed her through a curtain to a cozy little room that seemed to function as office, storage room, and parlor. I was settled on a chintz sofa and given a glass of cider and a cookie.

I was about to chomp down on a carob chip when a second woman came through the doorway. Unlike her co-owner, she was not willowy. She was a short, rosy little thing, and very pregnant. She was Poppy, I was told, and delighted to meet me.

"Do you think we ought to take this check?" she asked Rainbow.

They looked it over and decided to take it. Poppy waddled away, leaving me no choice but to chomp. I put it off by asking, "Are you and Poppy the official owners?"

"Oh, no. Zachery and Nate went into Starley City in the truck to pick up a shipment of bottled spring water. We get it all the way from Colorado, and hope to sell a lot of it. They should be back before too long, and eager to meet you. We haven't met too many people, although we've had a reasonable number of customers since we opened. Once we get settled, we might throw a party for the entire town so we can meet everybody."

I could imagine Ruby Bee with a carob-chip cookie and a cup of mint tea. Not a pretty picture. "A barbecue?" I asked politely.

She gave me a shocked look. "We're strict vegetarians. Zachery won't even eat dairy products. Poppy used to avoid them, but now she'll eat yogurt, if we remind her."

"Is Zachery the prospective father?"

"Possibly, although Poppy changes her mind daily. She's sure it's either Zachery or Nate. Both of them are going to participate in labor and delivery, of course, and we'll all share responsibility for child care and make joint decisions about the future." She gave me a warm, twinkly smile. "We're just like a big, extended family. We've been together for over a year now, ever since we met at a yoga retreat during the summer solstice. Our relationship is very spiritual."

"That's great," I murmured. I couldn't bring myself to ask about the meditation sessions in the backyard, so I stuffed the cookie in my mouth, polished off the cider, and told her I was pleased that the Emporium was back in business. She twinkled at me as we went back into the main part of the store, where I spotted Raz Buchanon studying crystals and several of the high school girls giggling over posters. Maggody might be taken aback at being served soybean hot dogs and bottled water, but I figured that after a time, no one would worry about Rainbow, Poppy, and their male companions. Except for Kevin Buchanon—unless Earl chopped down the sweet gum tree.

I whiled away the rest of the afternoon with the directions to the beeper, which I kept thinking was like one of those in-house ankle bracelets used when the prisons were sated. The wearer couldn't go more than fifty feet from his home. I could go anywhere I wanted—and the sheriff's dispatcher could find me so I could call in for a report. Isn't technology wonderful?

I was wondering how much abuse my beeper could take (and how much I could give it without being accused of beeper abuse) when the telephone rang. It was Ruby Bee, and she was blithering worse than a mockingbird.

"Slow down," I said patiently. "Or take a deep breath, two aspirins, and call me in the morning." When I'd lived in Manhattan with my hotshot Madison Avenue husband, I'd made witty repartee about the international trade deficit, Supreme Court decisions, and potent political figures. When I drove past the Maggody city limit sign, my brain atrophied. Bathroom jokes are big around here, along with traveling salesmen, ethnic slurs, and sexual perversions.

"You need to get right down for supper," Ruby Bee gasped. "You really do, Arly. I made a cherry cobbler this afternoon, and there's still a big corner of it left. When can you get here?"

"It's not even five o'clock. I'm not hungry, and I want to file all the reports the deputy left for me. Besides, I've been pigging out on carob chips and other organic stuff; I may swear off carbohydrates and grease and seek transcendental peace through fasting and intense meditation."

"Rather than your own mother's pork chops and fried okra? What has gotten into you, young lady? Have you been over to those hippies' house?" Ruby Bee is not into fasting and meditation.

"Not I. But it's too early to eat. What's the big deal, anyway?"

"You just get your smart-aleck self down here right now."

The receiver clicked in my ear, with a finality that unsettled me. In that I couldn't think of a particularly good reason to stir up trouble with Ruby Bee, I checked my lipstick, stuck the folder in a drawer, hung a Closed sign on the PD door, and walked down the highway to Ruby Bee's Bar and Grill.

The parking lot was thick with pickup trucks and good ole boys slapping each other on the back and kicking each other in the fanny. I joined the jocular group as we shoved our way through the door for that timeless tradition known as Happy Hour (in another life it was known, if I recall correctly, as the cocktail hour—martinis, hors d'oeuvres, crystal bowls of peanuts, politically correct conversation). Ruby Bee serves dollar draws and free popcorn, which suits everybody just fine.

I struggled through a row of denim backs along the bar, perched on a stool, and waved to Ruby Bee. When she came over, I requested a light beer and a bag of potato chips.

She sucked on her lip for a minute. "I thought you came here for supper, Arly. You don't want to ruin your appetite with junk food, do you? You just go sit in the last booth, and I'll bring you a nice plate of pork chops, okra, beans, and mashed potatoes. The cobbler will go right nice with vanilla ice cream, don't you think?"

"I'll eat after a while. I'm feeling a bit nostalgic for the cocktail hour. I realize I can't have chilled shrimp and paté, but I have hopes potato chips will ease my longings."

"You just go sit where I told you."

"I don't want to just go sit where you told me. I want a light beer and a bag of potato chips. If I have to go buy 'em at the Kwik-Screw and sit on the gravel beside the highway while I eat 'em, I will."

Her eyes narrowed, and she did some more chewing on her lip. Finally, looking about as guileless as a fox in the henhouse door, she said, "If I give you a light beer and a bag of potato chips, then will you go sit where I told you?"

I thought of all sorts of things to say, not to mention questions that deserved being asked. But obedient child that I am, I said I'd take my light beer and bag of potato chips and go sit in the last booth. I'd even consider the pork chops et al in a half hour or so. But when I got halfway across the room, I noticed there was someone already in the last booth. Not thinking much about it, I aimed myself on a tangent and started for another booth.

Estelle grabbed my arm. "Come on, Arly, there's someone I want you to meet." She propelled me to the last booth and shoved me down on the plastic bench across from a man with blond hair and, not unreasonably, a startled expression. "David Allen, I don't believe you've met Arly. She's Ruby Bee's daughter, divorced, and the chief of police. Arly, David Allen just moved to Maggody last month; he's widowed and the guidance counselor up at the high school. David Allen, Arly. Arly, David Allen. If I can't bring you two anything else, I'll just leave you to get acquainted."

She sailed away, leaving both of us to blink across the table at each other. I put down my beer and extended my hand. "Hi, I'm Arly Hanks, and I think I've just been set up by my mother the professional manipulator. My apologies."

"Oh, no apology needed," he murmured, flashing a pair of dimples as he shook my hand. Blue eyes, broad shoulders, about forty. And not bad at all. "And please don't give Ruby Bee a hard time about her manipulations; I'm delighted to meet you." He realized he was still squeezing my hand, and released it with an embarrassed laugh.

"So you're the new guidance counselor," I said cleverly. "How do you like the traumatized teens of Maggody High?"

"They're remarkably like the traumatized teens of anywhere. The halls reek of angst—along with armpits, hair spray, and dollar-a-gallon eau de cologne. I took the job here so I could be within driving distance of my son, who lives with his grandparents in Farberville. I try to get over every weekend to spend some time with him."

"How old is he?"

"He'll be seven in November. He's already reading and was the star slugger of his T-ball team this summer," David Allen said with a flicker of parental pride. "I wish I could have him with me, but he has a kidney problem and needs dialysis treatments several times a week. His grandparents live a block from the hospital. Anyway, my bachelor existence would make both of us crazy. I'm big on pepperoni pizza and beer. He needs a woman's hand these days—someone to make him eat spinach and take a bath every night."

"It's fortunate that you found a job not too far away. Were you able to find someplace not too dreadful to live?" We police officers are trained in the delicate art of interrogation.

"I rented a house in that subdivision past the high school. I'm in one of the twenty-five houses jammed together in the middle of a forty-acre cow pasture. In fact," he said, wiggling his eyebrows at me, "I live on an honest-to-God cul de sac. Impressed?"

"Immensely. I live in a dingy apartment above the antique store."

We continued on in that vein for most of an hour, comparing notes on the citizens of Maggody and the mysterious local rituals. It turned out David Allen was forty (as I guessed), a Vietnam veteran, a graduate of Farber College, and a football fan. His wife had died a couple of years back from cancer; he didn't say much about it, and I didn't ask. His one vice, he admitted, was spending too much money on model rockets, which he launched in the pasture behind his house and usually lost. My one vice, I admitted, was lying in my bed in the dark and thinking up ways to needle my mother. He invited me to watch a launch; I did not invite him to lie in my bed. We had made our way through pork chops and cherry cobbler and were into coffee when he gave me a frown.

"There is something I ought to discuss with you

in your professional capacity," he said in a low voice.

Dearly hoping he wasn't going to mention outstanding felony warrants, I put down my cup. "I don't fix traffic tickets, David Allen, but I can put in a good word with the municipal judge when he comes next Tuesday night."

"It's about this psychic woman. One of the girls was in my office all teary about a friend who was upset enough by the psychic to talk about suicide. I don't understand why anyone would take that sort of thing seriously, but I do take suicide threats seriously, especially with adolescent girls. Do you know anything concerning this Madam Celeste?"

"I know she's the talk of the town and the darling of the beauty-parlor crowd. I just got back from a long vacation, and I'm still in culture shock. I haven't had time to do any investigating. What did she tell this girl?"

He related a crazy story about the girl and her boyfriend being incompatible due to their numerological analysis. "I think it's total nonsense," he concluded with a sigh. "I wish the girl did."

I didn't much like the idea of the pyschic upsetting the girl, even if it was done in such an absurd way. And David Allen had a point about the suicide threats. "I suppose I ought to check her out," I said without enthusiasm. "I'll also see what the laws are concerning this sort of thing. It may be illegal, although I doubt it. Maggody's local statutes were written in the middle of the last century. Nobody's had any reason to read them since, much less update them. But I'll drop by Madam Celeste's house tomorrow and see what I think."

He reached across the table to squeeze my hand. "I appreciate your taking this as seriously as I do, Arly. If you have some spare time tomorrow evening, could you come by the house and tell me what you've decided about this psychic?"

Me with spare time? It wouldn't have been polite to laugh, so I settled for a nod and a smile. On the way out, I stopped by the bar and gave Ruby Bee a stern look meant to discourage any manipulations in the future. She managed not to see me. Estelle was busy studying the popcorn bowls. I could have climbed onto the bar, ripped off my shirt, and beat my breast while yodeling. Neither one of them would have looked up.

When I got back to the PD, I found Kevin Buchanon in the front room. He gulped, flapped his hands, turned scarlet when the broom, in compliance with the law of gravity, clattered to the floor, ran his hand through his crew cut, gulped some more, and shuffled his feet like an anemic tap dancer. "Uh, Jim Bob told me I was to come on in if you wasn't here," he mumbled. "I mean, I'm glad you're back, Arly. I just didn't want you to think I wasn't supposed to come in unless you was back."

I gazed at the gawky specimen of Buchanon inbreeding. "I'm not back, Kevin—it just looks like it. I am gone." I took my beeper and went home. Be it ever so humble, it ran rings around Kevin Buchanon.

3

The next morning, after a bowl of stale cornflakes and three cups of instant coffee (with instant cream), I drove over to Estelle's house, which was a quarter of a mile north of the Emporium on a county road that the county had disinherited along about WWI. The psychic and her brother lived a little ways farther up the road, just before a dilapidated chicken house and a rusted Nash set on concrete blocks that was the closest thing to a historical marker we had in Maggody. After that there were stunted pine trees and scrub, a low-water bridge across Boone Creek that provided excitement in the spring months, and ten teeth-rattling miles to Hasty. Hasty makes Maggody look like the Loop in Chicago.

Estelle's house was an old but tidy clapboard thing, and she'd done some landscaping with plastic flowers, concrete statues of gnomes and toads, and a genuine imitation marble birdbath. Wishing I had some plastic dandelions to poke into the flower bed, I went up onto the porch and lifted my hand to knock.

The door flew open and Estelle came outside, her purse clutched under her arm. "I swear, Arly, sometimes you're slower than sorghum at Christmas. I told Madam Celeste we'd be there at ten o'clock sharp, and she has a very busy schedule. Not to mention other folks, who have a business to run and Elsie McMay at ten-fifteen for a haircut, shampoo, and set. As you well know, Elsie practically has a stroke if she's kept waiting."

"I'm terribly sorry. Shall we walk or drive?" I asked humbly.

"Goodness' sakes, Arly, it's not more than a hundred feet up the road." Estelle took off at full mast, the hem of her lavender uniform flapping in the breeze. The red, dangling curls had been vanquished to hair heaven in favor of a beehive of admirable height—and not one hair trembled despite her pace. Which was leaving other folks breathless, I might add.

I caught up with her on the porch of Madam Celeste's house. In contrast to Estelle's house, the place was a sorry mess. Paint peeled off the sides in curling gray tongues or bubbled like alligator skin. The yard was a collage of crabgrass, wild onions, bleached patches of dust, and beer bottles. The only thing that saved it from essence of squalor was a satellite dish sitting in the side yard, although the weeds were getting a mite high around the base. Maybe they used it to beam down *The Grapes of Wrath* and *Tobacco Road.*

Before I could mention the possibility (or hightail it back down the road to my car), Estelle rang the doorbell. "You are going to love Madam Celeste," she confided as she straightened the belt of her uniform. "She is astounding, just plumb astounding—as long as you don't turn up your nose and act all snooty. The only thing you have to do is to believe in her powers, Arly."

"Is that all?" I said in a distracted voice. I was busy envisioning a heavy-set, elderly, swarthy Gypsy, complete with scarves, beads, gold hoop earrings, and a long, embroidered dress that hung down not quite far enough to hide swollen ankles. A mustache and bright-red lipstick. A hoarse Hungarian accent, if one was attuned to such things. A mole on her chin. Lugging a crystal ball, a Ouija board, and a floor lamp with a fringed shade.

A short woman with bleached-blond hair opened the door. "You are late," she snapped, one hand on her hip. "I have other appointments today, and there may not be enough time to do a complete reading. I really don't like to start and then have to quit just when I've begun to feel the cosmic force. It gives me a headache. But come in, come in."

"I'm so sorry," Estelle said, dragging me through the doorway. "This is Ruby Bee's daughter, Arly Hanks."

Two icy green eyes turned on me. "And this reading is for you—is that correct? Do you want cards, sand, an astrological reading, or a numerological analysis?"

Estelle leaned over and cupped her hand around my ear. "Take the sand, Arly; it's the most revealing," she advised in a hiss. "You might as well get your mother's money's worth."

"The sand, by all means," I said to Madam Celeste.

Estelle patted me on the back, then announced she simply had to dash off because of Elsie McMay. She preceded to abandon me to the clutches of the psychic. Madam Celeste appeared to be under forty, although there were some lines around her eyes—perhaps from all that peering into the future. She was shorter than Ruby Bee, but her waist was trim and her hips were contained in tight designer jeans. She wore a faded T-shirt and rubber thongs. No mustache, no mole, no scarves, no beads, no hoop earrings. The accent was odd; I couldn't place it, but it didn't sound like Budapest. She would have been attractive if her features had been less linear and harsh; as it was, she reminded me of a sharp-chinned cat, if that makes any sense to you.

"Are you ready to begin?" she said impatiently. "I don't have time to stand in the foyer all day while you goggle at me as if I, Madam Celeste, were a sideshow freak. Come along to the solarium." She wheeled around and stalked through a doorway, muttering under her breath.

I stalked after her, muttering under my breath. Odds are we weren't muttering the same things.

Forty minutes later, I came out of the solarium (which bore an uncanny resemblance to a breakfast room, owing in part to the tea-kettle wallpaper and the dinette set), armed with the knowledge that in the past I'd been treated unfairly but had shown courage. In the future I would see great changes in my life, make a meaningful career move, encounter two strangers who would have a profound influence on my life, travel, survive a test of character, and find great happiness down the line. Every time I'd asked for specifics, Madam Celeste had rubbed her temples and told me that it just wasn't coming through because of negative vibrations in the atmosphere. For those agog with curiosity, Mesopotamian sand is blue and looks like the stuff in the bottoms of aquariums. It was in a Tupperware salad bowl. She'd had me make a handprint in it, then done a lot of staring at it.

Madam Celeste opened the front door for me. "I hope you were satisfied with the reading, but I do not offer any guarantees. Sometimes I can see things as clearly as I see your face; other times I must battle negative vibrations, although I cannot say from where they emanated."

I wasn't going to tell her; after all, she was the psychic. "I have days like that myself," I said in my most sympathetic voice. "Ruby Bee said you came here from Las Vegas. That was quite a change, wasn't it?"

"Yes, of course it was." She gave me a wary look, no doubt thinking her newest client didn't have all her carob chips in the cookie dough, so to speak.

"But it must seem awfully tame here. Why did you trade Las Vegas for Maggody?"

"I had great trouble with the police there, if you must know. A woman came to me, very distraught, crying and twisting her hands, begging for me to help her. Her child, a dear little boy of seven, had disappeared over a month before. The police searched for him, but finally gave up and told her the case was as good as closed. To say such a thing to a mother—can you imagine such heartlessness!"

"Why did she come to you?"

Madam Celeste drew herself up (to about five-foot two). "Because I am a world-renowned psychic. I have studied with the greatest clairvoyants of the European continent. At that time I was working at one of the largest casinos, and creating much excitement and comment. This poor woman heard about me from one of her friends, and literally threw herself at my feet. After some discussion, I agreed to help the police find the child. The police, stupid scum that they are, laughed at me and sent me away—but in the end I was able to give the mother some guidance as to the location of the poor little boy's body several miles out in the desert. He'd wandered away and fallen into a ravine, where he could not be seen from above. The police were embarrassed, of course, and made wild accusations about me to cover up their stupidity."

"So you decided to come to Maggody, Arkansas?" I persisted. "Had you been here before? Do you have friends here?"

"I was drawn here by some unknown force, as if my destiny were to be unfolded and made known to me here in this peaceful little village," she said briskly, making me suspect she'd recited it many a time. She glanced at her watch. "Now I am very busy. You must leave so that I may prepare for my next appointment. It will be a most difficult session for me, and I must have time to arrive at the proper frame of receptiveness. I use your mother's credit card number, yes?"

I had a whole truckload of questions left, but I suggested she bill Ruby Bee time and a half for the additional few minutes, then went down the porch steps and along the road to my car. I hid out at the PD all afternoon and, with sly anticipation, went home for a can of chicken noodle soup just before Kevin's arrival. Conscientious enforcer of law and order that I was, I clipped my beeper on my belt as I scooted out the door.

Later that evening, I went over to David Allen's house and told him about the reading, which had been as perceptive and personal as a syndicated horoscope column in a newspaper. We agreed that the whole thing was apt to blow over, and on that optimistic note shared a six-pack and played Trivial Pursuit until midnight. It beat sitting at the front window of my apartment, counting the Mercedeses that went through town in one evening. If you're wondering, the world record to date was three.

"How'd she act?" Ruby Bee demanded as she wiped the surface of the bar. "Did she stop by afterward to say what happened?"

Estelle popped a beer nut in her mouth and chewed it pensively. Once she'd washed it down with soda pop, she said, "Well, if you want my opinion, I'd say Arly was a tad nervous when I took her over, but she settled down nicely after I'd introduced her to Madam Celeste. Nearly an hour later, I saw her come back and get in her car, but just as I put down my styling comb to run outside and ask her what happened, Elsie started telling me about her last obscene telephone call. I told Elsie she had a filthy mouth, and that sort of led to a prickly discussion. By the time I looked out the window again, Arly'd left."

"What all did Elsie say the caller said this time?" Ruby Bee put down the dishrag and propped her arms on the bar. "Four-letter words or sexual remarks or what?"

Estelle repeated the conversation as best she could remember. She and Ruby Bee decided that Elsie sure enough had a filthy mind—if not a filthy mouth. Anyone who relished those calls . . . Course the caller was mentally deranged and sure hadn't laid eyes on Elsie. . . . They were really getting into it good when the door opened and the newest barmaid trudged across the room. The light fixture above the dance floor quivered but held tight. The customers in the booth hunkered over and stuck their noses in their beers.

"Am I late?" Dahlia O'Neill said.

"Yes," Ruby Bee said, "but don't fret about it. As you can see for yourself, business is right slow. Put on an apron and go ask those folks in the corner if they want another pitcher."

Dahlia's mouth opened and closed slowly, like an immobile fish feeding on plankton. "I don't"—close, open, close, open—"recollect where the aprons is kept."

Ruby Bee studied the girl's monumental girth. "That's all right," she said kindly. "You don't need to wear an apron now. This evening when I get home, I'll run up a special one on my Singer Deluxe. If I have time, I'll embroider your name on the top of the pocket."

"That'd be real nice," Dahlia said. "Now what is it you want me to ask them folks over in the booth?"

Even though she figured it was too late, Ruby Bee couldn't stop herself from having Second Thoughts, not to mention a few Severe Misgivings.

* * *

Mason Dickerson got back to town about midnight. There wasn't a parade to welcome him; in fact, there were only two lights visible along the whole stretch of highway—and both of them were streetlights. Mason wasn't surprised. He took the opportunity to drive his BMW faster than the signs suggested, and whipped around the corner by the Emporium in a spew of gravel, dust, and chicken feathers.

He was in a fine mood. A little bleary from the wine, but his stomach was full and his sexual drive met for a while. For Mason, who was thirty-seven and healthy, bronzed to perfection, dressed with impeccable taste and proud of it, well groomed and always a gentleman, the lack of decent women in the podunk town was the most difficult thing to deal with. High school girls were too young and silly. Maggody didn't boast a sorority house with nubile occupants or a Junior League with perky young matrons in sable jackets and designer suits. They'd be married, anyways, Mason thought as he pulled into the yard and cut the engine. The three single women he'd thus far met in town had good reasons for their marital status; he had no inclination to alter it. Not, of course, that he had exalted standards. He just couldn't imagine kissing a woman who was hairier than a summer groundhog, or older than the hills. Or tipping the scales at three hundred pounds plus. Mason wanted a nice girl—nothing spectacular, but nice.

The house looked dark, but as he came inside, he saw a light in the back sitting room. He wondered if he could slip upstairs without being caught, then glumly decided he couldn't and went on to the kitchen. "You want I should bring you a beer or a glass of sherry?" he called to his sister.

"No. Why are you out so late? Do you realize it is midnight? Do you care that I have stayed up to worry about you, even though tomorrow I will have hideous dark circles under my eyes? Do you—"

Mason rattled the refrigerator door, drowning out the final rhetorical demand. Sarah Lou Dickerson Grinolli Vizzard had been in the sherry, he told himself as he took out a beer and popped the top. The bottle in the garbage can confirmed his theory, although he hadn't had much doubt. He once again considered flight, but instead went to the sitting room and poked his head through the door. "I'm right sorry you waited up, Sis. I didn't mean to worry you," he said.

"But you did," she retorted, her eyes harder than emeralds.

"I realize that now, and I'm truly sorry. I stopped for a drink and got to chatting with some folks. One thing led to another, and pretty soon we ended up eating enchiladas at a little place on the edge of town."

"For seven hours? How many enchiladas did you eat in seven hours?"

"Well, after dinner we went to a couple of bars to listen to music. Listen, Sarah Lou, I'm old enough—"

"Do not call me that. It is not my name." She found a glass of sherry on the table and drank the contents in one gulp. "I have told you never to call me that again. Sarah Lou is some child who lives in a hovel and wears hand-me-down clothes. She is some mindless woman-child who whimpers while her drunken husband beats her until her eyes are so swollen she cannot see. Sarah Lou is dead." She broke off with a scowl and pointed a finger at Mason. "Bring me another bottle of sherry."

Mason found a bottle in a kitchen cabinet and came back to the sitting room, still wishing he were upstairs in bed. "If she's dead, why don't you arrange a seance and see what all she has to say about the other world?"

"Do you think that amuses me, Mason? Do you see me smiling? Do you hear me laughing? Am I dressed in a clown suit?"

"I was just making a little joke, Sis. Lighten up, why don't you?"

"Do you think what I do is a joke?" She filled her glass and drank half of it. "It is not easy, you know. I have many feelings that you and the others cannot understand. I see auras; I hear voices. I know things that do not always make people happy—but I tell them the truth because I know the truth."

Mason figured that the truth was he was tired and she was drunker than a boiled owl. But, being the good brother that he was—and depending on her for his substantial allowance—he sat back and took a swallow of beer. "So, Celeste, did you have a good day?"

"No, I did not. My first client was late, and although she listened and asked questions, I could see that she was skeptical. This disturbed me. It ruined my day, in fact, and made it impossible for me to put aside her condescending smile and concentrate on more cosmic things."

"One of those biddies from the beauty shop?"

"Those women believe in my powers and pay very promptly for my services. Of course, I am worth every penny of it," Madam Celeste said, pouring yet another six inches of sherry into her plastic tumbler. "No, this was a woman not older than you. The daughter of one of my clients; she has been away on a vacation for several months. I took her as a favor, but now I think I should not have done so."

"Single?"

"She did not wear a wedding ring, but there was a faint mark as if she'd worn one once. The sand said she had been treated badly not too long ago; perhaps a divorce—I could not be sure."

This time Mason leaped to his feet and, with a small bow, filled Celeste's glass. "Allow me, Sis; I can see you're tired. This new client—she's my age and single? Does she have warts or anything?"

"She was pretty, in a cool way. Dark hair in a bun, dark eyes, the high cheekbones so common in the Slavic aristocracy. But why are you asking all these questions, my little brother? I can smell cheap perfume on you, so I know you have been with a woman. Are you still so very desperate?"

Mason squirmed as her eyes bored into him; he wondered if maybe she did have a line to an inky universe he sure couldn't dial direct. "Lay off it; I told you about that already. It was just a group having dinner and barhopping. Why does that make me desperate?"

"Because she's a cop, dammit." Celeste shot him an unfathomable look, then banged down her tumbler and left the room.

The beeper was an interesting little critter. Black, so it'd go with both my uniform and my cocktail dress. Two buttons, and a grill that covered its mysterious organs. The idea was that I'd leave the PD telephone on call forwarding so folks would end up with the sheriff's dispatcher. She'd beep me, and I'd know to call her for a message. Damn thing had a range wide enough to cover the county, so there weren't too many places I could hole up or hide.

I was sitting behind my desk playing with it when the door banged open. Mrs. Jim Bob marched into the room, her expression more rigid than Edwina Spitz in a bargain-basement girdle. There was a righteous glint in her eye, and her mouth was a white line. Mrs. Jim Bob is also known as Mizzoner, but only to a select few who have nothing better to do than to idle away the hours in the PD making up feeble puns.

Mrs. Jim Bob is not one to waste her precious time on pleasantries. Ungluing her lips, she said, "Arly, it has come to my attention that a most dreadful event has taken place."

"Jim Bob knock up Raz's oldest girl?" I flipped over the beeper to study its serial number and arrangement of tiny, shiny screws.

"My husband is in Hot Springs at a municipal league convention, thank you. He takes his responsibilities more seriously than some city employees around here, and he and the other members of the town council went to the meeting despite any personal or financial sacrifice."

"Raz's oldest girl is out of town, too. You don't think he took her along, do you? She's just the type to be impressed by a snooty hotel and a real live convention. I hate to imagine what she'd be willing to do for one of those laminated name tags. What do you bet she's never even heard tell of room service?"

She gave me a beady look. "I'll be sure and ask him about it when he gets home next week. He'll think your remark was real funny, Miss Chief of Police."

Needling Mrs. Jim Bob was not enough of a challenge to merit the effort. "So what dreadful event has taken place?" I asked.

"Robin Buchanon is gone."

"And that's dreadful? I think we ought to buy a bottle of champagne—no, let's get a whole dadburn case of champagne and invite the neighbors over for a celebration. I'll stop by the Kwik-Screw for a box of Ritz crackers and some onion dip, and we'll party 'til the sun peeks over the tallest tree in the national forest. What's more, you can offer the first toast." Good thing I hadn't made a New Year's resolution to stop needling her—those who claim the copyright to half the Bible are such easy targets.

"It is not a source of amusement—and neither are you. You know perfectly well that I wouldn't touch alcohol with a ten-foot pole. I am a good Christian woman. Now, are you going to stop being a smart aleck and listen, or do I have to call Jim Bob long distance all the way to Hot Springs and tell him that you're shirking your duty as chief of police?"

"Gee, do the telephone wires go all the way to Hot Springs?"

"You listen to me, Ariel Hanks—I am fed up with your remarks. Now once and for all, are you going to hear me out or not?"

I put the beeper away and took a pad out of the middle drawer. "Do you want to file a missing persons report, ma'am? We can have the FBI here within the hour."

She nibbled on her unsullied lips (cosmetics being a vanity that led straight to you-know-where). "Well, I suppose so. But that's not the reason I—"

"Victim's full name and address, please. Date of birth. Physical description, including any and all warts, moles, tattoos, and scars. Next of kin in case something terrible has happened. Name of dentist, should we need dental records for purposes of identification. When last seen and by whom." I poised my pencil and gave her a bright smile. "But you feel free to take your time, Mrs. Jim Bob. It's a long report, but if we hang in there, we can do it." If she wanted officiousness, she was going to get it. Ad nauseam and then some.

"I don't know those things any better than you do, Arly."

I threw the pencil in the trash can, scoring two points along the way. In an aggrieved voice, I said, "Then why don't you just tell me how I'm supposed to fill out the report and put it on the telex to the FBI? I'm trying my darndest to follow procedure, but I'm not getting any assistance from you, if you don't mind me saying so. Those FBI fellows get hotter than a peck of parsnips if they get called in on some wild-goose chase." I toyed with suggesting that Robin was shacked up in a Hot Springs hotel room, but lost my nerve at the last minute.

I could see she wasn't quite sure whether I was ribbing her or not. She twisted her gloves for a full minute, then concluded that I was and gave me a hundred watt frown. "You want proof? Well, you just sit there and I'll be back with proof!" She stomped out the door.

I was trying to unscrew the back of the beeper when she stomped back in the door, dragging a small figure who looked mighty miserable under a tangle of black hair.

"This," she said triumphantly, "is one of Robin Buchanon's bastard children." She shoved the figure forward. "You tell the policewoman what happened and be quick about it. Take your finger out of your mouth while you speak, so's she can understand you. And speak up nice and loud."

The child looked to be about nine or ten, and was blessed with the simian features of the Buchanon clan. He/she wore dirty, ragged overalls, with neither shirt nor shoes. "I ain't talking to no police," he/she said in a mumble I could barely hear from four feet away. I could, however, smell a sourness that was clear evidence of lack of familiarity with soap and water for quite a while.

Mrs. Jim Bob prodded a shoulder. "Stop that nonsense and tell the policewoman your name. If you don't, she'll lock you up in a dark, wet cell and let the rats eat your face until you feel more obliged to talk."

"I ain't talking."

You've got to admire spunk. Smiling, I said, "I'm fresh out of dungeons and rats today. Why don't you at least tell me your name? It can't hurt. In fact, I'll bet you have a real pretty name."

"Like shit you do."

Mrs. Jim Bob grabbed the shoulder and gave it a shake hard enough to make brain milkshake. "We will not tolerate that sort of language. Didn't your mother teach you anything at all, you filthy-mouthed heathen?"

"Yeah—not to talk to cops unless'n I wanted the shit beat out of me."

Needless to say (but I'm saying it anyway), that did not sit well with Hizzoner's wife. Only her sense of Christian charity stopped her from following Robin Buchanon's guide to rearing perfectly correct children. She huffed and snorted for a long time, while I studied the child, who was busy studying me right back.

"Is your mother missing?" I asked once everybody'd finished doing whatever he/she was doing.

"I dunno. Don't care neither."

Mrs. Jim Bob pushed her witness aside. "What happened is that I chanced to find this little heathen rooting through the garbage cans behind the store. I knew at once who he was and demanded to know how he had the audacity to steal right there in broad daylight. Once I'd assured him that he could go to jail for a long spell, not to mention other places for the sin of lying, he said that he and his brothers and sisters had been alone for several days with no food."

The child, who could by now be presumed male, gave me a sly look. "You cain't arrest me, because I didn't take nothing. The old bitch came out afore I could find sumpthin' worth taking. What was in those cans were meaner than gar-broth, anyways."

The old bitch started huffing. "You remember what I said about finding yourself locked in eternal damnation for the sin of cursing? If I hear one more foul word from you, I'm going to wash your mouth out with a bar of soap—and it won't be Ivory, either."

"Fuck you, lady."

We were having real success with this one. I gave Mrs. Jim Bob a wry smile meant to convince her of the futility of the situation (which was about as futile as they get), and said, "Well, I see no point in continuing this. The child is unwilling to make a statement. I can't take any action based on the information we have, so if you'll excuse me, I need to follow the school buses to the county line. We wouldn't want our youth jeopardized by those who fail to stop for school buses." Which would also allow me to breathe through my nose instead of my mouth.

"Don't be absurd. You must go to the cabin and investigate. If the mother is truly missing, then you must bring the rest of the heathens back to town."

"I shall presume all that heavy breathing has induced hyperventilation," I said. "Go home and breathe into a paper bag."

"It is your Christian duty. Think of those poor, starving children all alone in the forest."

I stood up and clipped on my beeper. "If it's anyone's Christian duty, Mrs. Jim Bob, it's yours. Feel free to think all you want about those poor, starving children all alone in the forest. Tell this child the story of Hansel and Gretel until you turn blue in the face. But you're crazier than a flea on an elephant if you think I'm going up there, especially on some vague notion that Robin may have taken a hike for a couple of days."

"More'n that," the witness contributed. "And the baby ain't had tit for a long while. He's a-cryin' and a-mewin' all the time."

I glared at the child. "What's your name?"

"Hammet."

"Okay, Hammet," I said through clenched teeth, "are you willing to tell me the whole story now? I'm hardly in the mood to sit here all afternoon and drag it out of you one word at a time."

Mrs. Jim Bob nodded as if she had singlehandedly pulled off a damn coup d'état in South America. "Of course Hammet will cooperate with the authorities. He doesn't want to go straight to hell on a freight train, does he?"

"Ain't never been on a train," Hammet muttered. "I heard 'em on t'other side of the ridge, though. How fast do you reckon they can go?"

This whole thing was going too fast for yours truly. "I will listen to the story," I said. "If it seems warranted, I will go so far as to borrow a four-wheel-drive jeep from the sheriff's office and try to find Robin's cabin out there in the middle of nowhere. If she has not returned, I will even fill the backseat with heathens and transport them back to town." I crossed my arms and stared at Mrs. Jim Bob. "Do you have any suggestions as to what I do next?"

She tried to pretend she missed the point. "Why, you do everything possible to find Robin and reunite her with her children."

"And until I find her?" I persisted, not missing a beat. "What do I do with the children until then?"

Mrs. Jim Bob paled. "Why, I'm sure you'll find a nice, warm, safe place for them to stay. They'll need food, beds, and clean clothing, of course, but they won't be any bother once they're fed and . . . disinfected."

I looked down at Hammet. "See this kind, Christian woman just brimming with charity? She lives way on the top of a hill, in a great big house with lots of bedrooms and bathrooms, and her refrigerator is bigger than the broad side of a barn. Ooh, it's just stuffed full of good things to eat, like meat and 'taters and cookies and ice cream. How would you and all your dear little brothers and sisters like to visit her?"

"I think," Mrs. Jim Bob said in a strangled voice, "that I'd best go see Brother Verber at the Voice of the Almighty Lord Assembly Hall. I feel a sudden need for prayer."

I let her stumble away. Then, after opening the back door and the windows, I sat Hammet across the room and we got down to business.

4

Don't think for a minute that Hammet Buchanon spilled out his little heart to me. For one thing, I wouldn't have bet a dollar that he had one; for another, he was about as credible as a televangelist claiming a hotline to God and requesting help with the phone bill. Hammet finally admitted he and his brothers and sisters had been alone for four or five days, and hadn't had much of anything in the way of vittles. When last seen, their mother was going 'seng hunting. I inquired where her patch was. He shot me a suspicious look and told me it weren't none of my goddamn business. What a cutie.

I considered various responses, then settled for a sigh. "Let's get you something to eat, Hammet. I'll call the sheriff's office to see if we can borrow a four-wheel and run up to the cabin. If your mother's still missing, I suppose we'll bring your siblings back to town and deal with the situation then."

"Ain't got none."

"None of what?" I said absently as I clipped on my beeper.

"Them that you said."

I thought about it for a minute, then realized what he meant. "Siblings are brothers and sisters, Hammet. How about a big, greasy cheeseburger and a glass of milk?"

He didn't budge. "Why ain't they brothers and sisters?"

"It's another word that means brothers and sis-

ters," I said, taking his shoulder strap to propel him toward the door.
"Why din't you jest say brothers and sisters?"
Cursing Mrs. Jim Bob under my breath (although I doubted I used any words not an integral part of the child's vocabulary), I dragged him out the door while explaining that there were often several words that meant the very same thing. I could tell he didn't believe a word of it.
We were still exploring the delicate issue of semantics as we went into Ruby Bee's. The proprietor's mouth fell open as I put Hammet on a bar stool, then hopped up on the next stool and gave her a bright smile. "Why, Arly," she said, "whoever is your little friend here?"
"Hammet Buchanon. He's one of Robin's children, and he's starving. How about a cheeseburger and a glass of milk?"
She wrinkled her nose. "Well, he's welcome to something to eat, but don't you think he might like to wash up first?"
I could tell she was thinking of a prolonged session with a sandblaster rather than a cursory encounter with soap and water in the rest room. "He hasn't had anything to eat in several days," I said. "Let's get him fed; then I'll take him back to my apartment and bathe him."
"The hell you will," contributed the object of the conversation. "Sure as cow shit stinks I ain't taking no goddamn bath. Done took one a while back."
Ruby Bee blinked, first at Hammet and then at me. "He has quite a colorful vocabulary, doesn't he? I'll start the cheeseburger right away. Would he like a bag of chips while I'm fixing it?"
"Would you?" I asked Hammet.
"Yeah, what the fuck," he conceded with a shrug.
Ruby Bee had enough sense not to roll her eyes and demand a "please" from this customer. She marched away, but I could hear her mutters all the

way through the kitchen door. After a minute I heard her shrilly repeating the conversation, presumably to Estelle. I wanted to escape to the kitchen and explain that none of this was my idea to begin with, but I settled for yet another sigh, then said, "I'm not asking you where the ginseng patch is. All I want to know is if you know where it is."

"Nope. Her never did say. Somewhere on t'other side of the ridge. It were grandpappy's oncet upon a time."

"How long does your mother stay gone when she's 'seng hunting?"

"I dunno. Don't care neither. She's a mean ole sow and I hope the bears et her for supper."

"How many brothers and sisters do you have?" I asked, hoping this sudden loquaciousness would last. I'd been at Robin's cabin on another matter, and I'd seen children hovering in the shadows. But at that time I was too concerned with an escaped convict, a kidnapped bureaucrat, and all sorts of crazy shenanigans to try to count those shifting, feral creatures.

"I has four"—he paused to give me an unfathomable look—"siblings, being Bubba, Sissie, Sukie, and Baby. Baby don't count for much 'cause he's too little to do anything exceptin' cry and shit in his britchins. He's about as useless as tits on a boar hog. You reckon we can jest leave him in the baby trough?"

"I doubt it, Hammet." I tossed him a bag of corn chips and spent the next five minutes praying Robin would be at the cabin when we got there. I could hand over Hammet, compliment her on her ginseng, and scoot right back down the mountain. Alone.

Ruby Bee came through the door, a plate in her hand and a disapproving expression on her face. "Here's your food," she said, banging down the plate in front of Hammet.

He bent down to sniff over the plate like a leery polecat. "What be this stuff?"

"A cheeseburger with lettuce, tomato, onions, pickle relish, and mustard. I might add that I am often told I fry the best cheeseburger on this side of Starley City," Ruby Bee said. She didn't sound real friendly.

"I ain't eating this crap." Hammet pushed the plate away and lunged for another bag of corn chips.

I caught his wrist and explained that he was going to eat the cheeseburger, one way or another, and that one of those ways included physical acts on my part and a great deal of discomfort on his. He offered a comment that implied I had engaged in a series of unnatural sexual encounters with various barnyard animals. Ruby Bee cut in with a few comments that might have come from the prissy lips of dear Mrs. Jim Bob. Hammet repeated the terse yet effective witticism that gave Mrs. Jim Bob the bout of hyperventilation. Ruby Bee slapped her hand to her heart and started hyperventilating. I suggested everybody shut up. Nobody did.

We were going at it real good when the kitchen door opened and out waddled Dahlia O'Neill. She was wearing her customary tent dress (which could have slept six—and probably had on more than one occasion) and an apron embroidered with daisies and her name. The sight stopped me in mid-word. Even Hammet broke off with a gasp, giving Ruby Bee the golden opportunity to swoop in for the last word. A favorite hobby of hers.

"I have never in all my born days heard such filthy language. You just eat that cheeseburger right now, young man!" She stepped around Dahlia and vanished into the kitchen.

"How ya doing, Arly?" Dahlia said.

"Fine," I croaked. "What are you doing here?"

"I'm the new barmaid. Madam Celeste—do you know her? Well, anyways, she told me that I needed to make what she called a career move, so I quit my job at the Kwik-Screw. Ruby Bee done hired me as a barmaid, and it's working out right nice. She, meaning Madam Celeste and not Ruby Bee, told Kevin the exact same thing, which is why he's cleaning the commodes at the high school and sweeping nights at the PD. You must of seen him, Arly—you being the chief of police and all."

"I've seen him," I admitted. Maybe Madam Celeste would counsel a career move for me. Something in the range of five hundred miles.

Dahlia beamed. "I figured out you had. You want I should get you a beer or something?"

"I'll take coffee, and Hammet'll have a glass of milk."

She figured out how to open the refrigerator under the bar for milk and, after a few false moves, how to coax coffee from the urn. All this in less than five minutes, too. Hammet tore into the cheeseburger with the grace of a hyena, splattering his bare torso and a goodly part of the immediate area with grease. By the time Dahlia put a glass in front of him, he'd polished the burger off and was peering from under his brow at the chips.

"I'll ask this woman to bring you a piece of pie—if you agree to a bath afterward," I said.

"Don't need no goddamn bath." He rubbed his palm across his glistening front, then carefully licked it.

"But are you willing to submit to one in exchange for a piece of Ruby Bee's homemade apple pie—with a scoop of ice cream?"

"I don't need no goddamn bath 'til next year. Creek's colder'n a well-digger's ass."

"My creek is not, however. My creek is warm, and it doesn't have any crawdads, snapping turtles, minnows, or rusty cans in it. Deal?"

He nodded without enthusiasm. Dahlia, who'd been listening to all this with a perplexed look, served the pie and even remembered the ice cream. His enthusiasm restored, Hammet tore into it.

"Why's he with you?" Dahlia asked, her cheeks puffed out like a bullfrog's on a summer night as she watched Hammet slurping his way through dessert.

"In the metaphysical sense, I have no idea. Mrs. Jim Bob gave him to me, and I haven't figured out how to pass him along to someone else." I nudged my ward. "You ready for a bath and an exciting ride in a jeep?"

We went to my apartment, and he did indeed take a bath while I washed his overalls in the sink, then dashed over to the Suds of Fun and stuck them in a dryer for a few minutes. When I returned, I threw them into the bathroom. I then called the sheriff's office to arrange for a vehicle worthy of logging trails, dried-out creek beds, animal carcasses, and whatever else I expected we'd encounter.

Hammet came out of the bathroom, his hair slicked down and minus a couple of layers of grime. "That's right smart," he said as he looked around curiously. "Havin' water in the house, I mean. It ain't bad, lady."

I told him he could call me Arly, which brought a shy smile. We went across the street to the PD to get my car, then drove over to Starley City. Hammet had a good time playing with the radio, which actually was functional for the moment. I filled out the paperwork at the county compound, took the keys to a spiffy red jeep, and had enough sense to grab a survey map before we set out into the vast, skimpily charted wasteland of Cotter's Ridge.

"I will see you for only ten minutes," Madam Celeste said through the screen door. "I have a busy schedule, and I do not like to be inconvenienced by intrusions. But stop that whining and come in."

Carol Alice Plummer glanced over her shoulder, then slipped inside. "Thank you kindly for taking me without an appointment, Madam Celeste. I'm in terrible trouble, and I just can't think what to do. You see, I told Bo what you said about us being incompatible because he's a four and I'm a six. Well, you'd of thought I said his foreparents were all white trash. He started fuming and swearing and—"

"Come to the solarium," Madam Celeste said, pointedly looking at her watch. "I have no time to listen to you dither."

Carol Alice followed the psychic through the dining room. "Anyways, Madam, Bo got so teed off that he told my pa that I was under some sort of magic spell. Then Pa got madder than a coon in a poke and said he was going to whip me so hard I'd forget all this tomfoolery and start worrying about cheerleading practice, like I used to do all the time."

Madam Celeste pointed at a chair. "Sit down and be quiet, you silly girl. You should not have repeated the details of your reading; in fact, I told you quite clearly that everything I reveal to you must be kept confidential."

"I had to tell Bo something when I broke up with him."

"You did not have to involve me in your petty love affairs. You should have told him nothing." Madam Celeste's eyes narrowed. "So both this miserable boy and your father are upset, yes? What do they intend to do?"

"I don't know," Carol Alice said, gulping. "Bo takes after his pa, who gets as mean as a diamondback rattlesnake when he drinks. And my pa ain't exactly Prince Charming, even when he's sober. Of course it's getting near deer season, so that might distract them. They're real big on hunting."

"What comfort for me to know they possess guns," Madam Celeste said coldly. After a minute of thought, she said, "I shall give you a reading right now, and for this one time will not charge you the regular fee. We will use the Mesopotamian sand, I think."

"Oh, that'd be great. Is there any chance the sand'll tell me that Bo and I can get married next June like we planned to do? Then Bo'd stop being so mad, and maybe Pa'd stop saying all those wild things about coming over here to have it out with you."

"I cannot say what the sand will reveal. The Mesopotamian sand can be very precise, or it can be general and only reveal trends. Here, make a handprint and allow me to study in silence."

Carol Alice managed to hold her snuffling to a minimum while the psychic gazed into the Tupperware bowl, but it wasn't easy. She hadn't told Madam some of the names Pa had used, nor had she mentioned that Bo and some of his football buddies had some right ugly plans. If only Bo had understood when she had tried her darndest to explain about the numbers and the vibrations and everything . . . Maybe, she thought with a wince, he was all riled up because he'd just finished telling her he had his uncle's Trans Am for the whole weekend. Carol Alice knew what that meant. After all, didn't she have a sister over in Hasty with living, screaming proof? She wondered if she'd sounded a mite relieved when she said she wasn't going out with him no more. She sighed noisily.

"Be still!" Madam Celeste snapped.

"Do you see something?"

Her eyes closed, the psychic sagged back in the chair and began to rub her temples. "Go away," she said in a dull voice.

"But what about me and Bo? Are we going to get married?"

"Leave. Go away. Get out of my house." Madam Celeste stood up and walked out of the room.

"That wasn't very nice," Carol Alice said to herself with a faint pout, looking at the bowl of blue sand. "I wonder what all she saw that got her so riled up? Jeez, everybody's awful riled up these days."

Mason came through the kitchen door, carrying a couple of sacks of groceries. "Hi, honey. Are you waiting for Celeste? Can I get you a can of soda pop or something to eat? I just bought some bologna."

"No, but thank you for asking. I don't know where Madam Celeste went—or why. We were having a reading, but she all of a sudden jumped up and told me to get out of the house. I didn't say nothing to upset her. I was just sitting here waiting to see if Bo and me can get married despite our numerological discord." Her voice dropped to a raspy whisper. "Do you think she saw something terrible about me in the sand? Like I was going to die tomorrow or get hit by a chicken truck or flunk out or get thrown off the cheerleading squad? Oh, Mr. Dickerson, what should I do?"

Mason stared at her over the spaghetti package. "Ah, I'm not sure, Carol Alice. Let me put down the sacks and see if we can come up with something. You're too pretty for anything terrible to happen to you." He put the sacks on the counter and joined her at the dinette table, hoping he could figure out how to stop her from bursting into tears right in the middle of the breakfast room. "Maybe I ought to look at the sand, do you think?"

"Can you interpret Mesopotamian sand?"

"Has Celeste given you a sand reading before?" When she shook her head, Mason produced a confident smile. "Of course I can interpret sand, honey. Is this your handprint? Look at this ridge right here by the edge of the bowl. You see what I'm pointing at? Well, that is the ridge of longevity, and yours is exceptionally high. That means you'll live to be as old as the hills, if not a sight longer."

"Well, that's good to know. What about me and Bo?"

"Look there—you can almost see the letters of his name right there on the ridge of matrimony. See where the grains kind of swoop in and out? That's the 'B' for Bo. This indentation is the 'O.' "

"I do believe I see what you're pointing to," Carol Alice said, feeling a tad brighter. "You do a better reading than Madam Celeste, Mr. Dickerson. Does it show how many kids we'll have?"

"Two of each, and all four of them the cutest things you've ever seen," Mason said, feeling a tad brighter himself, now that the girl was smiling. "Let's study the ridge of residence. Yep, you're going to live in a big house with ceramic-tiled bathrooms and televisions in all the bedrooms. And the kitchen—well, the kitchen is straight off the pages of *Better Homes and Gardens.*"

"Do I get to have a microwave?"

Mason assured her that she'd have not only a microwave (programmable, and with a browning unit), but also all sorts of luxurious things. He found the automotive ridge, which showed decisively she'd be driving a sleek red Camaro convertible before the first boy (Bo Junior, naturally) was in kindergarten. The ridge of financial expectations was high enough to provoke all sorts of squeals and hand clapping. They were having so much fun that both of them jumped like toad-frogs when a shadow fell across the Tupperware bowl.

"Get out of here," Madam Celeste said to Carol Alice. She then looked down at Mason, who was wishing he was on the ridge of elsewhere with a capital "E." "Mason, come to my study. I must talk to you."

Carol Alice fled. Mason toyed with putting away the groceries first, but abandoned the idea and went to the study.

"I realize I was spouting nonsense, but I was just

trying to cheer up the little girl," he said, scuffling his feet as though he were back in the principal's office for a spitball misdemeanor.

"Forget her; she is a foolish thing with equally foolish problems. Something happened while I was in the middle of the reading, something for which I was not prepared. I was concentrating very hard on attuning myself to the cosmic vibrations. Suddenly a picture flashed across my brain. It was a face, Mason. The eyes were open and unblinking. The skin was red with speckled blood. Flies were dancing on the lips and nostrils. It was very, very dreadful, this face I saw. There had been pain—and I could almost feel it myself. I wanted to weep, to cry out, to scratch and fight, to lose myself in blackness. Oh, God, Mason; it was so awful."

"Not that sweet little thing who was in the kitchen?" Mason said, shocked by her intensity.

"I do not know." Madam Celeste covered her face with her hands, and her voice was muffled as she again said, "I do not know."

"Why don't you lie down until the nausea passes?" Rainbow said with a motherly smile. "I'll bring you a nice cup of peppermint tea."

"Because she's supposed to be behind the cash register," Nate said from the doorway. His dark eyes glowered from under the shaggy curtain of black hair, and his mouth was twisted with frustration. Pushing back the hair with a brusque movement, he added, "We went over the schedule for the goddamn fiftieth time last night, and everybody agreed. You keep treating her like she was made of porcelain. Poppy's pregnant, not terminal. We're running a business, not a haven for unwed mothers."

Rainbow's motherly smile faltered, but held. "And she has an upset stomach and is seriously considering barfing all over the floor, Nate. That's not the way to encourage repeat business, now is it? Besides, we all love Poppy and we want her to rest."

Poppy managed a brave nod. "That's okay, Rainbow. I feel better, and I'll tend to the cash register until closing time. You stay back here and do the books."

"You're the color of creme de menthe," Rainbow said. "You'd better take the truck and go home. Stay in bed until I can get there to take care of you."

"I'm taking the truck," Nate growled. "She said she was better. You're supposed to bring the ledgers up to date for the accountant. Zachery's busy putting out the bottled water so we'll be able to use the back door. For Christ's sake, nobody can get anything done if Poppy goes home in the middle of the afternoon because her stomach is fluttery! You're doing this to make me angry, aren't you?"

Rainbow's motherly smile was being sorely tested, as was her temper, which she prided herself on never losing. "This is not the jungle of Vietnam, Nate, nor are we in the middle of a triathlon. I'll mind the register and bring the books home to work on tonight; I truly don't mind staying up late to get them finished. Poppy's going home in the truck. I have no intentions of making you angry, and you can run your errands later."

"The co-op closes later. If I don't get over there before they close, we won't have any layer grit tomorrow. I told some old coot we'd have it tomorrow morning."

There was not much communal harmony in the office as Zachery pushed aside the curtain. "Customer," he said, scratching his armpit as he tried to assess the situation through eyes befogged by a joint of exceptionally good pot. "Wants to know the price on six yards of velour."

"I'll see to it," Poppy said. She went around

Zachery, trying not to look too relieved at escaping the tension-laden room. Or to throw up.

Rainbow loved both men equally, because equality was the basis of their relationship, but at times she had to admit to a teensy amount of favoritism. Zachery was mild and dopey in a sweet way, with his wispy beard, ponytail, and soft brown eyes that never seemed to focus on much of anything. His face was lined with wrinkles, and his nose was perhaps on the large side, but he never complained.

Nate had the tendency to get too intense, as if he were still in the jungle with a machete between his teeth and they were the invisible enemy. She occasionally thought, although she'd never say a word, that he didn't seem to be meditating quite as seriously as the rest of them. More than once she'd had to remind him of his mantra, or gently admonish him to seek his psychic center. Zachery just needed a pat on the head or a kind word, and he'd offer to hang the moon for her. And he never forgot his mantra.

But they and Poppy were her family. Therefore, she loved them all. Once she'd rather sternly reminded herself of that, she turned on her best smile and gave Nate a kiss on his dear, pock-marked cheek. "There, everything is in proper alignment, and we can all share the energy."

"Yeah," Nate said.

Hammet had even more fun with the radio in the jeep, which sparked and spat and produced ear-shattering static when he turned it up as far as it would go. I kept my attention on the ghastly road, and my hands in a death grip on the steering wheel as we bounced up what was surely a creek bed pretending to be a road.

"Holy shit," Hammet muttered as a dispatcher somewhere sent a police car somewhere else. "Real folks is a-talkin' on this box."

"All courtesy of Mr. Marconi," I replied, trying to hold up the map to see how much farther we had to go. The ridge was crisscrossed by hairline roads, but most of them were abandoned logging trails that had disappeared a decade ago. I was pretty sure we were headed in the right direction; Hammet hadn't been any help because he'd never driven home.

"Yeah," he said. He flopped back against the seat. "You sure we're goin' right? I ain't seen this afore now."

"According to the map, we're going toward your house. As for the accuracy of the map and my interpretation, I don't know. We may end up on County 103, having wasted about six hours in the process."

"So you ain't so all-fired smart, huh?"

I gave him a very quick glance, but it was long enough to see his lower lip stuck out past the tip of his nose. "No," I murmured, "I'm not so all-fired smart. What's bugging you?"

"Macaroni, if you gotta know. Course you gotta know everything, don'tcha? Goddamn cops."

"Marconi was an Italian physicist who invented radios," I said without taking my eyes off the road. "He won a Nobel Prize about seventy years ago."

"So he's dead, huh? Big fucking deal. Ain't nobody what cares about some stupid old Eye-talian who's deader than a pump-handle."

"Well, the radio is a useful invention. It lets me stay in touch with the dispatcher when I'm out of pocket."

"Ain't nobody calling you on the radio."

"But they could, if there were an emergency," I pointed out mildly. "Before Marconi invented the radio, messages had to be mailed or sent on a telegraph wire."

"How'd he know how to make up this radio iffen

there weren't no radios around he could copy off of?"

I did my best to explain the concept of inventions. Hammet didn't buy any of it, but it got us most of the way to the cabin. As I parked in front of the ramshackle dwelling, I thought I might miss his company—in an extremely obscure way. I gave him a smile and a pat on the shoulder, then got out of the jeep. As I started across the weedy yard, two children who came straight out of the Hammet mold appeared at the door. Both were larger, but they had the same tangled black hair, piercing yellowish eyes, and protruding brows.

"Hi, there," I said, stopping at a safe distance. "I've brought Hammet back from town. Is your mother here?"

Hammet tugged on my sleeve. "That be Bubba and Sissie," he whispered. "Sukie's likely to be hiding inside. She's right shy of strangers."

The boy, thirteen or fourteen and leaner than a fence post, stared at me for a long while, then said, "Why do you be a-wantin' to know?"

Hammet edged forward, but he clung to my sleeve. "She be the cop down in Maggody, Bubba, but she ain't all bad. She got me some vittles, and says she'll get y'all vittles, too, iffen we go to town with her."

"I ain't goin' to town."

"Me neither," Sissie said, sticking out her chin. "Besides, Her'd whup the tar outta us iffen we wasn't here when she come back."

"Iffen you starve dead, Her won't find anybody left to whup," Hammet said, expressing my sentiment with succinctness.

Bubba declined to debate the point. "I ain't goin' nowhere. Ain't none of us goin' nowhere with no goddamn motherfuckin' police lady. Hammet, you get your ass in the house iffen you don't want me to stomp it right now."

"You're forgetting who stomped ass last time," Hammet replied smugly.

The two were exchanging alarmingly militant looks when another child came to the doorway, a finger in her mouth. "Baby's a-cryin' again," she lisped through the unappetizing finger.

"Git inside," Bubba snapped.

I realized that we needed a social worker, a referee, or perhaps a few National Guardsmen with great big guns. I would have settled for Mrs. Jim Bob with a Bible. One lone (expletives deleted) chief of police was going to have a potentially volatile situation on her hands, as we say in official jargon, if she tried to force any of the Buchanon offspring into leaving. I considered a plea for reason. I considered a passionate appeal to whatever intelligence Bubba possessed. Once I recovered from that momentary flight of fancy, I went back to the jeep and sat down on the fender.

"There's a lot of food in town," I said.

"Yeah," Hammet said, nodding. "Cheeseburgers and sweet milk and corn chips. All you wants, and you don't have to give 'em money or root through no garbage cans." He shot me a quick look. "You don't hafta take a bath, neither."

"I'm awful hungry," Sukie said through her finger.

Sissie looked up at Bubba. "Baby's doin' poorly. Iffen he dies, Mama'll be madder than a brooder hen tryin' to hatch a rock. And I'm awful hungry, too."

"But we cain't just go off with some cop lady."

Sensing Bubba's indecision, I moved in for the kill. "How about apple pie, kids? Does everybody like apple pie with ice cream? Soda pop? Okra and collard greens oozing in pot likker? Pork chops with red-eye gravy? Mashed potatoes? Soft white bread? I know just where we can get plates piled high with all that—and no baths." Okay, I lied.

Pretty soon we were all in the jeep, bouncing

back down the mountainside. Sukie was squashed next to Hammet in the front seat, listening blankly as he explained how Mr. Macaroni invented the radio before anyone else even owned a radio, which was a goddamn noble thing for Mr. Macaroni to have done in the first place.

The two older children sat in the backseat. The baby, wrapped in a piece of quilt and disturbingly quiet, lay in Sissie's lap. I was occupied with trying to figure out how to deal with Ruby Bee when I strolled in with my bevy of Buchanon bush colts and ordered two gallons of collard greens. I suspected it wasn't going to play well.

5

Mrs. Jim Bob's knees were getting sore, but she kept her lips tight and her head bent to a pious tilt, trying not to ponder the heretical idea that Brother Verber was a mite long-winded. Especially when she had things to discuss. She couldn't help but notice the floor of the church was dusty, which went to prove she'd been right all along when she said Perkins' eldest was doing a poor job of cleaning. She stole a quick peek at the windows above the choir loft, then hastily closed her eyes. Yes, they were streaky, just as she'd imagined they would be. And Perkins' eldest carrying on about how she always used ammonia when she wiped the windows. Everybody knew ammonia didn't streak.

"Amen," Brother Verber said in a deep, melodious flow of vowels and consonants, clinging to the final sound until it tickled his nose. He just loved it when his nose tickled, even if it meant a sneeze was coming.

"Amen." Mrs. Jim Bob stood up and brushed off her dusty knees. "I appreciate you taking the time to pray with me, Brother Verber, and it did warm my heart. Now I'm hoping you can offer some counsel about a difficult problem."

"You know better than anybody that that's why I'm here, Sister Barbara. What sort of problem do you want to discuss?"

"It concerns something that has arisen between Mr. Jim Bob and me."

"Problems of an intimate marital nature?" Brother Verber said, striving for the proper balance of sympathy and distaste. Sometimes, he knew, he sounded too enthusiastic when asked to counsel his flock about what all they did in the privacy of their bedrooms. And the stories he heard were enough to make a grown man blush. It was hard to imagine some of the lurid, disgusting, filthy animal practices he'd heard about over the years. In fact, only last week he'd been obliged to order some magazines (to be delivered in plain brown wrappers) so he could study the photographs and be more understanding of his flock's depravities. His old magazines were falling apart from all the studying he'd done.

Mrs. Jim Bob sat down on a pew and took out a tissue to wipe her forehead. "Brother Verber, you know I would never permit Jim Bob to even hint at anything unnatural or contrary to my Christian upbringing. When I agree to fulfill my marital obligations, we do it precisely like the Good Book says we should, and we don't dillydally about it, either. I wouldn't consider some unspeakable atheistic variation."

"Of course you wouldn't," Brother Verber said, swallowing his disappointment. He plopped down next to her and patted her knee with a pudgy hand. "Now, you take all the time you need to mull over this problem, then just let it come right out. I'll sit here quietly and wait." He patted her knee some more in order to encourage her to mull.

"I have had a disagreement with my husband, long distance since he's still at that municipal league meeting all the way down in Hot Springs. I told him about something I intend to do. He ordered me not to do it. I told him that it was the morally correct thing to do. He raised his voice, Brother Verber. He went so far as to yell at me over the telephone. All the operators in Hot Springs probably heard him." She took a swipe at her eyes with the tissue, then tucked it in her cuff.

"What is this thing you intend to do?" Brother Verber asked. He patted her knee a little bit higher to show his support in case she changed her mind and wanted to talk about a delicate sexual matter. "I know in my heart that anything you want to do will sit right pretty in the eyes of the Lord. Surely your husband knows that, too. But you're going have to tell me all about it, so's I can make an informed counsel of the matter."

"That is not the point," she said as she inched down the pew. "The point is that I intend to disobey my husband for the first time in thirty years of marriage. I took a solemn vow to love, honor, and obey him. The very thought of disobeying him rips my soul, Brother Verber. Rips it like it was wet tissue paper."

Brother Verber did some inching so he could pat her knee to show his soul was ripping as fast and furious as hers. "I see you have a very complicated problem. You did the right thing to bring it to me. But I still don't know what you're talking about, so you'd better just spit it out, Sister Barbara."

Sister Barbara inched for a few seconds, then said, "I am going to take some poor, starving, motherless orphans into my home. I am going to feed them, bathe them, and instill Christian morals and values in them. I am going to see they receive an education so they can make something of themselves in the future. And I'm going to wash their mouths out with soap until they learn to speak in a civilized fashion!"

"I think that sounds beautiful, Sister Barbara. More than beautiful. I think that sounds downright saintly." He inched down the pew so he could pat her saintly knee. "Why would Jim Bob object to something so charitable?"

"I am speaking of Robin Buchanon's bastards."

Brother Verber's hand halted in mid-pat. His florid face turned even redder, and the pores seemed to widen on his nose until they resembled lunar craters. "Say what?"

"Robin Buchanon's children. It seems the disgusting slut has disappeared in a totally irresponsible way. They have been alone in that primitive shack for the best part of a week, with no food or moral guidance. I almost cry every time I think of those poor, abandoned, dirty, starving bastards."

Brother Verber tugged on his lower lip as he tried to digest her proposal for sainthood. He'd seen those nasty little brats in the past, and they were by far the nastiest little brats he'd ever had the misfortune to see. The lot of them should have been drowned at birth. "I'm beginning to understand," he said cautiously. "Jim Bob doesn't want to open his home, his hearth, and his heart to the little waifs?"

"He started swearing before I even finished my explanation," Mrs. Jim Bob said with a sniffle of outrage. "His remarks were uncalled for and rude. I was quick to tell him so, but he kept right on with his curse words."

"He swore at you?" Brother Verber said incredulously. He started patting her knee again to express his dismay. "What precisely did he say?"

"Nothing a good Christian woman can repeat, especially in the House of the Lord. Brother Verber, if you don't mind, I'm afraid I'm going to have bruises all over my upper legs if you don't stop patting me."

"My deepest apologies, Sister Barbara. I was carried away with my heartfelt response to your story of verbal abuse and outrage. I was doing a terrible thing. I cannot believe I was doing such a terrible thing. Why, if you were to come by the church tomorrow and lift your skirt to show me horrid black-and-blue marks all up your thigh, I'd be so ashamed I couldn't live with myself." With a look of anguish (or something like that), he moved away from her and hung his head to stare over his girth at the floor. Which was dusty, he noticed.

"I would never do anything to cause you that kind of grief," she said solemnly.

"No, it's clear I deserve to be confronted by my venereal sin of overenthusing. I feel mighty badly about this, Sister Barbara, mighty badly. I fear I've taken a step in the direction of eternal damnation by causing you the tiniest bit of pain, just when you were inspired to do something selfless along the lines of an African missionary converting savages to the Lord. Do I hear Satan putting a check by my name in his ledger of sinners? Are the angels wringing their hands at my unforgivable actions? Are the sweet baby cherubims crying out their sweet little eyes?"

"My leg is fine," Mrs. Jim Bob said, sorry she'd ever brought it up to begin with. "I just mentioned the possibility of bruises, that's all. Why, I'd be offended if anyone suggested your tender hand could cause me pain and suffering."

"Is it too late to pray for salvation?" he said in a hollow voice.

Mrs. Jim Bob glanced at her watch. "Well, actually it is. I've got to run along now, Brother Verber. I'm afraid Arly's already fetched those poor little bastards and will be looking for me." She stood up and gazed down at his bent head. "Why don't you come by the house this evening, Brother Verber? I'll have a nice, fresh pecan pie and a cup of coffee for you. You can be thinking about how I can get around this 'love, honor, and obey' problem."

He gave her a watery smile. "Will you allow me to ease my mind about those bruises I may have inflicted on your knee?"

Mrs. Jim Bob nodded, then hurried down the aisle and out the door before he suggested a "before" and "after" view of the knee in question. Which he seemed to think went all the way to the bottom hem of her girdle. She drove down the highway, turning her head the opposite way as she passed the Emporium since it was owned by a bunch of drug-using, naked devil worshippers, and slowing down as she came to the PD.

Arly's car was gone, which meant she wasn't back with the bastards. At the Kwik-Stoppe-Shoppe, Mrs. Jim Bob parked and went inside to buy several bars of good, old-fashioned lye soap. After a moment of consideration, she told the pimply clerk to put the entire case in the back of her car. She then drove home, went to her bedroom, sat primly on the edge of her twin bed, and unclipped her nylons in order to inspect the damage.

"Well, it wasn't worth fifteen dollars," Estelle concluded tartly. "I'd estimate more like fifteen cents."

Ruby Bee moved the popcorn bowl down the counter to a more convenient location. "So all she did was tell you to keep wearing aquamarine? Except for your beautician's uniform, that's all you wear these days—and no man with a funny accent has stopped you on the street or offered to fly you across the ocean on a jet airplane to Paris, France."

"I don't know what got into Madam Celeste," Estelle said, shaking her head. She tossed a piece of popcorn into her mouth and sucked off the salt. "She kept looking out the window, and she didn't hear half of what I said to her. It got right tedious having to repeat myself over and over, like my tongue was the needle on a scratchy record. In the middle of a description of the man with the accent—she thinks he has a mustache, by the way—but in the middle of this, Mason came in and asked—"

"What kind of mustache? A big handlebar, or one

of those pathetic little things that look like they're drawn with an eyebrow pencil?"

Estelle frowned over the bar. "I'll thank you not to interrupt me, Ruby Bee Hanks. I don't happen to know what kind of mustache, because Mason came in and asked Madam Celeste how she felt. She said she was feeling better, but then she upped and told me she had a headache and that the session was over. Just like that. It was all I could do not to say something, if you know what I mean."

"Not one hint of what kind of mustache?"

"Not one hint; I already told you that. I felt as if I'd been swept out the door like a ball of cat hair. What's more, she had plenty of time for Carol Alice Plummer. I chanced to meet her while I was walking down the road, and she—"

"Who'd you meet?"

"Don't mess with me, Ruby Bee. You can see with your own eyes that I am upset. If you're going to interrupt every single sentence that comes out of my mouth, I'll just go home and talk to the mirror. At least I won't be interrupted all the time."

"I didn't hear to whom you were referring," Ruby Bee said indignantly. "I can't follow your story if I don't know who we're talking about."

"Carol Alice Plummer, if you must know, Mrs. Hard-of-Hearing. You know her—her pa works at the body shop in Starley City, and she's a right cute girl with medium-light ash-blond hair. I seem to recollect she's a cheerleader and keeping company with the Swiggins boy what's on the football team."

Ruby Bee slid the popcorn bowl back within reach, having surreptitiously moved it while she was being yelled at most unfairly. "So Carol Alice came out of Madam Celeste's house just before you got there? Did she have anything to say?"

"I will tell you if you give me half a chance. She was bouncing down the road like her heels were rubber, with a kind of dreamy look on her face. I said good morning in a neighborly voice, intending to ask her if she might want to lighten a few dark streaks in her hair, but she went right past me. You'd of thought I was a ghost!"

"Well, I never," Ruby Bee gasped. "Isn't it a shame the way the young folks are reared these days? You'd think they learned their manners at the hog lot in Hasty."

"Or at Raz Buchanon's knee."

"Or from a carnival huckster with tattoos."

"Or from Robin Buchanon," Estelle contributed, enjoying the exchange. "Or from a traveling vacuum cleaner salesman. Or from a—"

Ruby Bee stuck up a finger. "Did I tell you what happened earlier today? It was most puzzling." When Estelle shook her head, Ruby Bee related the confrontation with the puny, vile-mouthed Buchanon child.

"I can't believe he talks like that," Estelle said, tossing off her beer with a snort.

"But the strangest thing is why he was with Arly. She never did say anything about why he was in her custody or what crime he had committed. If you'd heard him, you'd probably guess murder or armed robbery." Ruby Bee took a handful of popcorn and pensively chewed it. "It's outright mysterious, if you ask me. Why on earth would anybody want anything to do with Robin Buchanon's bastards? They're such dirty, nasty things that the social worker crossed them off her clipboard and never mentioned them again. The school wouldn't take them, as sure as I'm standing here. I thank my lucky stars I don't ever have to see any of them again. But I sure would like to know why Arly had that savage with her."

"Why don't you ask her when you see her?"

Ruby Bee had to agree that was likely to be the

best plan. She even wondered why she hadn't thought of it first.

The patches of sunlight twitched and flickered as the breeze rippled the oak leaves. Although it was October, the heat had swelled all afternoon and was hot enough to raise a sweat, had anybody been hiking on the north side of the ridge. Nobody was. It was calm and quiet, just the way it's shown in a primary-level picture book. If you listened real hard, you might be able to hear a train way down at the bottom of the hollow. Once the leaves were gone, you might even have a fair chance of seeing a flash of silver or the dull red of the caboose rumbling loyally on the tail end of the train. But except for a hoe and knife, and a rotting gunnysack beside them, there was nothing to prove civilization was right down at the bottom of the mountainside.

You wouldn't have to listen too hard to hear the flies buzzing, though. The big old blue-green ones were the loudest as they danced on the clotted nostrils and crawled on the dried-out lips of the body still lying there, undisturbed by anything except that drawn by instinct to decomposing flesh.

The two eyes could have been glass for all they saw. The mouth, opened in a moment of surprise, was shaped for all eternity to offer the first syllable of a common curse word. The rest of the body had been gnawed by predators, but not so fiercely that you couldn't recognize the various parts of it. One foot lay twisted under a thin wire stretched between two almost invisible metal stakes. There were other wires around the half acre that should have been thick with ginseng but wasn't, and those wires were attached to funny-looking contraptions whose purposes were not at all funny.

"Why, here's Arly now," Ruby Bee chirped. "Were your ears burning a while back? Estelle and I were discussing a minor puzzlement, and we decided you were the one to clear it up for us."

I came across the ten-by-ten dance floor and leaned over the bar to put my hand on my mother's shoulder. "You know, Ruby Bee, you're the most compassionate woman in Maggody. You're probably the most compassionate woman in all of Stump County, for that matter."

"I am?" she said, easing from under my hand.

"Yes, indeed. That's why I thought of you when I needed help. I knew I could count on Ruby Bee Hanks to do the decent, charitable thing." None of this was easy, but it was the best I could come up with. I licked my lips and plunged back in. "You've always taught me to care about less fortunate folks, and you've been an inspiration to me all my life."

"I have?" She retreated down the bar to get the beer tap between us.

"Cross my heart." I drew an "X" on my chest and tried to look just a shade misty at all those warm memories I didn't have.

Ruby Bee (now the Sister Teresa of the bar-and-grill industry) studied me for a full minute. "You didn't just drop in to spew out the compliments. What do you want from me, Ariel Hanks?"

(A small digression. If you don't know by now, I was not named after the etheral character in *The Tempest*. I was named after a photograph taken from an airplane. Ruby Bee loved the sound of it, and she never was one to win blue ribbons at the district-wide spelling bee. As a whole, the Hanks clan has always gone in for exotic-sounding names. The fact that there was a German measles epidemic about the time Ruby Bee was born is not mentioned in her presence. Work on it.)

"Do you remember that little kid I brought in earlier? He was starving, and your good cooking saved him from death," I continued.

"That awful creature with the filthiest mouth

I've heard in all my born days? Is that the one you're referring to, Miss Smarty Pants?"

I hung my head. "I am sorry you had to hear some of those words. He's had a tragic upbringing, little Hammet, and he just doesn't know what to say in the presence of a fine, moral, kind, generous woman like you. He was so ashamed of himself that he cried all the way home."

"I can imagine," Ruby Bee said, her arms crossed and her voice chilly. She was all the way down to the cash register by now. "So why are you telling me all this and buttering me up like I was a hot biscuit from the oven?"

I told her how Robin had disappeared and the children had been without food for more than three days. I added very firmly that I intended to deliver them to Mrs. Jim Bob as soon as they were fed—and that I'd promised them the best home cookin' in the county in order to lure them off the mountain. I tossed in a quick aside that Mrs. Jim Bob's cookin' was hardly comparable to certain other folks' efforts. I concluded with a vividly drawn picture of malnourished children outside in the jeep, almost too weak from hunger to walk through the door of the most outstanding grill in all of Arkansas. I did not mention that said victims were probably ripping up the seats of the jeep, if not ripping off the radio for a transaction at the pool hall.

She didn't look especially pleased, but she grudgingly said they could come in for a plate lunch special—if they minded their manners and washed up first. I went back outside and gathered up my little herd of heathens, not bothering to warn them to watch their language. It would have been as successful as throwing rocks at the moon.

Hammet, however, had most likely related his previous encounter with the proprietor, because no one said a word as they followed me to the bar and sat down on stools. Sissie was carrying the baby, but she put the bundle on the floor before she took a seat. The bundle didn't stir.

I picked up the baby and drew back a corner of the quilt to gaze at a gray, translucent face and two closed eyes. "What's the baby's name?"

Sissie flashed some mossy teeth at me. "We jest calls him Baby. Do you reckon we can get some milk or something for him?"

Ruby Bee came out of the kitchen, armed with a dish towel just in case a savage leaped across the bar. "What do they want to eat?" she asked me.

"Whatever's convenient," I said before Hammet could offer an editorial. "Lots of it, please. Piles of it. Mountains of it. These kids haven't eaten in a long time."

She barked an order to Dahlia in the kitchen, then came around the bar to get a closer look at the baby. "That baby looks mighty unhealthy, Arly. What do you aim to do with it?"

"I don't know; I've never had any experience with this size infant. I suppose I ought to try to get some milk in him. You don't have a baby bottle in the back room, do you?"

"Why, this poor little thing needs a warm bath, clean clothes, and formula. You stay here and help Dahlia serve the plates. I'll have Estelle stop by the Kwik-Screw for a bottle and some formula, or at least condensed milk. I'm taking this baby over to my unit."

I handed over the baby, wondering if Bubba or Sissie might object to their brother being carried away by a stranger. Hammet raised an eyebrow, but none of the others so much as turned around as Ruby Bee went out the door. They were, I think, a bit bewildered by the appearance of Dahlia O'Neill. All three hundred pounds plus of her.

Dahlia was taken aback herself, but managed to dish up the plate lunch special and serve Bubba, Sissie, Sukie, and Hammet—who tore right into it as if he hadn't eaten in a week. There were some grunts and snorts, not to mention a good deal of smacking and slobbering, throughout the meal, but no one said a word, obscene or otherwise. Dahlia stared at them, coming out of her reverie every once in a while to dish out another mound of black-eyed peas or mashed potatoes.

I took the opportunity to go over to the pay phone and call Mrs. Jim Bob to tell her the success of my mission, depending on how you gauge success in this situation. "I've got them," I said brightly when she answered.

"You do? Well, it's a relief to know that the little bastards are safe now."

She didn't sound all that enthusiastic, but I didn't allow that to faze me. "Yep, I've got four of them over at Ruby Bee's right this minute. They're almost finished eating, so we should arrive at your house within thirty minutes."

"Have they—ah, have they bathed?"

I glanced across the room at grimy necks, hair snarled with twigs and dried leaves, clothing that the ragman would have turned up his nose at, brown feet, and eight hands glistening with grease. "They look right smart, Mrs. Jim Bob. We'll see you in a few minutes."

I hung up the receiver, then went out the door and around back to see how Ruby Bee was doing with the baby. Estelle drove up as I reached the covered walkway, and she grabbed a plastic sack before joining me.

"What is the emergency?" she panted. "Why in heaven's name does Ruby Bee want condensed milk and a baby bottle? I left Edwina Spitz in the chair, setting lotion dribbling down her neck, to dash over here."

I began to explain, but she scuttled around me and went into Ruby Bee's unit, no doubt inspired to hurry by Edwina Spitz's impending fury. By the time I caught up with her, she was sitting beside Ruby Bee on the couch, and the two of them were cooing and making silly faces at a bundle wrapped in a clean blanket.

"Isn't he the sweetest little thing?" Ruby Bee said with a saccharine smile. "I could just gobble up those darling little toes like they were jelly beans. What's his name, Arly?"

"I don't know. The Buchanon children refer to him as Baby."

"Why, that's disgraceful!" Estelle said, bending over to touch a waving hand.

"Can't help it," I said. I waited while they fussed around and eventually got enough warm condensed milk into the baby to satisfy some maternal thermometer that was beyond me. I then mentioned that I was taking the infant to Mrs. Jim Bob's. I was informed that I was not.

If you think I argued the point with those two, you overestimate me. I went back to the bar and gathered up the kids, with a short explanation that the baby would stay with my mother for a few days. Bubba shrugged and belched. Sissie nodded and belched. Sukie stuck a finger in her mouth and belched. Hammet opted for a no-frills belch.

On that pleasant note, I herded everyone out to the jeep and drove out Finger Lane to the Buchanon driveway, which had red-brick pillars on either side and a wrought-iron grill spanning them like a rusty banner. A number stuck on one pillar proclaimed their residence as "Number Four." I was impressed, since I hadn't known we had house numbers in Maggody.

The house was an imposing red-brick box, with a white colonnade and other pretentious stuff. A circular drive, and a discreet sign indicating deliveries were to be made in the rear. Barbered shrubs. Flower beds lined with red bricks. One was supposed to presume it was an antebellum plantation house. If I hadn't known that it was built ten years back, when Jim Bob bought the land for a pittance from an elderly widow with failing eyesight and no family, I might have fallen for it. Ha, ha.

The Buchanon children were making all sorts of noises as they stared at what was by far the fanciest house they'd ever seen. They all gasped when Hammet pointed at the glass in the windows. Sissie said it were higher'n a mountain. Sukie said it were a fuckin' monster house. Bubba, the eldest and therefore most sophisticated, said it weren't neither as big as a mountain, and iffen she said it was he would whup her ass.

I saw a curtain twitch, so I knew Mrs. Jim Bob hadn't fled the county. I turned around to Bubba and said, "I have to decide what to do about your mother. Hammet says she's been gone for nearly a week, and that she said she was going to hunt ginseng. Right?"

"Reckon it's close enough."

"She don't normally stay gone when it's dark," Sissie contributed. "She allus comes back before—" She broke off as Bubba glowered at her hard enough to produce spontaneous combustion.

"Thank you," I said hastily. "Now, no one knows where her secret patch is, which means I can't drive up there to see if she's still there. Do any of you have any idea why she might have gone off like this?"

"Bet a bear et her," Hammet said helpfully. "Probably kilt him."

Sukie's eyes filled with tears. "My mama ain't dead, motherfucker."

"I'm sure she's fine," I said. "Now, this is where you all are going to stay until I find your mother. The woman who lives here is very nice, and she wants you to have food and clean beds. She may seem a bit testy, but she does want to take care of you. Come along and I'll introduce you."

I had to pound on the front door for a long time before it opened to a slit and one eye peered out at me. "I thought they had bathed," hissed a disembodied voice.

"Did I imply that? Sorry, Mrs. Jim Bob, but I knew you'd want to supervise that yourself, since your standards are so much higher than mine." I gave the children a smile and patted Hammet on the head. "Okay, guys, here you are. I'll let you know the instant I find your mother. See you in a day or two, okay?"

Nobody looked real happy, but nobody bolted. They were still standing between the Grecian columns as I drove away, but the door had opened another inch or two, and I presumed Mizzoner wouldn't dare leave them on the porch for forty-eight hours. Why, that would get her kicked out of the Ladies' Missionary Society quicker than the congregation could shout "amen" at the end of one of Brother Verber's knee-busting prayers.

6

The *Ommms* drifted over the fence in the late-afternoon light. Kevin Buchanon, agonized by indecision (not to mention tortured by temptation), leaned against the sweet gum tree and told himself not to do it. "Don't do it," he said aloud, hoping it would help. "Kevin, you know you don't want to get your ass whipped. You know better. Don't do it."

He squinched his eyes closed real tight and tried to concentrate on a vision of his true love, with her warm, soft, monstrous-big bosoms that liked to suffocated him on more than one occasion, and her marshmallowy expanse of rippling body flesh, and her always sincere invitation for him to crawl up that heavenly path between her legs and do anything he wanted. Not to forget her kindly words of instruction and willingness to learn him all kinds of wondrous things.

It didn't help. He shinnied up the tree to the first branch, then wiggled around until he was standing up. He still couldn't see what was going on next door. Scrabbling and grunting, he climbed up several more branches, and took a minute to catch his breath before he turned around to see what he could see.

"Oh, lordy, lordy, lordy," he said in a low whoosh, as his stomach flopped over like a catfish in the bottom of a johnboat. They were naked as the day they was born, all four of them. The men were hairy and uninteresting. But the women—well, that was different, at least in Kevin Buchanon's wide, unblinking eyes. The one with a bun in the warmer was a smidgen rounder, as to be expected. The other one, that being the one with the ripe round perky bosoms, each just a handful, and that flat belly that went all the way down to that dark, fuzzy—

"Kevin Fitzgerald Buchanon! You git down from there right this minute! You pa's going be home any time now, and you know what he said he'd do if he caught you up in this tree again!"

He made it to the ground with only a few scratches and a rip in the seat of his jeans. "Gee, Ma," he said, his Adam's apple rippling furiously, "I was just making sure they weren't doing nothing illegal that I ought to report to the chief."

"What's Arly got to do with you being a low-down peeping Tom?"

"She told me to keep an eye on them. Since she doesn't have a deputy anymore, she asked me to do my civic duty and help her." He was real proud of the inspired reference to civic duty, his ma being big on patriotism and a one-time secretary of the county DAR. The rest of it had been planned over several hours of commode scrubbing. Ad-libbing was not his forte.

"Arly Hanks has a sight more sense than that, young man. I've known her since the day she was born, and I've never seen any signs she's mentally retarded. Which is more than I can say about some folks, present company included. You'd better go in the house and pray for forgiveness of both your sins: lusting at naked ladies and lying to your own mother."

"She did so, Ma. It's supposed to be a secret, though, and I'm not supposed to say nothing about it to anyone, including my own flesh and blood. I swore on the Bible and everything. She says those hippies are breaking the law, and all we need is evidence so we can lock 'em up tighter than ticks on a hound dog's tail."

"Commence your prayers," Eilene Buchanon said, unmoved by the importance of his secret assignment to rid the local environs of dastardly crime. "If you pray real hard, mebbe I won't have to tell your pa that I caught you up in the sweet gum again. His belt's hanging by the back door where it's right handy. He'll be home shortly." She went back to the kitchen to stir the corn bread batter. Kevin trailed after her, explaining her civic duty not to tell anybody, including Pa and especially Pa, about the secret assignment.

Across the fence, the chanting stopped. Poppy lay back on the blanket and massaged her belly. "It's kicking. Does anyone want to feel it?"

"Of course we do," Rainbow said, nudging Zachery. "We all love you and we all love our baby. Isn't that right?"

Zachery obediently crawled across the blanket and put his hand next to Poppy's. "Like, wow. I feel it. Do you think it's all excited by the meditation vibes?"

Rainbow smiled as she joined him next to Poppy's supine body. "That's an intriguing thought, Zachery. I don't know why the baby wouldn't sense the cosmic harmony and want to move with it. What do you think, Nate?"

He lit a cigarette. "Probably taking a crap. Listen, I need the truck in the morning. Got to talk to a man in Farberville about some personal business. I'll drop you off at the store on my way out of town. I should be back by the middle of the afternoon."

"That's impossible," Rainbow said gently. "Poppy has an appointment with the midwife just before noon. I'm going to drive her over and wait."

"Change it. I need the truck. I'll bet you enjoy hassling me all the time, don't you? Gives you a real kick."

Rainbow's smile trembled as she struggled for sympathy, cooperation, and lovingness. "But Nate, the midwife is an old granny woman who lives in a shack on the county road. She doesn't have a telephone, so we can't call to change the appointment. But let's vote on it, shall we? That way we'll follow the communal spirit and strengthen our harmony. Who feels Poppy's need is greater than Nate's?"

Nate threw down his cigarette and stalked into the house. A few minutes later the truck's engine rumbled to life. A cloud of dust blew over the fence, eventually settling like cocoa powder on the three naked occupants of the backyard meditation garden.

"Like, wow," Zachery said, using his finger to draw a happy face on Poppy's belly. Kevin would have loved it.

I had a pleasant evening and a reasonable night's sleep, although I had to remind myself a couple of times that the Buchanon brood was in good hands. Granted they were pious, self-righteous hands, but at least not gnarled and hirsute talons. Mizzoner, the mayor's wife, had good intentions. The Buchanons were tough enough to deal with her.

The next morning I dawdled at the PD for a couple hours. I was about to get in the jeep when David Allen drove up in his four-wheel wagon. "Aren't you supposed to be counseling the youth of Maggody High?" I asked. "Don't they need scholarship applications for welding schools and the mud-wrestling academy?"

"I've taken a break. Do you have time to do the same and join me for a cup of coffee?"

We went into the PD, and he looked around while I started a pot of coffee. "This isn't exactly Scotland Yard," he said, grinning at me. "You could put two of these in the auto-repair shop at the high school and still have room for a Trans Am with a bent axle."

"Did you run away from school to tell me that?"

"No, I ran away from school for two unrelated yet intensely compelling reasons. One is that a terribly sincere girl named Heather Riley has made her seventy-third appointment with me, and I felt a sudden urge to leave. She cries so much, I wear an inner tube while I listen to her. I have no idea what her problems are, either, beyond muddled references to harelips and imperiled virginity. I'm not sure if she wants to lose or acquire either or both."

I handed him a cup of coffee and sat down behind my desk. "And the second compelling reason?"

"You were right about the psychic, and I wanted to drink a toast to your keen grasp of the sociological interactions of the town." He took a sip of coffee and made a face. "At a later time and with champagne. Your waterbed or mine?"

I let it go over my head, which wasn't hard since I was sitting down and he was standing up. The Macaroni law of physics. "So the psychic is no longer upsetting the fragile psyches of the senior class?"

"Carol Alice Plummer is not going to commit suicide. She is sporting an eighteenth-of-a-carat diamond ring, and checking out bridal magazines from the school library. As far as I know, she's not even pregnant; it may be the first wedding ceremony in Maggody in which the groomsmen are not armed. Her fiancé, one Bo Swiggins, who has no neck but does have a sly sense of humor, has sworn to win the homecoming game in her honor. For the gripper, as he is reputed to have said in the locker room."

"Then I can see your professional life is under control, David Allen. I wish I could say the same about mine, but I never lie before noon. In fact, I'd better get back to business."

"Issuing tickets at the stoplight?"

"No," I sighed. I told him about the disappearance of Robin Buchanon and the subsequent problem, collectively known as Bubba, Sissie, Hammet, Sukie, and Baby. "I'm going to drive back up to the cabin and see if she, like a distaff General MacArthur, has returned. I'm not taking any bets on it, though. At the same time, it's hard to envision her deciding to head off across the mountains to points unknown. Her sideline's portable, but her major occupation isn't."

"Turning tricks and making moonshine," he said, nodding. "I'd been in town less than twenty minutes when one of the good ole boys in the subdivision dropped by with a mason jar of the vilest field whiskey I'd ever tasted. Not to say we didn't drink it, of course, but it left scars all the way down my throat. As for her sideline, the ole boy got all choked up when he tried to describe her talents in that arena. Only a couple of the boys have had the nerve to actually go through with it. One of them has never been seen again."

"I see you have no compunctions regarding prelunch fabrications. Actually, I'm worried about her. I'll hunt around for her still, but I doubt I can find it any more than I'll stumble across her family ginseng patch. And why would she be lurking for almost a week at either of those places, anyway?" I leaned back in the chair and propped my feet on my desk. "I can't come up with any theories to explain her disappearance. I wouldn't dream of trying to delve into her possible motives to pull this stunt; she's unlike anything I've ever met. All I know is that she left the cabin with a hoe and a gunnysack, and the children expected her back before dark. Nearly a week ago. She's a mountain woman, not the sort to twist an ankle or grab the wrong end of a copperhead. She probably fries up a mess of copperhead for Sunday brunch."

"I have an idea," David Allen said, perching on

the corner of my desk and giving me an impish grin. "Why don't you consult Madam Celeste?"

"That's the stupidest thing I've heard all morning," I replied with an impish grin of my own.

Mrs. Jim Bob perched on the corner of her bed so as not to wrinkle the bedspread. She'd been there most of the night. Her best linen skirt was crumpled so badly, it looked as if an army tank had run across her lap. One of her nylons had come unclipped and hung around her ankle like dead skin. Her hair was uncombed. Her best blouse was splattered with something; she couldn't remember what. Her own blood, maybe, unless it was ketchup or mud or something even worse. She didn't care what it was.

The bedroom door was locked. She was pretty sure it was, but she continued to get up every fifteen minutes or so just to check. It came to about fifty times she'd checked thus far, but she didn't care. There was water in the master bathroom, and a grayish candy bar in Jim Bob's night-table drawer. It wasn't like she was going to die. On the contrary, she could barricade herself in the room for a long time, and those despicable creatures couldn't get their filthy hands on her no matter how hard they tried.

Downstairs, somewhere, she couldn't tell exactly, came the sound of shattering glass. For a while she'd tried to envision what each explosion was—the pseudo-Ming vase on the dining-room table, a window, the screen on the television. She hadn't thought to keep a list, and by now she couldn't recollect what all might still be intact. Not much, though.

She went over to the window and stared down at the driveway. Brother Verber hadn't come by for a piece of pie, but it was just as well, since the bastards had chanced upon the pie within a few minutes of storming the house. That was when she was still clinging to the premise that she was in control. Oh, she'd tried to be nice about it and not scold the little one too sharply about the smudge on the new beige carpet. A slap on the hand had stopped the whining. And, she'd told herself at the time, it was important to establish that they were there only out of the goodness of her heart, for which they should be deeply and eternally grateful.

It hadn't turned into a nightmare until she'd announced that the stink was unbearable and that it was bathtime, no ifs or buts. She'd ordered the oldest, a surly thing who was way too big for his filthy britches, into the mud room off the garage. Of course, by the time she'd hustled him there, the others had scuttled into hiding like cockroaches caught in the light. And every time she found one and started dragging it toward the bathroom, another one would leap on her back and claw at her and screech unspeakably vile things at her, as if she weren't engaged in doing her Christian duty to get them one inch closer to godliness.

Which got her back to Brother Verber and his no-show. He was the one who'd counseled her to bring the bastards into her home—or what was left of it. He'd been full of praise for her self-sacrificing, saintly, charitable generosity. Why, if he'd said not to do it, she might well have heeded his advice. But he'd been right enthusiastic. He didn't seem to think it was a sin to disobey her husband, even though she'd said "love, honor, and obey" in a clear, steady voice and had certainly meant every syllable of it at the time.

Which got her back to Jim Bob.

She retreated to the bed and sank down on the edge so as not to wrinkle the bedspread. At last she took the telephone book and looked up a number. She didn't much want to admit things weren't going real well, but she didn't see what else she could do—if she wanted to be the mayor's wife and live in a fine house on top of the hill, complete with professional landscaping and new beige carpet. Her finger was trembling so hard, it took her a long time to fit it in the little circles, but she did.

"That is the second stupidest thing I've heard all day," I said. "The only reason it's not the stupidest is that I've already heard it."

"But it makes perfickly good sense," Ruby Bee said. She plopped a spoonful of yellow goop into Baby's mouth, then wiped the little chin with a dishrag. "Madam Celeste has the ability to help you find Robin Buchanon, and you're downright mulish not to ask her to assist in the investigation. I told you how she advised Gladys Buchanon to look in her top dresser drawer for her glasses, and there they were. Now, you can't close your eyes to the significance of something like that."

"Watch me." I closed my eyes until it got boring. When I opened them, I saw Ruby Bee bent down in front of the high chair, shoveling in more goop. "It's out of the question, and I don't want to discuss it further. Madam Celeste is a quack, as in duck."

"She is not," Estelle said in a scandalized voice. She was sitting at the bar, smiling approval at each successful spoon of goop. "Wipe his chin, Ruby Bee; he's liable to chap. Now, Arly, I don't know where you get off saying that sort of thing. Did you hear the story behind Madam Celeste's move to Maggody?"

"Something about a lost boy," I said. "Right out of a book about flying children, pirates, and fairies. I just came by to check on Baby and let you know where I'll be for the next six hours of my life. I did not come by to argue about something that is out of the question."

Estelle held out her hand to inspect her scarlet fingernails. "Well," she said airily, "isn't it timely that you'll have the opportunity to tell Madam Celeste yourself."

"No, I won't. I'm going up to Cotter's Ridge to see how many chiggers and ticks I can find. I'm going to come back to my apartment and take a long, hot bath and read a trashy thriller until my toes shrivel up. If I see fit, I may go hog wild and open a can of chicken noodle soup." I did not add that I would then go over to David Allen's house for a rematch and a bottle of champagne. Nobody's business.

"Tomorrow," Estelle continued in the same complacent voice. "That's when I told Mason to tell her that you were coming. At eleven o'clock, and try not to be late this time, Arly. You can see that it upsets Madam Celeste."

"No."

"Estelle as good as made an appointment," Ruby Bee said.

"Estelle can cancel it," I said, starting for the door.

"Madam Celeste has a very busy schedule, and I don't aim to do anything to upset her," Estelle said.

I stopped and turned back with my firmest expression (my ex-husband used to refer to it as "the Ice Queen Clone"). "This has nothing to do with me. I am not going to allow Madam Celeste to muddle up this investigation. I am not going to allow you two to muddle it up, either. You may make and break appointments to your hearts' desires, but I do not even want to hear about it. Am I making myself clear?"

"Like Boone Creek," Ruby Bee sniffed.

"In April," Estelle snorted.

I turned my back on the pair and stomped out the door. It would have played better if my beeper hadn't started chirping before I made it to the jeep. In that it was the first time it had done anything except disrupt my lines, it took me a few seconds to punch the button that indicated I'd received the message. And of course the radio in the jeep was dead, owing to someone's inquisitive, dirty little fingers.

I went back inside the bar and over to the telephone, ignoring all the raised eyebrows and smirky smiles aimed in my direction. I called the dispatcher and asked for the message, which turned out to be Mrs. Jim Bob Buchanon, an emergency, call as soon as possible.

"What kind of emergency?" I asked the dispatcher.

"I don't know, Arly. She sound pretty weird, though, like a character in one of those zombie movies. The last time I had a call like that was from an eighty-four-year-old woman who'd just put two loads of buckshot in her husband's face. Seems he'd been fooling around with some girl at the community college. Night school, naturally. She pled temporary insanity 'cause of unbridled passion, and the jury hooted so hard the judge threw it out of court. It was about a month after Hiram's barn burned."

I thanked the dispatcher for the bit of trivia (although I doubted it would come up in the edition David Allen and I played) and replaced the receiver. I knew darn well what Mrs. Jim Bob's emergency was, but I didn't know how to handle it so that it wouldn't result in a jeepful of Buchanon bush colts.

"Isn't he the sweetest thing?" Ruby Bee cooed.

"He's such a darling," Estelle simpered. "It's just awful that no one seems to have taken the time to give this cutie pie a name. Now, look at that tiny nose. Isn't that the tiniest little nose you ever laid eyes on?"

I took my thirty-five-year-old nose out the door, telling myself I'd deal with the emergency at Hizzoner's house when I got back to town. The justification for the cowardice was the premise that

I'd find Robin at the cabin, sick with worry about her children and frantic to dash back with me so she could clutch them to her bosom. It put a strain on my powers of imagination, but I clenched my teeth and gave it my best as I drove toward Cotter's Ridge. At fifteen miles over the speed limit. I wasn't going to issue a citation to myself, after all.

Mrs. Jim Bob glared at the telephone, but it still wouldn't ring. Somewhere below there was a thud that shook the house, followed by a screech and some howls. Mrs. Jim Bob kept her eyes on the telephone, willing it to ring. Making all kinds of promises to the Lord if He'd make it ring. Making promises in Jim Bob's name if He'd make it ring, and telling herself she would take it upon herself, Barbara Ann Buchanon Buchanon (they were second cousins once removed), to see he carried out every last one of them. The telephone remained silent.

When she'd called earlier, she was promised that the message would be beeped to Chief Hanks pronto. She'd told Jim Bob that the purchase of the beeper was a waste of municipal funds, but he'd snickered and said he'd have preferred a choke collar, but couldn't convince the other councilmen to agree. Well, it was obvious who was right and who was wrong. The beeper was a waste of money—since it didn't work.

Thinking of that brought her back to Jim Bob, for the umpteenth time. He was going to be furious, both at the fact that she'd defied him and at the destruction of the house. He could be meaner than a pit bull terrier with mange. She certainly couldn't call him all the way down in Hot Springs to get his advice about the horrid frenzy going on downstairs. Arly didn't seem inclined to return her call. Besides, she told herself with the slightest hint of a wicked smile (because she was not a wicked woman;

everybody knew that), the bastards needed a strong moral hand to slap them into a semblance of civilized behavior. And who was the shining beacon of morality and righteousness and decency in Maggody?

Wincing at a particularly loud crash, she dialed the number of the Voice of the Almighty Lord parsonage, which was a mobile home parked out behind the building. The line was busy. Sighing, Mrs. Jim Bob dialed the dispatcher to try again.

The cabin was as vacant as a dead man's eyes. Having expected nothing to the contrary, I forced myself to poke around for clues. What kind of clues did I think I'd find? Nonexistent clues. The cabin was a two-room shack, the front room a general-purpose living room, library, kitchen, sleeping area for the children, and den. A living room because of a couple of hickory chairs with splintery seats; a library because of a family Bible and a few tattered picture books; a kitchen because of a wood stove and a bucket of greenish water; a sleeping area because of the straw pallets. A den because it was fit for animal occupancy.

The back room was Robin's bedroom. The bed was a contraption of sticks lashed together with rope, the mattress stuffed with corncobs. A pile of clothes reeked in one corner, and two complacent mice scratched in the other. Over the bed hung a small square of cross-stitch that said, God Bless Our Happy Home. Robin probably traded a jar of hooch for it.

She wasn't there, though, and the stove was cold. There were a lot of cobwebs, but I had no idea how long they'd been there. Years, maybe. Dirt and grime and grease. Dried leaves on the pinewood floor. A tin plate with some unidentifiable smears of a meal long past. If you noticed I didn't describe the bathroom, it's because it was at the end of a path out back and I wasn't in the mood to open the door for a quick search.

It got to me. I went outside and sat down on the edge of the porch, still amazed and depressed that people could live that way. It was more than thirteen hundred miles to Manhattan—it was more like a million miles. Had my ex, who thought he was dealing with a primitive culture when his martini lacked an olive, been given a tour of the cabin and adjunct, he would have assumed he was hallucinating and dashed off to his analyst to discuss the implications. Had Robin been given a tour of the Manhattan co-op, she would have laughed herself silly at what we felt was vital to a civilized existence.

I reminded myself that Robin Buchanon had chosen her lifestyle. She had enough relatives in the county to throw herself on one of them, to live in the back room or up in the attic. Or down in the root cellar, for that matter. But her children hadn't made the decision to live in incredibly grim poverty, isolated from normal people, deprived of any chance for an education and thus unable to escape from a lifetime of this. Perhaps I'd done them a disservice by bringing them off the ridge, I thought bleakly. Especially Hammet, who seemed to have a quick wit and a curious mind.

"Aw, hell," I said aloud, startling a lonely hen that had wandered around the corner to peck at the packed dirt. She gave me a beady look, then produced a single cluck of disapproval and stalked away.

I decided to see if David Allen might be able to do something for the children, who were legally required to attend the local school, even if said school was not delighted to have them and willing to waive the long-standing truancy. However, for the moment I needed to search the area for Robin's still and the ginseng patch. Both were probably in an eighty-acre section. I reluctantly rose and started into the woods, glad I'd had the sense to wear boots and a heavy jacket.

Mason opened the door cautiously. "How you doing, Celeste?" he asked in a low voice. "Can I fetch something for you—a soda pop or a sandwich?"

She sat in front of a round table. Tarot cards were spread in front of her, each a brightly colored depiction of an ancient symbol. "Come in, Mason," she said without looking up.

"Ah, sure." He entered the solarium and sat down across from her at the dinette table. "Have you figured out whose face you saw when you were with Carol Alice?"

"No. But there are many swords in the cards these days, which tell me there will be trouble. The King of Wands appears every time I deal the cards; he will not go away and he is always reversed. I do not like it." She tapped a card with a picture of a bearded monarch.

"He doesn't look all that nasty," Mason said.

"You see him from your side of the table. To me, he is reversed, which indicates the presence of at best an unreliable man, at worst a sly liar."

Mason laughed, albeit uncomfortably. "Not your baby brother, I hope. I may forget to watch the time once in a while, but I'm a terrible liar. You know how my face turns red and I start to stammer."

She glanced up for a brief second, her expression enigmatic. Returning to the cards, she said, "I am not sure who it represents. He is surrounded by the Nine of Swords and the Moon, which warns me there is trickery and deception in this town. There is much mischief afoot in this little town of Maggody, but I do not know who is behind it or why." She tapped a picture of a skeleton holding a scythe. "And Death is here, grinning at me."

Mason stared at the card, reminding himself he

didn't believe in this crap. "Is someone going to die?" he heard himself say with a gulp.

"It does not always mean that someone will die. There will be changes, however, and not necessarily for the best. And the King of Swords, reversed, speaks to me of violence. I do not like what I see, Mason, but the cards do not lie to me."

He couldn't think of much to say, so he settled for a nod and repeated his offer to fetch her something to eat or drink. He was relieved when she ordered him away with an irritable demand to be left alone. Fine with him, he thought as he went out to his car. He'd go over to Ruby Bee's and see if anybody wanted to discuss pro football over a beer.

As he backed out of the driveway, he spotted the red-haired beautician coming toward the mailbox. He rolled down the car window and said, "Good morning, Miss Oppers. How are you this fine autumn morning?"

"Did you tell Madam Celeste that Arly wanted an appointment tomorrow morning?"

"You have my deepest apologies, because I forgot all about it. Do you want me to run back inside and ask her if that'll be okay?"

She stood there chewing her lipstick for a long while. "No, that's real kind of you, Mason. But I can see you're leaving, so I'll just tap on the door and have a word with Madam Celeste myself. Things are a little more delicate than I'd first thought they'd be."

Mason considered warning her about his sister's present mood, since her moods weren't all that good even when she wasn't upset. He settled for a smile and another comment about the crisp sunshine and glorious foliage of the trees. He then got the hell out of there and went in search of a beer.

My beeper beeped sporadically all afternoon. That was the only thing that happened, except for a minor heart stopper over a six-foot black snake and a slight sensation of paranoia that came from being alone in the middle of nowhere, with only squirrels, birds, gnats, mosquitoes, and a horde of unseen critters for company. I didn't spot any pay phones among the scrub oak, so I didn't call the dispatcher. Maybe I was psychic, since I knew precisely what the message would be.

No still, no ginseng patch. No sign of Robin Buchanon. No sign of anyone else, for that matter. I spent an hour working my way to the top of the ridge in a zigzag. I sat down on a log until the sweat dried, then moved half a mile east and zigzagged back down to the cabin. Robin hadn't come back in my absence. A spider had started a web in the jeep. A bleached sow with an amiable expression ambled out of the brush and went past me without so much as a grunt of acknowledgment. The hen, perched on the porch rail, watched me closely as I eased the spider out with a stick, started the engine (I will admit to a small word of prayer as I turned the key), and drove down the road to town.

As I went past Ruby Bee's, I noticed a silver BMW parked among the pickup trucks, but I was too sore and itchy to waste more than a second wondering why anyone with that sort of income would have such wretched taste in their choice of watering hole. I did feel obligated to stop at the PD, despite the knowledge that Kevin Buchanon might stumble through the door while I was there.

The beeper chirped as I parked out front. I told myself I was going to have to grit my teeth and do the right thing, but I wasn't feeling any tingles of anticipation as I called the dispatcher. Who told me that Mrs. Jim Bob Buchanon had left eleven messages concerning the escalating state of emergency.

I was about to call her when Kevin did indeed stumble through the door. Telling myself I really ought to adopt this psychic stuff and set up shop in some distant city, I managed a civil greeting.

"You look downright awful, Arly. Did something happen to you?"

"I look like someone who spent more than three hours fighting briars and mosquitoes up on Cotter's Ridge. As soon as I make one call, I'm going home to clean up." I picked up the receiver, hoping he'd take the hint.

Subtlety was not his forte. "Was you looking for Robin Buchanon? Dahlia says the dirty slut done run off and left her babies all alone. Dahlia says the littlest baby was near starved to death. Dahlia says you ought to lock Robin up and swallow the key."

"I'll take Dahlia's suggestions into consideration. Now, if you don't mind, I need to make a call."

"Sure thing. Don't pay me no mind, Arly." He sat down and stared at me as though prepared for small green antennas to slither out my ears.

"You can sweep the back room."

"Okay." He didn't move. Well, his Adam's apple bobbled and his eyes blinked and his lips twitched and his fingers plucked at the hem of his plaid shirt. His rear end, on the other hand, might as well have been epoxied to the chair.

"Is there anything else, Kevin?"

"Whatcha going to do about finding Robin? Do you want me to go with you next time to help you search for her? I could ask Dahlia to pack some samwiches and RC colas so we could search all day."

I held back a shudder. "No, but thank you for the offer. I realized this afternoon just how futile it is to think I can find anything in that many square miles of woods. I'm going to take the jeep back to the sheriff in the morning and see if he can send over some deputies to help. If we have to, we can try for a helicopter from the state boys. By noon tomorrow, the whole case will be out of my hands."

I'd decided all that on the drive home—while scratching the innumerable red spots and watching the blood well up in some of the deeper lacerations on my hands.

"But we can find her ourselves," Kevin protested. "I know we can."

"There is no 'we,' Kevin. I am paid to serve as chief of police and you are paid to sweep the floors and empty the wastebaskets. Those are entirely different job descriptions."

"I'll be a deputy for free. You don't have to give me no extra money. It's my civic duty, and—"

"Please sweep the floors," I said with a sigh.

"But I know we can find out where Robin's holed up. Mebbe Dahlia can come with us to help search. If you want, I can call her right now and ask her if she can come along."

"The search is over," I said in a stern voice, trying not to even imagine Dahlia O'Neill trudging through the woods. It was an ecological nightmare. "I am going home. When you finish your chores, you go home and spend a quiet evening in front of the television with your ma and pa."

"But gee, Arly, don't you—"

"Good night, Kevin." I let the door slam for emphasis.

I heard his whines as I cut through the parking lot and waited on the side of the highway while a battered pickup truck ran the light. Then, clutching my coat tightly around my shoulders, I trotted across the street and took sanctuary in my apartment. With the door locked and the telephone off the hook.

7

I took a bath that lasted as long as I'd vowed it would. I put on jeans and a shirt, stuck a few bobby pins in the bun on my neck, took it down and did it again, applied some makeup, and remembered that I hadn't called Mrs. Jim Bob. I was debating whether to call or drive over there when I heard a timid tap on my front door.

Hammet stood on the landing. "Howdy, Arly," he said, giving me a smile meant to disarm me via candor and charm. "I thought to come by and see how you was doin'."

I took him inside and put him on the couch. "That's neighborly of you, but I suspect there's more to it than a sudden urge to pay a social call. Does Mrs. Jim Bob know you're here?"

"Her? Course she does. She done telled me to visit you as long as I wanted to. She said I could stay here all night iffen I wanted to."

"What's going on over there, anyway? Are your brothers and sisters raising hell?"

"My siblings happens to be behavin' like they's supposed to," he said indignantly. "Last night ever'body took baths and had some grub. Today we jest hanged around, mostly a-playin' and things like that. What do you think we'd be liked to do? Skin the hide offen that kindly ole woman or somethin'?"

Something like that, yes. "I've been getting frantic messages all day. It was reasonable to assume she was having problems," I said, looking down at him. He gazed up with a dopey, angelic expression that almost—but not quite—convinced me he wasn't lying through his teeth. Which I suspected he was. "Why don't I call Mrs. Jim Bob and let her know you made it over here safely?" I suggested.

"She done knows that. I ain't going to get et by a bear in town."

"Let's tell her anyway." I headed for the telephone, but before I could dial the number, there was another knock on the door. Pretty soon I had David Allen on the sofa next to Hammet, who was delighted to make the acquaintance of this unexpected (read: timely) visitor.

David Allen grinned at me. "I was going to surprise you with an invitation for an exotic cocktail at a bar in Farberville. Something with seven kinds of liqueurs in a plastic coconut shell with lots of fruit and an umbrella. But I've got a better idea: how about a hot fudge sundae with oodles of hot fudge sauce, whipped cream, nuts, and a maraschino cherry? What do you say to that, Hammet?"

If he expected Hammet to clap his hands in childish glee, he was in for a long wait. Hammet studied him, then said, "What be all those things you says?"

"You've never had a hot fudge sundae?" David Allen said, clearly dismayed. "But that's disgraceful. Criminal. Unforgivable. Come on, you two. I have a paternal obligation to get this child into the presence of seven thousand calories. To the wagon!"

Somehow I got bustled out the door, put inside his wagon, admonished to buckle my seat belt, and swept away into the sunset. I had a quick glance at the PD as David Allen dove around the corner, and something was not right. Before I had a chance to pinpoint it, Hammet Buchanon draped himself over my shoulder from the backseat and demanded to know why anybody'd be fool enough to put hot stuff on ice cream, which was supposed to be cold stuff. And who invented it, anyways? One of those

Eye-talians, he bet. David Allen was clucking like a hen.

"When we get where we're going, I aim to sit right here in the jeep," Dahlia said. "I don't aim to wander around in them woods and get spiders in my hair like I did last time. But you better hurry, 'cause it's getting dark. Arly's going to kill you if we run into a old log and wreck the jeep." She gazed at her beloved, feeling a twinge of sadness on account of his inescapable fate. "She's going to kill you, anyways, for stealing the jeep. It's not even hers."

"I didn't steal the jeep. I borrowed it so we could help in the investigation of the missing woman what got lost in the woods, which is my civic duty. Yours too, honeybun. All we have to do is find Robin Buchanon and bring her back to her poor little baby. Arly won't be mad, 'cause it'll mean me and her solved the case without having to call the sheriff." He gunned the engine, sending the jeep bouncing up the trail like a clubfoot rabbit.

"How do you know how to go about finding her, Kevin? There's a lot of trees and bushes. She could be anywhere on the ridge, you know, unless she's over at Starley City a-whorin' on a street corner. How're you going to find her?"

"I don't rightly know, angel," Kevin admitted, beginning to wonder if his plan was a mite shaky. "But Arly must've searched by the cabin, so I figgered we ought to take one of the trails from the other side of the ridge."

"It's gettin' dark, Kevin."

"I see that, sweetie pie, but we cain't turn around now. We just got to hope this trail will take us to the ridge road."

"Why cain't we turn around?"

Kevin gave her a manly smile, since he was a man who was brave and fearless and willin' to take a risk now and then in the name of civic duty. "Because the trail's too narrow. Now you hang on real tight. We'll get somewhere before too long, and you just wait and see if we don't find Robin Buchanon."

Dahlia took a sandwich out of the basket between her feet. She disposed of it in three mouthfuls, licked her fingers, then carefully folded the wax paper into a neat square and tucked it back into the basket. "I trust you, Kevin," she said with a bovine gaze of deep emotion. And a dainty belch.

Kevin took one hand off the wheel to pat her knee. The jeep promptly hit a rut deep enough to drown a mule. Before either of them could so much as shriek, the jeep lunged across the weeds and buried itself in a thicket of firs and scrub oaks. Branches slashed at arms and necks. Fir needles slapped faces with the fury of a spinster schoolmarm. The engine, which had squealed in midair, died as the jeep bounced into an unyielding tree. The silence was louder than anything preceding it.

"Oh, lordy!" Kevin gasped. He looked wildly at his beloved, who seemed to have lodged herself on the floorboard in front of the seat. All he could see was her broad back and one leg hanging out the side of the jeep like a fat white salami. "Dahlia! Are you okay?"

"Git me outta here," came a muffled voice. "I got my face in the chicken salad and it's trying to get up my nose and kill me."

It was not easy, what with her being wedged so tightly, but Kevin managed to get her free and settled back on the seat. Her face was bright red, her cheeks puffing in and out at an alarming rate, and her hands fluttering with distress. "What happened?" she demanded when she got her breath back.

Kevin tried to explain, but he could tell she wasn't impressed. In fact, right when he was describing how he'd battled the steering wheel like their lives depended on it, she bent down to see if the sandwiches had been squashed beyond eating. Luckily, they had not, and that was the only reason Kevin Fitzgerald Buchanon was allowed to live.

Once she finished a tuna salad on rye and a pimento cheese on white, Dahlia gazed at Kevin. "What d' you aim to do now? We're stuck plumb in the middle of the woods, and I reckon the jeep's busted. It's miles and miles to town, no matter which way we go. And I ain't gonna walk."

"I never said you had to walk," he protested.

"Ain't no bus service."

"I never said there was bus service, my lamb chop."

"Then what do you aim to do?"

Kevin studied the woods all around them. All tangled and snarly, and on the shadowy side. Getting darker by the minute. Estimating was not his forte, but he hazarded a guess they was more than ten miles from town. He eyed his beloved. She wasn't going to walk, and he doubted he could carry her more than a couple of inches.

She plopped a sandwich in her mouth, and through the chicken salad said, "It's getting cold, Kevin. I heard tell more than one time there was bears and wolves in these here woods. I'm supposed to be at work at nine o'clock. Call for help on the radio; tell them they got to come get us."

Gripped with ambivalence yet unwilling to disobey, Kevin fiddled with the knobs, but the radio remained silent. "It's broken, my angel. Lemme see if I can fix the jeep. There's a toolbox under the seat."

Dahlia worked her way through the remainder of the tuna sandwiches while Kevin crawled around under the jeep. She had just decided to tackle the pimento cheese when she heard a droning noise from somewhere up the ridge. She thought about telling Kevin, but chose not to interrupt him. She also thought about pimento cheese but ultimately chose chicken salad, and was on her third as the noise grew so loud it started to alarm her. "Kevin! Something's coming."

He wiggled out from under the front of the jeep and got to his feet. "You're right, my darling. I hear it, too. But what do you reckon it is?"

"I was thinking that it sounds like that crazy lunatic in *The Texas Chainsaw Massacre* when he commenced to cutting off everybody's head. Now what do you aim to do?"

He came around to the passenger's side, a wrench held in his decidedly sweaty hand. "I ain't going to let some crazy lunatic attack you. If he so much as makes a move in any of your directions, I'll bash him on the head until he sees stars and begs for mercy." He could see she was impressed, although he had a few doubts himself. However, there wasn't anything to do but stand there, prepared to defend his woman from a chain-saw lunatic.

A light cut across the tops of the firs. The drone, now a heartchilling buzz that implied decapitation and worse, grew louder and louder. Kevin sucked in his gut and raised the wrench. The light bounced in the branches. Dahlia solemnly ate the last of the chicken salad, wondering if she'd ever see pepperoni pizza or cherry cobbler again. The buzzing became a million angry hornets. Kevin stepped forward. Dahlia let out a belch of sheer terror.

A motorcycle crashed through the underbrush. The driver, disguised by a bubble helmet, wore a black leather jacket and boots. Kevin stumbled backward, lost his balance, and sprawled across Dahlia's lap. The driver leaned over to cut off the engine. Dahlia goggled, just knowing in her heart this madman from hell was reaching for the chain saw.

He came up emptyhanded. Taking off the helmet, he said, "Kevin Buchanon and Dahlia O'Neill? What in blazes are you two a-doin' up here?"

"Merle?" Dahlia said as she tried to remove Kevin's shoe from her rib cage. "Merle Hardcock? What are you a-doin' up here?"

"I was practicing my cross-country technique," Merle said. He smoothed down his wispy white hair and gave Dahlia a conspiratorial wink. "Got to get ready for the big one, you know."

Dahlia didn't know anything, including why Merle was winking at her like he had a gnat in his eye. "For goodness' sakes, Merle; you liked to give me a heart attack. Kevin and I came up here for a picnic, but we had a small variety of problem with the jeep."

"Like running into a tree?" Merle cackled. "You two can get on with your picnic, but it's getting dark. I got to hustle ass back to town and find Arly."

Kevin freed his head from under the steering wheel to peer across Dahlia's broad thighs. "Why do you have to find Arly? Is it police business?"

"You might say that." Merle let out another round of cackles. "It's a dead body, so I'd say it was likely to be police business."

"I am on assignment for the chief," Kevin said in his best official voice. He pulled himself up and ordered his Adam's apple to stop bobbling like a yo-yo. "You better tell me what you found, Merle Hardcock. You just tell me whose body you found and where you found it—and for your sake, I'd like to hope you didn't tamper with the scene. I'll report to Arly."

"From your tree phone?" Merle put on the helmet, muffling the cackles. The motorcycle came to life with a thunderous roar, then edged past the jeep and plummeted down the trail.

"Well, holy shit," Kevin said in disgust.

Dahlia unwrapped a pimento cheese sandwich.

Celeste lay in her bed, surrounded by plump feather pillows in lacy cases. A satin cover was pulled to her chin, but she was awake and staring at the ceiling. Mason eyed her from the doorway, then came a few feet into the room. "Would you like a glass of sherry or a cup of tea, Sis? You're looking a bit pale."

"Can you do nothing but play waiter? Do you realize that you spend a great deal of time in doorways asking me if I should like something to eat or drink? Do you aspire to be a waiter in a ritzy New York restaurant?"

"I don't mean to offend you," he said soothingly. "I just feel responsible for you at times. Besides, you're always occupied with important things like giving readings and—"

"Shut up, Mason."

He hung his head, trying to look properly chastised while he decided how to escape her room. "I was just trying to help," he mumbled.

"Yes, you will help. Tomorrow morning, as the sun first rises, you must go to this Arly Hanks and bring her back here. Although she is skeptical, she will listen to what I have to say to her. The miasma of violence grows like a cancer in this putrid village. She is the chief of police, and she must do something before it is too late."

"Now, Celeste, we don't want to get involved with the police, not after what happened back in Vegas. You were six inches from jail, and damn lucky the judge's wife turned out to be one of your clients."

"I will not discuss that incident, Mason. You and I both know that I took money from the child's mother only because she insisted. I provided the information. I had no knowledge of the location until I saw it in a trance." Celeste gave him a cold look. "Do you understand what you are to do, my little brother? Knock on this woman's door before dawn and bring her to me."

"I don't even know her. I can't go banging on her door at dawn, demanding that she come with me. That's crazy, Celeste. She's liable to pull out a gun and shoot me in the stomach."

"I want her here," Madam Celeste said, her eyes narrowed to slits. "One of my clients came this morning to tell me how some local woman has disappeared. It seems this policewoman is too proud to ask for my help, but I shall give it to her despite her petty jealousy. And I must see her immediately. Death is very near. We cannot waste one minute."

"Does this have something to do with the face you saw?"

"Mason, I have known asparagus stalks more perceptive than you. Will you do what I tell you to do—or will you return to Hickory Ridge, Mississippi, to sell used cars?"

Mason's hand curled into a fist, but he prudently kept it behind his back. "This is crazy," he persisted. "She's not going to go wandering off with a total stranger, especially at that hour of the morning. Nobody in her right mind would."

Madam Celeste closed her eyes and put her fingers on her temples. "I am having a vision, Mason. It is of . . . of a '77 Chevy with less than ninety thousand miles. It has had only one owner. The interior is immaculate. The price is painted on the windshield, and it is an excellent deal."

"All right, all right. That's not real funny, you know. I will go over to this policewoman's house and ring the bell. After I explain why I'm there, she can decide for herself if she's willing to come back here with me. But I'm not going to drag her out the door and into my car. That's called kidnapping or assault or something, and I'm not having anything to do with it."

"I shall be in the solarium when you return with her. Now, I must rest because it will be most difficult for me in the morning. Stop fidgeting and leave me alone."

Mason went downstairs and into the kitchen, wishing he had stayed in the army long enough to learn something more useful than how to hurl grenades at gooks. He'd been offered further electronics training if he reenlisted, but he was too eager to get as far away from the army as he could. So now he was qualified to sell used cars, dig ditches, twiddle his thumbs, or do as Sarah Lou Dickerson Grinolli Vizzard, a.k.a. Madam Celeste, ordered.

He looked out the window at the chicken house across the pasture. The roof had caved in on one end, and the sides were boarded up with scrap lumber, old signs, and sheet metal. There hadn't been a chicken there for twenty years, but it still reeked so badly of manure that he could smell it on sultry days when the wind came up the valley. He was about as useful as an old chicken house, he thought as he took a can of soda pop from the refrigerator and went to the living room. He fiddled with the TV controls until he picked up a sumo wrestling match from Tokyo. The lack of action lulled him to sleep before the soda was half gone.

Hammet, David Allen, and I ended up at the drive-in movie, where we were treated to nonstop violence, bloodshed, an improbable storyline that included the removal of vital anatomical attachments of almost everyone in the cast, and enough fake blood to fill a swimming pool. Hammet adored it. He ended up in the front seat, crouched in a ball and yelling encouragement to the mass murderer. David Allen kept the popcorn coming.

In the middle of one of the more grisly scenes my beeper beeped. "Damn it," I said under my breath, remembering that I still hadn't called Mrs. Jim Bob. Approach avoidance at its zenith.

David Allen reached across Hammet. "Let me have that insidious cricket. I know the perfect place for it."

"You can't throw Jiminy out the window. He's official police equipment, I'm sorry to say."

He took the beeper, wrapped it in a handful of napkins, and stuffed the bundle in the glove compartment. "See? No violence to the little chap."

"I wish I could ignore it, but I've been ignoring it for too long. I need to find a telephone to get the message. I was about to do it earlier, but you two abducted me."

"You're going to miss a particularly fine decapitation."

"The sacrifices we have to make in the line of duty. Can I bring back anything from the concession stand?"

"I wants some more candy bars," Hammet said, not taking his eyes off the screen. "And another sody and a hot dog."

I went to the concession stand and asked where to find a pay telephone. I listened to concise directions, then made it halfway to the door before hearing that the phone was out of order. I inquired if I might use the office phone. I was informed that only the manager could permit it. I asked to speak to the manager. I learned the manager was home with a stomach virus. I showed my badge. I was told that only the manager could permit the use of the office phone by an unauthorized party. I argued some more. I gave up when told that the manager with the stomach virus who was the only one who could permit the use of the office phone by an unauthorized party also had the only key, so it wasn't going to do a damn bit of good to stand around and argue the point. Did I wish to purchase anything before the concession stand closed?

Wishing I had a chain saw, I bought drinks, candy bars, and a hot dog, then went back to David Allen's wagon and watched the last dozen people get their heads cut off. It suited my mood perfectly.

Brother Verber, dressed in pajamas and a robe, stared at the simulated walnut paneling above the television set, unmindful of the chatter from the sitcom. He kept trying to convince himself that he wasn't being cowardly, but he was losing the argument. Poor Sister Barbara had come to him in her hour of need. He'd comforted her and offered spiritual guidance—or at least he'd intended to do a bushel of comforting and guiding until he'd learned the name of the mother of the poor little orphan bastards. Just thinking the name made him a mite sweaty under his elastic waistband.

But, he told himself as he peeked at the television on the off chance that the blond girl in the miniskirt might cross her legs, Sister Barbara was a strong woman, with a solid Christian sense of duty and a pair of fine, muscular thighs from all that pious praying. She could handle those awful bastards, and instill in them a healthy fear of the Lord and a feverish desire to battle the wickedness of their souls. Why, she didn't need any help from him. She was a battleship armed with cannons of righteousness. She was a rock of piety. She was an army tank that could run right over Satan and squish him into the mud. It was arrogant of him to think she needed his help. Sinfully arrogant.

Brother Verber got on his knees to beg the Lord's

forgiveness for his arrogance. He glanced a bit nervously at the telephone receiver dangling below the coffee table, then closed his eyes and settled his knees on the braided rug. It might well take hours of seclusion and prayer to regain his humility, he thought with a windy sigh. If the Lord chanced to be occupied with more important things (like striking down evolutionists and homosexuals and feminists), it might even take days.

It was nearly one o'clock before we got back to Maggody. Hammet, bloated from an incredible amount of junk food, was snoring in the backseat, while visions of blood-drenched sugarplums danced in his head.

"What do we do with him?" David Allen asked as we drove past the Emporium.

"I don't know. He's supposed to be staying with Mizzoner, but it's pretty late and supposedly she knows he's with me." I looked back at the little liar. "I guess I'll let him sleep on my sofa tonight. Tomorrow morning I'll go by there and find out what's happening, but I'm too tired to face it now."

David Allen slammed on the brakes as a black-clad figure on a motorcycle roared from out of a side street and vanished down the highway. "Officer, arrest that maniac!"

"I prefer to let that sort self-destruct," I said, turning around to make sure Hammet hadn't rolled off the seat. He hadn't. "I feel sorry for Hammet and his siblings. I've given up trying to find his mother. I searched part of the ridge today and realized how absurd it was to think I might find her. I'm going to call the sheriff and request assistance, which is what I should have done in the first place. If his posse has no luck, he can contact the state police for a helicopter. I should have called Social Services, too, and had them take responsibility for the children. Mrs. Jim Bob's on the anal-retentive side, but her gesture was generous. However, she and I are both amateurs and way out of our league. The professionals have institutions and foster homes for this situation."

"I think you did the right thing. This Buchanon woman may show up at any moment to demand her children. If they had been placed in foster care by an agency, she might never unwind the red tape in order to get them back."

"I know." I closed my eyes as we drove past the PD so I wouldn't have to think of all the things I was busily doing wrong.

David Allen parked beside my stairs. He took Hammet's inert form from the backseat and carried him to my door. Once we got him settled on the sofa with a blanket, I walked downstairs with David Allen.

He took his keys out of his pocket and gave me the look that meant he was deciding whether to risk a good-night kiss. I gave him the look that said no, don't even try, then thanked him for the ice cream and the movies. The look faded, and he told me I was more than welcome. Neither one of us could come up with anything more, so I said good night and went up to my apartment to lie in my bed and stare at the ceiling.

Ruby Bee padded to the refrigerator and took out a plastic baby bottle. She ran some water into a pan, set the bottle in it, and turned on the burner of the stove. Baby continued to howl as Ruby Bee waited a few minutes, then picked up the bottle to sprinkle some droplets on her wrist.

Once she was satisfied, Ruby Bee padded on into the living room and picked up the red-faced, screaming baby and retreated to the sofa. She managed to cut off the cries by inserting the nipple in the appropriate orifice, then sank back to gaze through befogged eyes at the level in the uptilted bottle. In that it was the third time that night that she'd fed the little darling, she was feeling less than charmed by the button nose, perfect flower-petal ears, and tiny clenched fists.

Maybe, she thought as she put Baby back in the bassinet and padded to bed, maybe Estelle should have an opportunity to have a sweet overnight guest tomorrow night. After all, she and Estelle were good friends, and it wasn't fair not to share all those special moments. It would mean so much to Estelle, especially since that foreigner with the mustache hadn't shown up as of yet. Why, it would be a big help in taking her mind off her disappointment.

A smile on her face, Ruby Bee drifted to sleep.

Celeste threw back the satin cover and switched on the bedside light. Despite the lateness of the hour, she pulled on a robe over her negligee and went downstairs to the solarium. She sat down at the table and shuffled the tarot cards, then dealt them out and bent forward to study the results.

The King of Wands, the King of Swords, the Nine of Swords, and the Moon. Could they not for even one time stay away? It was as if they now were citizens of Maggody, these symbols of malice and violence, of deceit and trickery and fear. And Death was there, as always.

The psychic pushed the cards away and sat back, her eyes closed. She forced herself to recall the face she had seen earlier. It was definitely a woman, she decided with a shiver, but it was impossible to see any features beyond those distorted with blood. Although there was an elusive impression of hair color, of age, of eye color, of cheek and brow and jaw . . . all was dominated by blood. By flies. By the pervasiveness of decay.

She gathered up the cards and once more dealt them, hoping for some sign to identify the face.

The faces on the cards gazed back at her through glassy, two-dimensional eyes. They seemed to be smiling.

Poppy took the milk carton from the refrigerator, then tiptoed across the kitchen to get a glass from the cabinet. She flinched as the cabinet let out a tiny squeak. It wasn't that she didn't want company, she told herself as she eased the cabinet closed. She was committed to the concept of sharing, of oneness and wholeness and cosmic harmony and the manifestation of collective energy and all that; if she weren't, why, she'd still be waiting tables at the Pizza Hut and living in that drab apartment over the bowling alley. It was just that it was tiresome at times, all that determined family sharing and everything.

She was standing by the window when the door opened behind her. Nate gave her a guarded look as he went to the kitchen table and set down a paper sack. "What's wrong with you?" he said, scowling.

"Nothing. The midwife told me to drink a lot of goat's milk."

"Good for her." He sat down and took out a hamburger. "Get me a beer, will you?"

Poppy tried not to pout as she took a beer from the refrigerator and placed it in front of him. "That's poison, you know. The meat is from animals raised on chemicals, and the bread's all preservatives and artificial flavors."

"Name one," he commanded through a mouthful of chemicals, preservatives, and artificial flavors.

"Oh, things that cause cancer. Where've you been all night?"

"Out. I had to see a middleman about a deal. Why are you skulking around the kitchen, for that matter? I thought pregnant women were supposed to sleep twelve hours a night so they weren't too tired for their morning nap."

Poppy almost stamped her foot, but thought better of it. "Rainbow says I need to—"

"I don't care what she says. God, I'm about to drown in her cheerful, warm, cozy, sugary smiles and suffocating cosmic awareness. As soon as I work out this deal, you can kiss my ass good-bye, 'cause I'll be driving down that long country road."

Poppy couldn't think of anything to say. On the other side of the kitchen door, with her ear pressed against the wood, Rainbow couldn't think of much herself. But her smile was far from toasty warm and her eyes were cold. Silently she moved away from the door and returned to bed. She snuggled next to Zachery and tried to meditate to the rhythm of his gentle snores.

8

I was sleeping quite peacefully when a hand touched on my arm. In that I had had no companion in my bed for nearly two years, I almost choked on a mouthful of pillowcase as I opened my eyes.

"There be somebody at the door," Hammet said. He was fully dressed and regarding me with a sober expression.

"Who is it?"

"I din't open it yet. You want I should get your gun and blow 'em to smithereens?" He took a step toward my dresser, his hand outstretched and his little yellow eyes bright with eagerness to make his day.

"No!" I said as I scrambled out of bed. "Just give me a second to wake up, then I'll see who's at the door. What time is it?"

Hammet looked at the clock, then at the floor. "I dunno, but I reckon the sun'll come up afore too long. I ain't heard a hoot owl in a long whiles."

I made a mental note to teach him how to tell time, although I doubted his mother would give him a Rolex for Christmas. I was reaching for my bathrobe when I heard an insistent knock on the front door of the apartment. After a glance at the clock to confirm the absurdity of the hour, I pulled on the robe and stalked across the living room.

Hammet trailed after me, reiterating his offer to blow the intruder to smithereens iffen I wanted him to. After assuring him that such actions would be premature (and defining "premature" when I saw his lip creep forward), I opened the door to stare at a man with dark hair, brown eyes, and an apologetic smile. He took in my robe and bare feet while I took in his sports coat, starched shirt, discreet silk tie, and creased slacks. It probably took me longer to do the taking in, but I wasn't standing at his door before the sun rose.

"I'm Mason Dickerson," he said. "I know this is crazy, but I wonder if I might ask you something?"

"You jest did," Hammet said. "Asked her somethin', I mean."

"Well, yes, you're right. But it really is important, Miss Hanks. I realize it's early and I'm a total stranger, and by all rights you ought to slam the door in my face or shoot me. . . ."

I joined him on the landing before Hammet could offer to comply with the latter part of the suggestion. "Mason Dickerson," I said slowly. "You're Madam Celeste's brother, right? You're her business manager or something like that?"

"Something like that. If it's not too much trouble, she would like you to come over to our house. I'll be happy to drive you over."

"At six o'clock in the morning?" I shook my head, wondering if Hammet might be on the right track. "I have a personal policy of declining social engagements before sunrise. Unless this is an emergency involving official police business, tell Madam Celeste to call me in a couple of hours."

"Yeah," Hammet contributed from the doorway. "It's too fuckin' premature to be visitin' folks."

Mason shrugged helplessly. "You know that and I know that, but my sister refused to listen to any argument. Look, I'm sorry to disturb you. Please just go back to bed and forget about this, Miss Hanks."

"What's all this about?"

"I don't know. One of Celeste's crazy visions." He moved down a step. "Something about a dead woman. Celeste thinks she has information that'll be useful to you, but the whole thing's nonsense and I'm sorry I bothered you." He retreated another few steps.

"Wait a minute." I told Hammet to go to the kitchen and fix himself a bowl of cereal. Once he was gone, I studied Mason while I tried to jolt my brain into a functional state. "What are we talking about—a dead body or a vision of a dead body? And while we're on the subject, whose?"

"I really don't know any more than I've told you. Celeste wanted you to come by the house because she has something to tell you about some woman who may be dead. But Celeste has been kind of screwy since she was a child, and you don't have to listen to her if you don't want to. Please accept my apologies, and forget I was ever here." His face was red and his voice cracking with embarrassment. He kept looking at the top of his car as if he wished nothing more than to be in it and speeding down the highway.

I felt sorry for him, and I was also feeling a little bit curious about this peculiar invitation, especially since he seemed so eager to cancel it. "Why don't you come inside for a cup of coffee while I try to decide what to do? Now that I'm awake, I suppose it won't hurt anything to hear what your sister wants to tell me, although I am fairly skeptical about this sort of thing."

"So am I," he murmured. "But thank you for agreeing to come. Celeste can be difficult when she doesn't get her way."

He had come back up to the landing when a motorcycle roared around the corner. A figure in a helmet braked in a shower of gravel, then imperiously gestured for us to come downstairs. Telling myself this was a truly bizarre dream, I did as requested. As I reached the bottom step, I realized the figure was covered with mud and dripping like a faulty faucet. Ruby Bee's idle gossip came back to me.

"Merle?" I said tentatively.

He pulled off his helmet. "Morning, Arly. How are ya?"

"Fine, thank you. What brings you here at this hour?" I fully expected him to pull a dormouse and a March hare out of his pocket and suggest a tea party. I wouldn't have raised so much as an eyebrow.

"I came by last night, but you was out," Merle said, forgiving me with a toothless smile. "Good thing I caught you this morning, 'cause I'm going to be right busy later today over at the creek. I built a ramp outta some scrap lumber, but I jest ain't having any luck so far. I believe I'm gonna have to recalculate my angles."

"Why did you come by last night and again this morning?" I asked, optimistically ignoring the reference to his daredevil antics.

"To tell you what I found yesterday evening just afore dark."

"And what did you find?"

"A dead body, Arly. I found me a dead body. I found some other bodies, too, but they was wanting privacy so's they could commence to court, so I don't reckon I ought to carry tales about 'em." Merle loosed an ear-shattering cackle. "No, sir, them two kids was sweaty when I happened across them, and real red-faced when they realized they'd been caught."

I looked back at Mason, who was white and clutching the railing for dear life. Taking a deep breath, I said, "The dead body, Merle—tell me about the body."

"Don't you want to hear about the two that was

having themselves a fine old time in the front seat? They was doing it in a funny way, but these kids today have some newfangled notions on how to go about procreatin'. Mrs. Hardcock, bless her soul, would of been right scandalized. She always wore a flannel nightgown and covered the face of the alarm clock with a towel when I came a-sniffin' at her."

"Merle, I want to know about the body. Are you going to tell me, or do I have to drag it out of you word by word?"

I had to drag it out of him word by word. Once I learned that he had happened across a dead, bloodied body on the far side of Cotter's Ridge, I ordered him to wait for me at the PD. I told Mason, who was quivering like a molded salad, that I would get back to him later and sent him home. Then, bewildered and thoroughly apprehensive, I went upstairs and told Hammet the news. He shrugged and asked if were Her. I said I didn't know for sure, but that it was likely. He then wanted to know iffen she'd done been et by a bear, and if so, was the bear dead, too? And if that were the case, was they gonna skin the bear and who would get to keep the hide? All in all, he handled it with aplomb.

Aplombless, I dressed, gulped down coffee, called the sheriff's office to report a suspicious death and arrange for a backup, and somehow managed to function like the cop I was supposed to be, although my brain, like Merle's motorcycle, had not yet cleared the creek. I left Hammet in front of the television, enthralled equally by cartoons and commercials, and trotted across the deserted highway to the police department just as the sheriff's deputy drove up in a four-wheel wagon. I ordered Merle to get in the backseat, then climbed in next to the deputy and tried my darndest to explain something I didn't know anything about.

An hour later, after jolting up a wretched logging

trail on the north side of Cotter's Ridge while Merle shouted directions in one of my ears and the deputy shouted questions in the other, we parked and got out of the vehicle. Merle led us to a clearing, then stopped and wordlessly pointed at a crumpled and very still figure on the far side. From where we stood, I could see it was what remained of Robin Buchanon. I wasn't totally surprised, but I had to battle the sudden explosion of icicles in my stomach and the flood of sourness in my mouth.

"Goddamn it," I muttered under my breath, thinking about her children. Hammet in particular, since I hadn't been fooled by his casual remarks earlier. A mother is a mother is a mother, even if she's a moonshining, whoring, abusive mountain woman. "What the hell happened to her?"

The deputy caught my arm as I started forward. "Booby traps," he said, pointing down at a thin wire almost lost in the leaves. "The trip wire's attached to some sort of detonation gizmo. The woman must have been in too much of a hurry to watch the ground."

I shook my head as I looked at the rows of four-foot plants. "I'll bet she was. This must have been the family ginseng patch. She'd have been furious when she saw the marijuana plants, and rushed forward to rip them up." I eased around the perimeter of the clearing, keeping an eye out for wires, buried cans and buckets, dangling fish hooks, and other charming devices, most of which were brought home from the Vietnamese jungle, along with a fondness for marijuana. I won't say much about the odor, but it wasn't anything you could miss, not even from a good fifty feet away. Covering my mouth and nose with a handkerchief, I knelt down at a prudent distance and forced myself to examine the pitiful body. "Yeah, her foot's caught on a trip wire. There's the booby trap in that branch. I saw a diagram of one in a manual at the academy, but I don't guess I've ever seen a real one."

The device was a Rube Goldberg contraption involving the trip wires, a spring-coiled door hinge, a nail, a square of wood with a hole bored in it, and a shotgun shell that had been detonated. That's all I'm going to tell you, and there are no diagrams in the back of the book. Do not go down to the basement and fool around with the above-mentioned items unless you have a perverted secret desire to go through life minus eyes and a smattering of fingers.

The deputy came over to peer at the booby trap. "It's only number six bird shot, but she caught it square in the face. It was probably rigged just to scare the living daylights out of some innocent trespasser, which it sure as hell would of. Bird shot won't kill you unless you get it in the eyes. If she'd been half a dozen inches taller or a few feet farther away, or even turned the other direction, she'd be squawking like a wet hen while she picked pellets out of her bottom."

That wasn't much comfort for Robin Buchanon.

"I'm going to nail the son of a bitch who booby-trapped this patch," I said. My voice must have sounded a mite cold, because the deputy and Merle exchanged cautious looks and stayed quiet. I sucked in a breath through the handkerchief, then continued. "It's one thing to grow a little dope out in the National Forest; God knows it's the number-one cash crop in this part of the state. But this booby trap changes things. We're not going to rip out the plants and haul them to the county incinerator, moaning all the way about lack of manpower. We're going to catch the bastard and hang him on murder one and everything else in the book. He's going to drown in the felony charges we'll come up with."

I stood there and glowered while the deputy radioed in his report. Merle squatted under a tree and did not cackle. After a great deal of staticky conversation, we were told to handle the preliminary investigation ourselves because they doubted they could find us. They had a point.

The deputy and I gingerly examined the scene for evidence, of which there was damn little. Robin's tools and gunnysack were labeled and put into plastic evidence bags, then stashed in the back of the vehicle. The tiny fragments of cardboard from the shotgun shell were treated in a similar fashion. The device that had killed Robin Buchanon was bagged, with a few expressed hopes that fingerprints might be found. The plants were measured, counted, and assessed at more than ten thousand dollars, wholesale alone, although they were short enough to indicate they had been planted as late as midsummer. Retail (a.k.a. street value) could be as much as ten times higher. Six more booby traps were located around the perimeter—and very carefully left intact.

At that point the deputy and I grimaced at each other. He returned to the vehicle for a body bag, and we forced ourselves to slide the remains into it. Then each of us found a private spot in the forest in which to vomit. I knelt for a long while afterward, thinking all sorts of crazy things that I still can't put into words. Which goes to show I was about as hard-boiled as the heroine of a Jane Austen novel.

Once the vehicle was loaded, I went back to make sure we hadn't missed anything. The marijuana plants were swaying just a bit in the breeze, like proud, bushy, green plumes. Once the investigation was closed and the son of a bitch was doing a string of consecutive sentences for murder, manufacture of a controlled substance, trafficking, reckless endangerment, and an assortment of federal charges, the patch would be cleared and burned. Maybe the ginseng would come back, I thought with a wry smile. If it did, I'd bring Hammet et al to the spot and show them their family legacy. Their mother's estate, so to speak.

I went back to the wagon. Merle was perched on the edge of the backseat, not real pleased by the bags (and odor) behind him. Sympathizing, I got in the front, rolled down the window, and told the deputy I was finished for the time being. As he drove our makeshift hearse down the road, I stared out the window. "This is my case, you know," I said without turning my head.

"So the sheriff figured you'd say. It's as much your jurisdiction as anybody's, and you did know the deceased. He may be being so generous because we're shorthanded, overworked, and underpaid. Ain't none of us had a decent vacation in the last six months."

I considered suggesting they take so-called vacations instead, but decided it wasn't worth the effort. I leaned back and closed my eyes.

"Looky there," Merle said suddenly, bruising my ear as he stuck his hand out the window to point at a clump of firs. "Do you recollect how I said earlier that I'd seen some kids courting along the road? Looks like they couldn't get their jeep to working again."

I'd forgotten about the courters. And I didn't like the word "jeep," which brought to mind the one that was supposedly parked in front of the PD. Because it now occurred to me—a mere three hours after the fact—that it hadn't been there earlier, when I'd raced over to meet the deputy. It hadn't been there the night before, when David Allen had driven us past too quickly for me to decide what was wrong. That flash of insight was a mere fourteen hours after the fact. Perspicacity is not among my sins.

The deputy jammed on the brakes. "It's under those firs. You got to look real hard to see it, but you can see a flash of red and the sunlight glinting on a taillight."

"Red jeep," I said, sighing. "Just for the record, Merle—who were these two lovebirds you met last night?"

He confirmed my worst fears. The three of us pushed through the brush to the jeep, which was empty of all signs of humanity except for a square of wax paper on the floorboard in front of the passenger's seat. At that moment I caught myself wishing the twosome had been et by a bear, but I put the fantasy aside and yelled their names. Pretty soon the deputy and Merle started yelling, but nobody waddled or stumbled out of the woods.

"They're damn lucky they're not here," I said through clenched teeth. "I've got a murder investigation on my hands; the last thing I need is a missing team of car thieves. If Kevin fell out of a tree in front of me right now, I swear I'd strangle him. If I could get my hands around Dahlia's neck, I'd strangle her, too."

"Shall I call in a grand theft auto?" the deputy suggested. "Destruction of government property? Malicious mischief? How about we put out an APB on 'em?"

"Do that, and stress that they're liable to be armed and dangerous. Maybe some trigger-happy cop'll save me the bother." I leaned back against the hood of the jeep and rubbed my face until it hurt. "This whole mess is too damn much for me. I've got a murder, a bunch of orphans, a stolen vehicle, two missing morons, a town full of loonies who communicate with dead ancestors, and a psychic who seems to know more than I do. I don't return my calls, my lipstick's crooked, and my mother thinks I'm a stagnant pond. I don't need this, guys."

I didn't burst into tears, but I toyed with the idea all the way back to town.

Mrs. Jim Bob nibbled a corner of the candy bar with her small, even teeth. Although her stomach was grumbling, she carefully refolded the wrapper and put the candy bar back in the bedside drawer. Rationing was essential, she told herself in a firm voice. She was in no danger of drying out too badly, what with the bathroom tap. But thirty-six hours into the siege, she was getting hungrier by the minute and she was having a hard time not just jamming the candy bar into her mouth.

She dialed the sheriff's department and dully asked to speak to Chief of Police Arly Hanks.

"I'm sorry, Mrs. Jim Bob," the dispatcher said, "but she still hasn't called in. I swear I've been beeping her since your first call. I don't know what else I can do for you, dear. Are you sure there isn't anyone else who can help you?"

Mrs. Jim Bob wasn't about to admit she was at the mercy of four children, that she couldn't exercise her authority or even sneak past the little heathens to the kitchen for a meat loaf sandwich and a glass of iced tea. Why, the dispatcher, one LaBelle Hutchinson, was by far the biggest gossip in the whole county, and more than likely to tell the whole world about Mrs. Jim Bob's dilemma. LaBelle belonged to every auxiliary and missionary society in the county and it wasn't because of her dedication to all those worthy causes. She just knew everything that happened, from marital squabbles to drunken teenagers stealing the family car to filthy child abusers, and she wasn't above preening in the limelight while her tongue wagged harder than a duck's tailfeathers.

Mrs. Jim Bob caught herself wondering how to find a filthy child abuser, since she knew some candidates worthy of abuse. She scolded herself for such un-Christianlike thoughts, then told LaBelle to keep trying to locate Arly. She dialed Brother Verber's number, but it was still busy. The telephone company had run a check sometime in the now murky past, and assured her that the line was not out of order. They were real snippy about it, too.

She replaced the telephone receiver and went to the bedroom door to make sure it was still locked. As she returned to sit on the corner of the bed, she heard what sounded like an elephant thudding into the living-room wall. She didn't even wince, being long past the wincing stage.

"Well, at least it proves you were right," Mason said, keeping his distance.

"Did you have doubts?" Celeste snapped. She sat at the dinette table, a cup of tea in front of her. The tarot cards were pushed to one side, their corners bent and soft from a hard, all-night workout. "I told you to bring that woman here, and you did not. That is why I have doubts, Mason—doubts about your ability to follow simple directions."

"She was going to come; I told you that. Then this strange guy on a motorcycle showed up, making weird noises and alluding to a body up in the woods somewhere. She's a cop, Sis. She had to go investigate. She did seem a little unnerved about the coincidence, though, and said she'd be by to talk to you this afternoon."

"What coincidence, Mason?"

He realized he'd put his foot squarely in it, but it was too late. "Not the coincidence of your having the vision. The coincidence of me appearing at the door just when that crazy coot showed up with the news."

"I saw a dead woman's face. A dead woman was

subsequently found. There is no coincidence."

"Of course not," Mason said, easing toward the door. "Well, I have a few errands to run this morning, so I'll see you around lunchtime."

"Errands, Mason? Are your errands more important than what I have determined about the dead woman? You run along, little brother; I shall save my revelations for this policewoman."

Mason came back to the table and sat down across from her. "What revelations, Sis? For all we know, this woman got bit by a snake or fell off a cliff. If you start telling the cops all kinds of wild stuff, they're liable to think you're involved in a crime. You know what happened in Las Vegas."

"But I am involved. I know more than the police, just as I did in the earlier matter."

"Like what?"

She picked up the deck of cards and idly riffled them. "I put myself in a trance last night while you engaged in transcendental vegetation in front of the television. Once I was able to contact those who assist me from the other world, I learned that this death was the result of a crime."

"You talked to the dead woman?" Mason tried not to let his face twitch, but he didn't have much luck. "You asked her stuff about how she died?"

"I was not able to communicate directly with her; there is a period of adjustment, especially for those who have died a violent death. But I made inquiries of my spiritual guides, and one was able to tell me of the death. This woman was innocent of crime, and had the misfortune of stumbling into someone else's evilness."

"What kind of evilness?"

"Something illegal. Although to me it remains hazy, it seems to involve bushy green plants—marijuana, I would guess." Celeste put down the cards and scowled. "But the vision was inverted, upside down, as if the plants were rooted in the sky. It disturbs me, in that I cannot make sense of such an inexplicable idea, but the very inversion is linked with the woman's death."

"She was killed by a marijuana plant hanging from the sky?" Mason said, feeling an uncomfortable wetness in his armpits. "How could that kill her?"

"I told you that I am struggling to understand, Mason. Stop gaping at me as if I were an exotic fish in an aquarium. There was an explosion—a great burst of light and pain, but I could not see from where it came. I must talk to this policewoman, however, and find out what she knows. Perhaps that will help me as I seek the truth."

"Celeste, she's not going to tell you the results of an official investigation. When's the last time you met a cooperative cop? Why don't you forget about this and concentrate on Carol Alice's impending marital woes or the hairdresser's mysterious boyfriend?"

She studied him in silence, then snorted and picked up the cards. "Go fetch Arly Hanks, Mason. And get it right this time, unless you want a one-way bus ticket to the used-car lot."

Mason left the house. He drove by the police department, but there were no cars parked out front, and he assumed the policewoman was still up in the woods. Just as well, he thought with a sigh. Celeste had lost her marbles on this one, and it might be wiser to let things simmer for a while. In fact, it might be smart to stop at Ruby Bee's for a plateful of eggs and grits. That way he'd hear the up-to-the-minute gossip on the dead woman and could decide what to do about Celeste once he had some idea of what was going on. It'd be downright smart.

* * *

Merle, the deputy, and I spent a long afternoon at the sheriff's office, filling out reports and stashing the baggies in the evidence locker. Robin's body was sent to the state crime lab, but we all knew what it would take the state boys several days to determine. The birdshot had entered her brain through her eyes, and had killed her within seconds. It was sheer bad luck on her part that she'd caught it like she had.

I had a little explaining to do about the jeep, in that it wasn't mine to begin with and it was my responsibility. We decided to leave it for the time being, so we wouldn't arouse any suspicions from our dope growers. As for the jeep thieves—well, we decided to let them continue doing whatever they were doing. Hitchhiking out of the county. Procreatin' under a bush. Starving to death in the woods. (Guess which was my favorite theory.)

The sheriff, a gruff old boy with a surprising amount of common sense, took me to his office and settled me across the desk from him. He then tried to tell me, gently but firmly, that we didn't have the manpower to stake out the marijuana patch until the growers showed up. There'd been a spate of robberies all over the county. A fellow in a ski mask was causing all kinds of grief to the convenience-store industry. They'd had a tip about an impending armed robbery at a bank branch in Emmet, and they figured they'd have to keep three men undercover there for a week. So, the grandfatherly lecture concluded, we were just going to have to rip out the plants and burn them.

I hit the ceiling. I pointed out that we had a murder on our hands, which was a damn sight more important than a bunch of convenience-store robberies or the possibility of a bank job. I pointed out a lot more things, and the sheriff pointed out some more, and pretty soon we were both yelling and jabbing the air like woodpeckers.

Things went on in that vein for most of an hour. The sheriff knew me well enough not to pull any chauvinist tactics, but he wouldn't budge one goddamn inch. Oh, he agreed with me left and right, admitting that murder was a damn sight more important, etc., then repeated his contention that he just couldn't put two or three deputies up in the woods for what might be weeks to catch a couple of weekend gardeners. If they weren't already tipped off and heading for Mexico. Or sitting at home in front of the television, willing to abandon that particular patch.

"But no one knows we found the body except for Merle, who hasn't told anyone else, Mason Dickerson, who knows very little, and police officials," I said, turning on the earnestness. "I'll stake out the field myself. It's about harvest time. Give me this one weekend." I turned on the charm for good measure. "Come on, Harvey, you know this will make you look good. You can claim all the credit at the press conference afterward—a big dope bust and a murder rap would sound right nice 'long about reelection time, wouldn't it? If we can't pin murder one on the perps, we'll surely get a manslaughter or negligent homicide. Voters just love to know those homicidal maniacs are behind bars."

I was so overcome with my boundless earnestness that I nearly clasped my hands in supplication as I stared at him. He chewed on a stubby, cold cigar for a long time, then asked me what I thought I'd do if a truckload of boys showed up to harvest the marijuana. Big, nasty, stupid boys, armed and ornery. Did I think I could politely ask them to handcuff each other while I read them their rights?

It was a setback. I thought about that unappealing scenario, then said I'd merely observe from a prudent vantage point, and we could nail them when they spread the plants to dry in someone's backroom or barn. We argued some more over minor issues (mostly involving the newspaper and television interviews), and at last he granted me the weekend. The cigar bobbled as he warned me that, should nothing happen, he would send up his boys to destroy the plants. We shook on it, and that was that. I'd just won the dubious honor of hunkering behind a bush for two days by my lonesome, with no backup should things turn nasty, with no one to talk to as my toes froze and my nose dripped.

It was the best I could do for Robin's offspring.

9

Mrs. Jim Bob nearly had a stroke when the telephone rang. She stared at it for three or four rings, almost scared to answer it in case it was possessed by the devil hisself. At last she snatched up the receiver and banged it against her ear. "Arly?" she squawked.

"Sorry, honey, this is LaBelle. I just thought you might like to know what's going on. It's been right crazy all afternoon, since Arly and one of the deputies got back to report. Why, when I took my coffee break a while ago, you'd have thought the department was a dadburned beehive."

"Arly's at your office? Let me speak to her right this minute, LaBelle."

"I'm afraid I can't oblige you. I was going to grab her and give her your messages in person, but first she hightailed it to the backroom to do official business, and then she holed up with the sheriff. I stepped away from my desk for one tiny minute to take care of a personal need, which has been happening more than I care to admit since I came down with this pesky bladder infection. Anyway, when I came back, she and Merle Hardcock had gone off in another one of our department vehicles. It seems to me she already has one, but—"

"Gone off where?" Mrs. Jim Bob demanded, fighting off a wave of panic that made her dizzy and queasy and a lot of other unpleasant things. "Why was she with Merle Hardcock? What's going on over there? Did she say she'd call me?"

LaBelle licked her lips so loudly, Mrs. Jim Bob could hear it. "Well," she said at last, "I can't tell you anything about the murder, because it's confidential."

"Murder? What murder?"

"I am not at liberty to disclose that information to a civilian. I am privy to a lot of classified information due to my position, but I'm not supposed to breathe a word of it to anyone."

"Just like I'm not supposed to breathe a word of how you entered your sister-in-law's corn relish in the county fair, then took home that blue ribbon without saying one thing about who made it?" Mrs. Jim Bob figured that the emergency justified playing hardball this one time, although she doubted she could find the precise scripture in the Good Book.

"You promised not to repeat that," LaBelle gasped.

"I'm waiting to hear about this murder," Mrs. Jim Bob replied smugly. "I'd appreciate all the details, LaBelle. After all, you know everything that happens in the whole county, don't you?"

LaBelle felt obliged to agree.

When I returned, Hammet was still in front of the television. An empty can on the coffee table indicated he'd had lunch, although even he must have had a hard time with cold, condensed soup. I turned off the set, sat him down next to me on the sofa, and told him that his mother had died in an accident. I made it sound like a hunting accident, although I didn't out-and-out lie. No, I wasn't real proud of myself.

He looked at me for a long time, then said, "No bear, huh?"

"No bear. Just a terrible accident up on the ridge. It wasn't her fault, and I doubt she even knew what happened. Once I finish the investigation, I'll tell you more about it."

"I really thought she'd done been et by a bear. Are you sure there weren't no bear tracks?"

"No bear, and no bear tracks." I went to the kitchen and ate a handful of crackers, then changed into a clean uniform and went back to the living room. "Come on, we've got to go to Mrs. Jim Bob's to tell the others."

"What's gonna happen to us then?"

"I don't know. I suppose I'd better contact the social services office in Starley City and tell them about the five of you. They have special places where you'll be taken care of until something permanent can be arranged." Didn't sound like all that much fun, did it?

Hammet wasn't especially enchanted, either. "What does that crap about special places and permanent arranges mean?" he demanded, his brow lowered so that he was glaring up at me like a wild animal in the bottom of a pit.

"A social worker will take you to a foster home—somebody's house—to live for a few weeks. Meanwhile, she'll try to find someone who wants you to become part of the family. You'll have a mother and a father and some new siblings. A nice house, a chance to go to school, maybe a bicycle."

"I don' want any of that shit. What about Bubba and Sukie and Sissie and Baby? Is they goin' to this foster place, too? Is they goin' to get bicycles and go to school?"

"I don't know if all of you will be placed in the same foster home, or end up together," I admitted.

"Then I ain't going."

"I can't leave the five of you scattered around Maggody. You'll be better off in a permanent setting, as will your siblings."

"Sez who?" He reached across me to switch on the television, but I caught his hand.

"Sez everybody, Hammet. You all can't go back to a cabin in the middle of nowhere and exist on roots and berries. Ruby Bee can't raise a baby, nor can Mrs. Jim Bob take in all of you indefinitely. I'm happy to have you visit me here, but I'm not capable of taking care of you on a permanent basis."

"Why not?"

"Because I'm not—that's why. I work all day and sometimes half the night. I survive on Ruby Bee's generosity and canned soup, depending on my mood. I'm not used to worrying about anybody but myself these days."

"I ain't no bother. I can eat soup jest like you do, and I can chop wood and slop the hogs for you whenever you tells me to."

"No," I said gently. "You'll be better off in a stable family setting, with dinner on the table and clean sheets on the bed and motherly reminders to take baths and brush your teeth. I've never been a parent, Hammet—I don't know how to do those things."

"I reckon you're so all-fired smart you could learn—iffen you wanted to."

I studied him for a minute, then shook my head. "Let's go tell the others what's happened and try to figure out what to do. Once that's settled, I have to leave town for a few days."

"Goin' on a vacation? That's right nice what with my ma kilt and everything." He stalked through the doorway and down the stairs, his tangled black hair slapping his shoulders.

As I hurried after him, I fully expected to spot him halfway into the sunset (metaphorically, anyway, since it was still afternoon), but he had stopped at the bottom of the stairs and was talking to David Allen.

"Is this true?" David Allen asked me as I joined them.

"I'm afraid there's been an accident of sorts. I'm

going to do everything I can to clear up a few questions about it, but first I've got to decide what to do with the children."

"Siblings," Hammet hissed under his breath. He shot me a dirty look, then went over to David Allen's wagon and climbed on the hood. Hunkered down with his arms wrapped around his knees, he bore an unsettling resemblance to a turkey vulture on a high branch. I had a pretty good idea whose body he hoped to scavenge, should the opportunity arise.

David Allen glanced warily at Hammet, then turned back to me. "Well, it's dreadful, and I feel really rotten. Let me know if there's anything I can do to help you. For what it's worth, I'm trained in crisis intervention and child psychology. Have you made any effort to contact the fathers of the children?"

A rather obvious question that simply hadn't occurred to me. I was aware of the biological requirements of reproduction, but somehow one did not associate paternal contributions with Robin Buchanon's offspring. I realized David Allen was grinning at me. "No," I said, "I haven't made any effort to locate the fathers. They must have fathers, though. I mean, they have to have fathers out there somewhere, don't they?"

"If they don't, *The National Enquirer* will pay a fortune for the story."

I glanced at vulture-boy. "Do you and the others ever hear from your fathers? Do they visit or send money once in a while?" Said member of *Falconiformes Cathartidae* spat on the gravel and shook his head. Shrugging, I continued, "I'm not sure we can pin paternity on anyone, but it's a fine idea. I suppose someone ought to question the children, and in particular Bubba, about the identities of the visitors to the cabin. He's the eldest, and may be able to help us."

"Bubba don' know shit." Guess who.

I gave David Allen a beguiling smile. "But I think a professional would be able to deal with the situation better than some bumbling amateur trained in fingerprints and traffic citations. They'll respond to someone who's adept at eliciting information from recalcitrant adolescents, don't you think? Besides, I did want to talk to you about enrolling the older children in school, at least for the moment. This will give you a chance to assess the possibilities." I looked at the sun, which was sinking toward Cotter's Ridge. "And I've got to leave town for a few days, and I'd like to pack up and get going before dark."

"Going on vacation?"

"No," I said, wounded that everyone seemed to have such a high opinion of my dedication to duty, "it's official business, but I can't discuss it until I get back. I sure could use your help, David Allen."

"Then you'll get it. I'll take Hammet over to Mrs. Jim Bob's and break the news to the children. We'll figure out what to do for the moment, and I'll see what, if anything, we can determine about absentee fathers. You just run along and do whatever you're planning to do."

I felt guilty, but I didn't want anyone to know where I intended to spend my weekend. Merle had sworn he wouldn't breathe a word about Robin's body, and he was so daft I doubted anyone listened to him, anyway. He'd also said he intended to spend several days on the banks of Boone Creek, recalculating angles, which suited me just fine. I thanked David Allen several times, meaning every word of it, and went so far as to ask him to have a word with Ruby Bee. I then tried a tentative smile in Hammet's direction.

"See you in a couple of days," I said.

He got in the passenger's side of the wagon and studied the windshield-wiper blade. David Allen went around to the other side and got in, then called to me. "I forgot to give this back to you," he said, holding up the beeper. "You don't want to leave home without it, do you?"

Looking at the blasted thing made me remember how irresponsible I'd been. It was the icing on the cake of incompetency, and the cake seemed to be growing extra layers every minute. I took it from him and clipped it on my belt. "I sort of forgot to return Mrs. Jim Bob's calls—maybe forty or fifty of them thus far," I said with a wry smile. "There's not much of a reason for me to call her now, since you'll be there in a few minutes and be able to tell her in person what's going on. I just don't have time to get entangled in her problems right now. Would you please tell her how busy I've been and offer her my apologies?"

David Allen assured me that he'd smooth it over, and he and Hammet drove away in the direction of Mizzoner's manor. I went back to the apartment, sat down and made a list of the paraphernalia I needed to take with me on this little camping jaunt, made a list of all the people I needed to talk to (but wouldn't until I got back), loaded up said paraphernalia in the sheriff's vehicle, and locked the apartment door behind me.

Then, wondering how someone as incompetent as I seemed to be, not to mention coldhearted and self-centered and all sorts of other charming things, could have survived thirty-four years without being locked away in a home for Nazi war criminals, I drove down the highway toward the road that led to the ridge. Although I knew the words to a few camp songs, none came to my incompetent, coldhearted, self-centered mind.

"Isn't he just the most darling little creature in the whole world?" Estelle said, squatting down in front of the high chair to tweak a sweet little pink toe.

"He sure is," Ruby Bee said. She leaned against the edge of the counter and fought back a yawn. "Why, last night he gave me the dearest smile while I sang him some lullabies in the rocking chair." She didn't see any reason to mention how many lullabies it'd taken for the baby to go back to sleep, but there'd been a good dozen more than there were sweet little pink toes.

"Who do you think he favors?"

"He favors the Buchanon clan," Ruby Bee said, trying not to sound testy, which wasn't easy on four hours of sleep. "Any fool can see the family resemblance. He's got that unfortunate, chimpanzee-lookin' forehead, black hair, and those yellow eyes what remind me of a weasel."

Estelle stood up and put her hands on her hips. "I beg your pardon, Rubella Belinda Hanks. I am capable of seeing that he has that Buchanon look to him, but thank you kindly for pointing out the obvious. I was referring to the pappy. You do recollect how there has to be a pappy, don't you? He does contribute something to make the little baby, so he might well look like him, too."

"I know all that, but thank you kindly for reminding me of something I learned at my mother's knee. I swear, these days they talk about it right in the classrooms of the schoolhouse, just like it was arithmetic or state capitals."

"Does that have something to do with the price of tea in China?"

"Not particularly," Ruby Bee conceded as she struggled with another yawn that darn near dislocated her jaw. "Do you think you can take Baby over to your house this afternoon? I've got to inventory my napkins and paper products, and I'm way off schedule 'cause Dahlia didn't come in last night."

"Did she call in sick?"

"Nope, not a peep. I know she's likely to have been in the shed with Kevin when God passed out the brains, but I was a mite disappointed with her. Thursday night's not a busy night, and I really did plan to leave her out front so I could go in the back room to count napkins and paper products. I need to put in an order before the weekend. What about you taking Baby?"

"I would if I could, but I absolutely have to redo Elsie's perm. She's been squealing about how she looks like Shirley Temple, and I've got to admit you can see a passing resemblance if you squint."

"Can't you put the crib in your bedroom?"

"Can't you put the crib in your storeroom?"

The two looked at each other for a while, then both turned to look at the sweetest little thing you've ever seen, who was turning red and screwing up his mouth in preparation to howl.

"You know," Ruby Bee said, deftly inserting a bottle into the baby's mouth, "this precious punkin does have a pappy out there who loves him. If Arly never finds Robin Buchanon, someone's going to have to take Baby and give him a home. It'd be criminal to deprive his pappy of the chance to raise him and wait up till all hours when he's out drinking beer with his friends."

Estelle climbed on a stool and nodded. "Downright criminal. I think we owe it to the little angel to help Arly find the father. We could even learn the identities of the fathers of the other children—just in case." She wiggled her eyebrows, not wanting to alarm Baby with the dire scenario.

"I'm sure Arly'd be real grateful. I don't know exactly how to go about it, though. Robin did have a reputation for . . . having a lot of friends." Ruby Bee wiggled her eyebrows, too. "Men friends."

"She sure did. She must have known half the county—and in the Biblical sense, if you follow my drift. I don't see how we can find out who all was blessed enough to father any of the children."

The baby bottle now depleted, Ruby Bee wearily

took the stool next to her. "Me neither. It ain't like we can go over to the county hospital and ask to see the birth certificates. I have a hard time seeing Robin in a hospital bed with a doctor hovering over her. She'd have had a midwife—if she had anything at all. It's just as likely that she dropped the younguns while hoeing potatoes in the field. Might not have even noticed at the time, for that matter."

"But that's a beginning," Estelle said, straightening up.

"What's a beginning, for Pete's sake? Searching potato fields?"

"The midwife out on the county road. We could ask her if she went to Robin's cabin to assist in the delivery of any of the babies. Then, if she says she was there, we can ask if Robin said anything about who the fathers were. That's a fine idea of yours, Ruby Bee. I'm right proud of you for coming up with it."

"I suppose so," Ruby Bee said with a sigh. "I just hope Arly doesn't get all hot and bothered and commence to thinking we're interfering again. She like to have had steam coming out her ears last time."

"We're not trying to find Robin Buchanon; we're just making discreet inquiries about the fathers. It's not even near the same thing as interfering in one of her so-called police investigations. After all, if fathering a bastard was a crime in Stump County, the jail'd be so jampacked that the convicts would have to make reservations to serve their time."

"I have a bad feeling about this. Maybe I'm having one of those premonitions like Madam Celeste has all the time, but I don't know if we're doing the right thing."

"Now, Ruby Bee, just look at that sweet sleepy baby. Doesn't he deserve to grow up with a loving pappy to take care of him? Besides, we'll just hop in my station wagon and run out to the midwife's house to ask. She's such a senile ole granny that she most likely won't be able to tell us anything. There's no point in acting all mystical and muttering under your breath like a psychic with laryngitis. Get your Closed sign and hang it on the door. We'll wrap up Baby and take him with us, and we'll all three be back in less than an hour. It can't hurt anything."

Ruby Bee nodded, but she was still having Severe Misgivings.

If I thought nothing ever happened in Maggody (and that theory was on the moth-eaten side by this time), I hadn't realized the extent of true nothingness. It was moderately amusing at first. I parked a good ways from the dope patch, and spent most of two hours lugging equipment from the four-wheel to a spot I felt was distant enough not to be seen should the weekend gardeners appear. I pitched a pup tent, unrolled my sleeping bag, lined up the cans of soup like little tin soldiers, spread out my gear, and generally got myself organized.

By then it was blacker than the inside of a cow, so I fixed a pan of soup on my stove, then crawled into the tent and dined on vegetable-beef and saltines while reading by flashlight. I didn't worry too much about someone seeing the faint light in the middle of nowhere, because no one would be dumb enough to approach the patch in the dark. The only person dumb enough to do that was sitting in a pup tent on the back side of Cotter's Ridge having an intimate experience with Campbell's finest. At some point I felt the need to put on heavy wool socks, and a little bit later a pair of gloves. Finally, dressed in every item of clothing I'd brought, I got into the sleeping bag and shivered until I fell asleep, reminding myself that this was my brilliant idea and that I was doing it for all the right reasons.

* * *

Hammet managed to delay the reunion for several hours, first by bursting into tears and wailing so loud that David Allen pulled over to the side of the road. Hammet then allowed how he jest couldn't face his siblings 'cause they would be so fuckin' upset it'd set him off again. He agreed that something to eat might help, and tried not to grin all the way down to Ruby Bee's Bar and Grill. For some odd reason it was closed, so David Allen offered to take him home for a quick sandwich and a soda.

That were even better, Hammet decided, letting his face crumple up again for good measure. Big tears rolled down his cheeks while he tried to figger out how to stay away from that thin-lipped ole bitch's house as long as possible.

"Look at all these here houses," he said admiringly as they drove through the subdivision. "Do you know all them what lives in 'em?"

"No, just the ones next to me. You do realize we're going to have something to eat, then go straight to Mrs. Jim Bob's house, don't you? I promised Arly that I'd break the news to everyone, and I feel guilty about the delay."

"Arly wouldn't mind. She's real nice about that sort of thing. Don't you think she's a right nice lady?" Hammet stole a quick look from under his brow. "And knockers—she's better built than a sow what's suckling a dozen babies. And she can cook real good, too, and she never talks dirty unless'n she's mad."

David Allen parked in his driveway and gestured for Hammet to get out of the wagon. "I can see you're smitten with her, but don't you think she's too old for you?" he asked as they went into the house.

"I never said she weren't old as the hills." Hammet wandered around the living room, examining the crumpled beer cans and old pizza boxes while his host went on to the kitchen. "You happen to be married?"

"Once upon a time I happened to be married. In fact, I have a little boy a few years younger than you. I'm fixing bologna and cheese—you want mustard or mayonnaise?"

"Where's your boy?"

David Allen poked his head out of the kitchen. "He lives with his grandparents in Farberville. Mustard or mayonnaise?"

"Both," Hammet said decisively, since he wasn't sure what either was. He recommenced to wandering. "Whose toys are these?"

"Mine."

"What does you do with them?"

"I launch them into the air, then try very hard to find them when they come down. Then I glue them back together and launch them again."

"Iffen you don't want to bust them, why do you launch them in the first place? Why not jest leave them on the shelf?"

David Allen stopped spreading mustard. "A good question. I enjoy the launch, and I have a radio thing to help me track them when they crash. It's sort of exciting . . . I guess."

"Mebbe if you was a kid," Hammet said, dismissing the crazy notion. "What happened to your little boy's mama? Was she kilt too? How come he don't live with you no more?"

"Because he needed a mother to take care of him, and the best I could do was a grandmother. He also needs to live near a doctor. As for his mother, she died from a nasty disease."

"My ma was kilt by a bear. She damn near kilt him first, but the ole thing was bigger than the broadside of a barn, and he had teeth sharp as knives, and big, long claws that could rip out your guts," Hammet said, proud of the way his ma'd tried to fight off the bear. "She din't die of some dumb disease."

David Allen came into the living room and put a

plate on the coffee table. "It would be more exciting if a bear attacked your mother, wouldn't it?" (*Techniques for Today's Intervention Therapy,* Chapter Three: "Denial as an Expression of Grief.") "But you and I both heard Arly say that your mother was killed in a hunting accident, didn't we?"

Hammet hadn't studied the technique in effect. "Yeah, she said that 'cause she thought it'd make me feel better than iffen she described how my ma's guts was all ripped into tatters by a fuckin' bear. There was most likely blood splattered up in the trees to the top branch. Arly probably had to look all over the place to find my ma's arms and legs—or what was left of 'em. Why, little Sissy'd start bawling and keening and carryin' on if we told her that." He snatched up the sandwich and jammed it in his mouth, regretting the reference to his sibling. He sure din't want to remind David Allen they wasn't doing what Arly'd told 'em to do.

"As soon as you're finished, we're going. We are not going to relate this wild story about the bear; instead, we're going to say as little as possible. Right, partner?" (*Ibid.,* Chapter Six: "Eliciting Cooperation from the Client.")

"You know," Hammet said through a mouthful of sandwich, "you could have your little boy here with you if you was to get married. You already knows how to be a parent and make little boys take baths and all that crap. All you need is a woman to be his ma. She doesn't have to know much about doin' it."

"That's a possibility, I suppose. You don't happen to have anyone in mind, do you?"

"Guess your little boy's right sad that he don't have any siblings." Hammet let out a lengthy sigh of despair over the plight of the siblingless boy. "He don't have nobody to play with or to punch in the mouth when he gets all riled. I bet he has to sleep by hisself in his bed, and gets colder than a widder woman's feet. He most likely—"

"He has several friends in the neighborhood," David Allen cut in, "and he doesn't mind being an only child."

"Only a child? If he's littler than me, he's got to be only a child. How old do you reckon I am?"

"Old enough to know what went on at the cabin," David Allen said, opting for a diversion. "Old enough to recognize the men who visited your mother on occasion, and old enough to tell me about them. I almost laughed when Arly suggested I talk to Bubba, simply because he's the oldest. Anyone with the sense God gave a goose can see that you're the smartest."

Hammet had that much sense, if not more. He figgered if he admitted he could recognize his ma's visitors, he might well find himself having to go live with one of the sumbitches. Instead of comin' up with a lie, he clutched his belly and doubled over, howling like a January wind coming through one of the cracks in the cabin. It ended the conversation, at least for the moment.

10

"And if you don't mend your ways, why—you'll all spend eternity in the blazing fires of hell," Mrs. Jim Bob concluded in a pious spray of spittle. Steeling herself to be charitable about the big rip in the upholstery of her sofa, she folded her hands in her lap and gazed at the nearest Buchanon bastard, who happened to be Sissie. "Now, just what do you have to say for yourself?"

"How do I know you ain't lying?"

"Because, young lady, I am a God-fearing Christian woman who was brought up to tell the truth if I didn't want to be beaten on the buttocks by my father's leather strap. I was not reared in some filthy pigsty by a woman with no morals or sense of decency. And now that's she dead and burning forever in the fiery furnace of damnation, you'd better heed what all I say to you." She turned to stare at Bubba, who held a sniveling Sukie on his lap. "And as for you, young man, you're likely to spend your life on this earth in a rat-infested prison cell if you don't mend your ways, not to mention enduring ever-lasting torment after you die some terrible death."

"Big fuckin' deal," Bubba said. "I still think you're a-lyin' about what happened to Her. We don't have to pay any mind to what lies you tell us, or listen to all this shit about devils and fires and furnaces." He pushed Sukie off his lap and stood up. "Come on, y'all. We're gittin' out of here. This holyfied lady's jest tryin' to bumfuzzle us."

Mrs. Jim Bob resisted an urge to smack the smirk off his face, because that wouldn't be charitable in his hour of grief. "If you don't believe me, I'll call Brother Verber to come over here and tell you all the details of how you'll burn in hell until you look worse than a charred marshmallow. But let me point out that you were brought here by the police, which means you're arrested and in my custody. For another thing, you don't have anywhere to go. Your mother is dead, and there's no one in this entire world who has one whit of concern about any of you. If you had any sense at all, you'd drop to your knees and beg my forgiveness for all the wretched, horrible sins you've committed against me, right here in my own home. I'm liable to throw you out myself, and let you sit in the cold night until you all starve to death."

Sissie looked at her brother. "Do you think Her is really dead? Iffen she is, we hafta do something."

Sukie got up off the floor and stuck a finger in her mouth. "Where's Hammet?" she whined, as saliva dribbled down her wrist like a brown crayon mark.

Mrs. Jim Bob stopped being righteous long enough to run a head count. "Where is that little heathen? Did he have the nerve to leave my house without asking permission?"

"You was upstairs," Bubba said. "He'll come back when he's a mind to." He wrinkled his brow for a minute, then frowned at Sissie. "Where the fuck is Baby? You was supposed to watch out for him, and I don't recollect hearing him howl for a long while. I ought to whup you up the side of the head for losing Baby."

He took a step toward her, his hand raised. Shrieking, Sissie dashed behind the sofa and lit out for the kitchen. Sukie began to moan and hiccup, sending more rivulets of brown down her arm to collect on her elbow. Bubba yelled at Sissie to get her ass back afore he kicked it across the county. Sissie yelled that he was gonna be shit-faced sorry, 'cause she was coming back with a goddamn butcher knife to carve out his heart and feed it to the hawgs. Bubba began to stalk toward the kitchen as he loudly opined that she had a fat chance of doin' that.

From her perch on the sofa, Mrs. Jim Bob took in the action. She was still in control, she told herself in a level voice. One or two of the bastards might have wandered off, but she was down from the bedroom and clearly held the upper hand. The bastards were orphans; they were at the mercy of her generosity and hospitality, not to mention the fact she could have all of them thrown in jail for what they'd done to her newly carpeted downstairs. If she was kindhearted enough to allow them to work off the damage, they'd be cutting the grass and scrubbing the floors until they were middle-aged. And cleaning those disgusting smears off the plate glass. And gluing together shattered dishes. And polishing the wood until it positively gleamed. And scraping food off the wallpaper, although the flocked swirls would never look all that pretty again.

"You!" she said, snatching Sukie's arm to dislodge the finger. "You are a nasty little orphan girl. If you don't beg my forgiveness, you're going to be right sorry for the rest of your life."

"Let go my hair or I'll kill you!" Sissie shrieked from the kitchen.

"I'm fixin' to rip out every goddamn hair on your head!" Bubba replied in kind. "And kick your butt till you cain't walk no more!"

"Oh, yeah? How about I cut off your dick?"

Mrs. Jim Bob tightened her grip on Sukie's arm. "Did you understand me, young lady? You just get on your knees and start begging."

Sukie lifted her free hand to consider which finger held the most promise. Once she made her selection, she stuck it her mouth. "Fuck you, lady," she said wetly.

Mrs. Jim Bob was formulating a reply when she heard a knock at the front door, although it was a miracle she heard it over the din from the kitchen. She went to the door, smoothing her skirt along the way, flipped on the porch light, and opened the door with a vague smile.

"Why, David Allen, how nice of you to come by for a visit," she said as she stepped onto the porch and closed the door behind her. There was no reason for him to be forced to listen to those vile screeches, she told herself. After all, someone who was unacquainted with the personal sacrifices she'd made by taking in the bastards would be likely to misinterpret what all was going on in her kitchen.

"Good evening," David Allen said, wondering what the holy hell was going on in her kitchen. It sure didn't sound like a meeting of the ladies' missionary society—unless they were role-playing heathen savages.

"I'm afraid I wasn't expecting company just now. Did you drop by unannounced to have a word with Mr. Jim Bob? He's out of town at the moment, but I'd be glad to take a message. Or is there something I can do for you?"

David Allen began to tell her about Robin's death, but she cut him off almost immediately. "I already know about the murder and the booby trap," she said. "I have informed the children, who seem to be taking it well. Of course, they were as aware as the rest of us that the woman was an ignorant, immoral, filthy-minded whore and therefore hardly a great loss."

"She were not," Hammet said from behind David Allen.

"There you are, you wicked, wicked child!" Mrs. Jim Bob said. "How dare you sneak away like some slimy snake?"

Before Hammet could point out that snakes wasn't

slimy, Sissie opened the front door. "There's some man a-bellowin' for you on this contraption. Sounds like a right ornery peckerwood."

Which ruled out Arly and LaBelle, who weren't men, and Brother Verber, who never sounded like an ornery peckerwood. Squaring her shoulders in much the same way the Christians had when ushered into the presence of lions, Mrs. Jim Bob told David Allen that he would simply have to come back in the morning when she could receive him. She went inside and locked the front door, then crossed the living room to the telephone in order to have a word with her husband, who was all the way down in Hot Springs at a municipal league meeting. At least she dearly prayed he was.

David Allen stood on the porch for a while, then finally got into his wagon and drove over to Ruby Bee's Bar and Grill, where over a beer and a cheeseburger he related his news to an interested party.

I woke up the next morning at some absurd hour, heated water for coffee on my camp stove, ate cornflakes from the box, and tidied up the tent. All that got me to seven o'clock. I brushed my teeth, combed my hair, and had another cup of coffee. That got me to seven-fifteen. I doubted my weekend gardeners would show anytime soon, so I went down to the jeep and made sure it was invisible under the scrub pines and branches I'd piled on it. Seven-thirty. I checked for tire marks along the road, just in case my boys were wily enough to notice. Seven-forty. I was back at the tent, preparing another cup of coffee, when my beeper beeped from somewhere inside the sleeping bag.

Although it was not my favorite sound, it was pleasant to reaffirm the existence of an outside world. I went back to the wagon (seven-fifty-five) and called in on the radio. "Somebody need me?" I asked optimistically.

"This is LaBelle, honey. The sheriff just wanted me to check on you and see how it's going up there. You caught any criminals as of yet?"

"Not as of yet," I said, watching a squirrel scamper up a tree and fling itself into space like a furry Frisbee. "But tell Harvey that I've set up camp and found a place from which to keep surveillance on the scene. I think odds are good that the perpetrators will show up today or tomorrow. If not, I'll drag myself back tomorrow night and admit defeat."

"I just know as sure as the sun rises that you'll nab them, Arly."

"Thank you, LaBelle."

"Oh, and Harvey says he feels rotten that he couldn't send a man up there for backup, but we're plumb busier than ants at a Sunday-school picnic these days. He also says for you to check in every four hours, so we'll know you're okay, that you haven't been eaten by wild animals or shot in the head by these awful dopers and left to bleed to death all by yourself up on the ridge. So you check with me every four hours, rain or shine. Can you remember all that?"

"Yes, LaBelle, I can. Did Harve really say all that?"

"Verbatim, honey. Oh, and Ruby Bee called to talk to you. She seemed to think your beeper was like a walkie-talkie and that she could holler into it and you'd hear her, but I had to inform her otherwise." LaBelle licked her lips as she pondered some folks' misconceptions about police technology. "Anyways, she said for you not to worry about her and Estelle interfering in the police investigation, because they're not."

The squirrel had stopped on a nearby branch to glare at me through little red eyes. I glared back so hard, he backed into the leaves. "Just what did Ruby Bee mean by that?" I said grimly.

"I really couldn't say. She just told me to give

you the message. Well, I've got to run, Arly. Harvey's bellowing for coffee, and he can be worser than a mangy old grizzly bear if he doesn't get it. You have a nice time up there in the woods."

Her voice faded in a crackle of static. I fetched a blanket, my book, a thermos, and my camera, then went to the spot I'd chosen and made myself as comfortable as possible, considering. I could see the patch and part of the road beyond it. I figured I'd hear a car engine long before it arrived, or even the snap, crackle, and pop of dried leaves if someone tried to approach on foot. Eight-fifteen.

After a while the birds, gnats, mosquitoes, and squirrels decided I was harmless and began to squawk, buzz, bite, and chatter. I leaned back against a tree trunk and considered the case. Robin Buchanon had a ginseng patch (e-i-e-i-o). She'd come to it about a week ago, with her gunnysack and hoe and expectations of digging up the roots to sell to a wholesaler. A nice autumn day, the family patch, an easy hundred dollars or so. Her only source of legal income, although it was hard to imagine that she reported it for income-tax purposes.

But someone had found the patch earlier in the year, probably toward the middle of the summer, and decided it was the perfect spot to grow a little dope. And why not? It was flat, with good drainage and a creek not too far away to provide water, and best of all, it was smack-dab in the middle of nowhere. The ginseng had been a scattering of low plants then, with no berries or distinctive leaves to hint at its value. So that someone(s) had cleared the ground and put in a half acre of marijuana.

The fact that there were booby traps was uncommon, but not unheard of. Plenty of ole boys thought they'd be right sly and put various traps around their patches to spook hikers and hunters, or those who failed to follow the philosophy of the Little Red Hen and hoped for an easy profit. The growers could hardly report the theft. I'd heard stories of punji pits, of baby rattlesnakes tied to the plants, of all sorts of crazy devices made from clothespins, detonator caps, gunpowder, and Plasticine.

So that didn't get me anywhere. Now that I thought about it (eight-forty-six), I was most likely wasting my time. True, it was the end of the harvest season and time to cut the plants. True, the perps were likely to do so on the weekend, since they could pretend they were out scouting for deer or taking a little nature hike. True, all I had to do was get a good look at them and maybe at the vehicle. True, true, true. It was also true that I was intending to sit on my fanny in the middle of the woods for forty-eight hours on the off chance they might show up. There was an equally good chance I'd nab wee green men in shiny saucers complete with Christmas lights and synthesizer music.

I wondered how David Allen had made out with Hammet, his siblings (I was beginning to regret my vocabulary lesson), and Mrs. Jim Bob. That arena of thought made me uncomfortable, so I moved right on to Kevin and Dahlia and the jeep. It wasn't too tough to conclude Kevin had taken up the junior G-man cause, and had managed to persuade Dahlia to accompany him on his harebrained mission. But what had happened to them? I made a mental note to have LaBelle check at the high school to see if he had shown up for work yesterday.

Dahlia, of course, worked for my mother, the same woman who'd sent the message that she wasn't interfering in the police investigation. Which meant that she was. Ruby Bee's easier to read than a *Reader's Digest* condensed book. But I couldn't come up with any theories to explain what she and Estelle might be doing. They weren't perched in a tree to assist in the stakeout, since no one knew about the dope patch except for the sheriff's department, Merle Hardcock, and yours truly. For that matter, only that select group knew there'd been a murder—or any other crime.

"What police investigation?" I muttered aloud, just to hear a human voice. Lord, within twenty-four hours I'd be singing hymns and having debates with myself. I threw a walnut at a squirrel that had ventured too near, then picked up my book and settled in. Nine-eleven. Over and out.

"And she claimed not to know where Arly is?" Estelle said in an incredulous voice. "You know as well as you know the nose on your face that LaBelle is lying through her teeth—which anyone can see are nothing more than mail-order dentures. Arly wouldn't waltz away in the middle of all this confusion, what with Buchanon bush colts all over town and Robin Buchanon deader than a doorknob up in the woods." She patted a stray wisp into place and propped her elbows on the bar. Lowering her voice to a husky whisper, she added, "I find that mighty suspicious."

"What?" Ruby Bee asked. "LaBelle lying, Arly waltzing, Buchanons all over Maggody, or Robin the victim of an accident?"

"All of it," Estelle said grandly.

"Don't wake Baby. This is the first time I've had a chance to sit down and take a load off my feet. Dahlia didn't come in last night, so I had to run myself ragged between the bar, the booths, and the kitchen. I suppose she's decided to quit. I'd have thought she had the common courtesy to tell me to my face, instead of just plain not showing up. She didn't even drop off the apron I made especially for her."

"Well, there's no point in fretting over her. Breeding shows, if you know what I mean. But what are we going to do about finding out the identity of Baby's father?"

"What can we do? The midwife says she never attended Robin's birthings, and wouldn't have anyway on account of Robin being the way she was. We wasted a good hour over there, all for nothing. The Bar and Grill was closed right in the middle of the Friday happy hour, which cost me a pretty penny. Then Baby cried half the night, and I couldn't get back to sleep, and—"

"We can't give up yet, Miz Throw-in-the-Towel."

It occurred to Ruby Bee that they certainly could give up if they wanted to. It also occurred to her that Estelle had failed to have a precious little overnight visitor, and therefore had had considerably more sleep than some she could name. Leaning against the counter, she pointed out all of the above in a voice that was reasonably polite, considering.

"That was an innocent oversight," Estelle said indignantly. "I had to hurry off because I had to finish Elsie's perm so I could have a session with Madam Celeste, if you must know. Some people are acting like real busybodies these days, aren't they?"

Ruby Bee let the insinuation slide by her. "What'd Madam Celeste say?"

"She didn't say anything because she refused to see me. Mason was real nice about it, though, and invited me to sit down for a soda or a glass of iced tea. He's the politest thing."

She and Ruby Bee exchanged looks that verged on telepathy.

"He's single, you know," Estelle said.

"He doesn't have a real job," Ruby Bee pointed out.

"But he's personable and polite," Estelle countered. "Politer than a door-to-door missionary with a handful of religious tracts. Dresses like one, too, in a nice jacket and tie, just like he was going to a funeral."

"Nobody said they have to get married," Ruby Bee said, nodding. "I suspect Arly's been keeping company with David Allen Wainright, although she's so tight-lipped that it's hard to get a word out of her. Anyway, it'd do her some good to have a couple of suitors for a change. I worry about her."

"And well you should." Estelle took a sip of sherry, then carefully dabbed her lipstick with a napkin. "Imagine a daughter leaving town without telling her own mother where she was going. And she never did ask Madam Celeste to help her with the investigation, you know. She just scooted out of town without bothering to cancel the appointment or anything."

"Just imagine," Ruby Bee said. "You'd think she'd never been taught any manners, or that she doesn't have enough sense to take help from someone who's maybe a teensy bit odd."

"Someone who's proved she can assist the police, who can find missing people as easy as snapping her fingers."

"Madam Celeste will be right offended if no one shows up to ask her for help."

"But Arly already knows what happened to Robin Buchanon." Estelle wasn't arguing; she was just building a case for any future defense.

Ruby Bee chewed on that one for a few minutes. "But," she said slowly, "she doesn't know who fathered all those children, and now that they're orphans, it's real important to find out. David Allen told me he was going to question the children today, but he didn't anticipate much success. He said Arly asked him to do it, too."

"Well, there you have it! That just shows that Arly would appreciate any assistance she can get. We tried the midwife, and that resulted in a big, fat goose egg if there ever was one. We know there aren't any birth certificates at the hospital. Robin sure isn't going to offer up any information from the funeral parlor."

"Do you think Madam Celeste could identify the fathers just by thinking real hard? Wouldn't we need to take her something so she could grasp the cosmic vibrations or whatever it is she does?"

It was Estelle's turn to chew. "We can't steal Robin's body and take it over there; the sheriff would have a fit. We just need something that belongs to Robin."

Ruby Bee stared at the storeroom door, behind which was a crib and the sweetest thing you ever laid eyes on. "Something comes to mind, now that I think about it. I just hate to wake him up and set him off howling and screaming the rest of the day."

"That little dumpling? We'll carry him out to my station wagon, and I'll drive slower than smoke off a manure pile. He won't notice a thing until we're back here, all safe and sound. And he can sleep better because we'll know the identity of his dear pappy, who loves him and can come pick him up to take home with him." Estelle picked up her purse and settled her sunglasses on her nose. "Fetch the baby, Ruby Bee. It's almost ten o'clock."

Ruby Bee fetched as carefully as she could, but Baby was screaming like one of those punk rockers by the time they drove out of the parking lot of Ruby Bee's Bar and Grill.

At ten o'clock I reported in to the sheriff's office. Once LaBelle finished informing me that I was supposed to wait four hours, which would make it twelve instead of ten, I asked if there had been any further communiqués from Ruby Bee or Mrs. Jim Bob.

"Not a word from either of them, honey. Nobody has any messages for me to send to you. You don't have to worry about that."

Rather than relieving me, the silence struck me as ominous. "Did you ever find out what was going on at Mrs. Jim Bob's house while she was putting in all those hysterical messages for me?" I asked.

"Can't say I ever inquired," LaBelle said with an audible sniff. "You know perfectly well that I am not supposed to discuss police business with civilians."

I scratched my nose as I tried to make sense of that remark. As I opened my mouth to point out that I was police, LaBelle informed me that she had to make a visit to the little girls' room and that she would look forward to hearing from me in four hours. I hurriedly asked her to check up at the high school to see if Kevin Buchanon had come to work yesterday, and to ask his parents if he was at home today. LaBelle made a gurgly noise and told me to take care, bye-bye.

I went back to my nest, telling myself that David Allen had things under control at Mrs. Jim Bob's house. He probably had a list of the fathers and was busy calling them one by one to tell them the good news. Mrs. Jim Bob was plying him with fresh coffee and pecan pie, while the Buchanons frolicked like puppies in the front yard. As for Ruby Bee, perhaps she wasn't in the midst of doing something she knew darn well would irritate me, if not enrage me. She was counting spoons or bathing the baby, or serving up heaping plates of chicken fried steaks, gravy, green beans cooked with salt pork, crisp fried okra, mashed potatoes, cherry cobbler. . . .

I abandoned my post long enough to get the box of cornflakes from my tent. Then, lecturing myself at ninety miles an hour, I returned to the post and stuffed said flakes into my mouth while keeping an eye on the pot patch. Just like it mattered. Ten-fifteen, if you're counting.

David Allen rapped again on the bedroom door. "Please come out, Mrs. Jim Bob. We've got to do something about the children."

"I don't care what you do with those filthy, satanic monsters. They've ruined my life. Let them rot in hell for all eternity."

"I realize they did a certain amount of damage downstairs, but—"

"Did you see the rip on the sofa?" she demanded

shrilly. "The mud on the new beige carpet? The smears on the walls? Did you smell the guest bathroom? Did you?"

David Allen tried to remember a chapter that dealt with the impending hysteria of a client. He decided there probably wasn't one. "We can clean all that up, if you'll just unlock the door and come out of the bedroom. Please, Mrs. Jim Bob."

"He's going to kill me," she answered, shrillness replaced with flatness.

"I won't let Bubba or Hammet or any of the children near you," David Allen said. "I promise that they'll keep nice and quiet so we all can talk about their futures."

"He's going to kill me. He said so, plainer than day."

David Allen came to the conclusion that it wasn't doing any good to converse through the door, and it was clear she wasn't coming out anytime soon. He went downstairs, where he found the four Buchanon children hunkered on the floor in front of the refrigerator amid a clutter of bowls and bottles.

"Having a picnic?" he inquired in a jovial, hearty tone meant to win their trust and ensure their cooperation.

The intensity of the slurps and belches increased, but no one bothered with a reply. He opened cabinets until he found a bourbon bottle pushed way back in a corner, and poured himself several inches of courage. Only then did he squat down next to Hammet and give him a comradely wink.

"What do you think, buddy? Shall we talk about fathers?"

Hammet put a handful of cole slaw in his mouth. "Ain't none of us know anything about that," he said in a jovial, hearty tone that sounded suspiciously familiar to David Allen's professional ears. "You ain't going to find our fathers, so there ain't no point in harpin' any more about it. When's Arly coming back?"

Bubba growled through a piece of chicken. "Who gives a fuck when the policewoman comes back? She's just a damn whore anyways."

Hammet slung a handful of slaw across the little picnic area. "Take that back, you shit-faced sumbitch, or I'll stuff that chicken wing up your nose!"

"Sez who?" Bubba said, rising to his feet. He ignored the strands of slaw dripping off his chin as he crushed a Tupperware bowl under his foot. "Wanna make me?"

David Allen decided the time was not appropriate for a discussion of paternity. He went to his vehicle and lit a cigarette. He did not glance up as a curtain fluttered in an upstairs room. When the cigarette was finished, he drove down the driveway without once looking back.

"Isn't he a living doll?" Ruby Bee held up Baby so that the little legs dangled like a ballerina's.

"I do not have time to admire babies," Madam Celeste said through the screen. "I am studying the cards. Come back later."

"But this is right up your alley," Estelle said. "This is just like that case back in Las Vegas when you found the poor little boy's body out in the desert. This is a police investigation."

"So now you are police? How interesting. When did you change professions?"

Estelle shoved Ruby Bee closer to the door. "You remember how Ruby Bee's daughter is the chief of police, don't you? We're just helping Arly while she's gone on a trip."

Celeste shook her head. "I do not know what's happening, but I do know that I am not a babysitter or even the sort to make stupid noises over a baby. Go away and leave me alone."

Mason came out of the den. "Hi, Miss Oppers, Miz Hanks. Wherever did you get that adorable little baby?" Ignoring his sister's hiss, he went to the screen door and opened it. "Y'all come right in so I can get a better look at this baby of yours."

While he bent down to tweak toes and make stupid noises, Estelle gave Madam Celeste her most meaningful look. "This baby's mother is the woman who was found dead up in the woods somewhere."

"That's right," Ruby Bee added, not sure her look was quite as meaningful as Estelle's, especially since she wasn't sure what precisely it was supposed to mean.

"So?" Celeste shrugged, apparently not sure either.

Estelle came a few steps farther into the hall. "We want you to tell us who's the father of this baby. We figgered the identity might manifest itself if you had the baby here with you."

"Why? What difference does it make?"

Mason straightened up. "Well, if the mama's dead, the baby sure does need a daddy, doesn't he?"

Estelle bobbled her head. "And you're the only person who can help us, Madam Celeste."

The psychic moved farther back until her face was distorted by shadows. "I am not an adoption agent or a social worker. I do not like babies, and I cannot work when one is in my presence. Or in my house."

Estelle took Baby from Ruby Bee and tucked him under her arm. "Well, I'll just stash this little sweetums in the car while you get settled at the table in the solarium. It won't do a toad's hair of harm for Baby to sit outside by himself for a few minutes. Think how happy he'll be to learn who his daddy is!"

Celeste told Mason to bring an extra chair to the solarium, then wearily gestured for Ruby Bee to follow her through the living room. She and Ruby Bee were both at the table when Estelle joined them.

"Do you think Baby'll be okay in the station wagon?" Ruby Bee whispered to Estelle.

"Do you think I'd put him there if I didn't?" Estelle retorted, offended by the very idea. "Nobody ever comes down this road anymore except for a occasional chicken truck headed for Hasty. We don't have caravans of Gypsies going up and down the road, looking for babies to steal. Baby's as safe out front as he would be in your storage room."

"Hush!" Madam Celeste said as she closed her eyes. "You are worse than a squawling baby."

Estelle snorted, but very quietly. Beside her, Ruby Bee tried to keep her mind on the matter at hand and not worry about Baby out in front.

Brother Verber woke up with a groan. His back hurt something awful from the night on the couch, and his knees felt like they were gripped by rubber bands. On the television set across the room cartoon characters moved their lips like amateur ventriloquists as they discussed invasions and wicked princes. He looked at the clock.

"Holy Jesus," he muttered as he sat up. His foot knocked over the glass of sacrificial wine, sending an odorous splash of red all over the braided rug and the pile of study material. It was nearly eleven o'clock. There was something he was supposed to do, but he couldn't for the life of him think what it was. A bedside visit to some dyin' member of the flock? A meeting with the church elders to talk about the behavior of the newest Sunday-school teacher, who'd been seen coming out of a coed skating rink in Farberville? A counseling session with some of the sexually depraved parishioners?

He used his handkerchief to wipe off the study material, wishing it was the counseling session, now that he'd had the opportunity to engage in some right serious research into the possibilities of depravity. On the cover of one of the manuals was a photograph of a young man wearing a black mask, a studded leather collar, and not much else. Noticing the model's rippling thighs brought it all back.

Brother Verber looked at the telephone receiver, which still dangled at the end of the cord. Sister Barbara was expecting him to come by for a piece of pecan pie. Or she had been expecting him more than thirty-six hours ago, anyway. But he hadn't gone because . . . (Brother Verber tugged his earlobe) . . . he'd felt the need of atonement for . . . (he scratched his stubbly jowl) . . . the sin of . . . (he squirmed like a nightcrawler in a coffee can of dirt) . . . arrogance. Yeah, that's why he hadn't gone by to praise her for her Christian zeal in taking in those bastards and trying to instill in them a healthy dose of decency and morality and humility and eternal gratitude.

It was because she was more pious than he was, and he'd seized the necessity of praying in solitude. It wasn't because he didn't want to lay eyes on those filthy bastards. It wasn't because he wished to avoid unpleasantness. No, he told himself, wincing as a lightning bolt flashed across his head, he was doing the correct thing by isolating himself in humble prayer without permitting the intrusion of the telephone to disrupt his concentration.

And since it was Saturday, he mused as he eased himself back onto the couch, he needed even more isolation so he could work on his sermon. In fact, he was going to need isolation all day long. Comforted by the necessity of all that impending isolation, he mentally ran down the list of his favorite sermon themes: charity covering the multitude of sins; the wages of sin being death; the effectual fervent prayer of a righteous man availeth-ing much; by their fruits ye shall be knowing them.

None of them struck just right. As he rolled over, he saw the centerfold of one of his study manuals. The woman was clad in the typical sinful black-lace underthings, which never seemed to go under things since these harlots never wore things over them. He picked up the magazine and held it a few inches from his nose. Looking at the photograph inspired him in more ways than one.

"Shall I continue doin' this, my angel?" Kevin asked, raising his head so he could see his beloved's face over the generous contours of her body.

Dahlia gave him a tender smile. "You're doin' right well. Why, one of these days you're going to know exactly what to do without me having to tell you." She opened her lips to allow the escape of a tiny burp. "I'm beginning to feel like I'm in heaven."

"You are? Gee, that's great, honeybun." Gulping nervously at what he felt was an epic challenge to his manhood (and perhaps a civic responsibility as well), Kevin returned to work.

Dahlia entwined her fingers under her neck and gazed at the ceiling. She thought about how she loved Kevin, for his devoted diligence, if nothing else. Some might say he was kind of a slow learner, but she figgered they had all the time in the world—and then some. After all, wasn't nobody ever going to find them. Not Kevin's sharp-tongued mother nor his mean ole pa, not her own granny with the scary quotes from the Old Testament and her glass eye that all the time fell out and rolled under the recliner like a marble, not thundering Brother Verber, not even Arly, who might throw Kevin in jail for what all he did.

"Just a smidgen higher," she murmured contentedly.

11

"I thought you were going to Starley City to get the crystal shipment," Rainbow said, coming into the Emporium office.

Nate was sprawled on the couch, a baseball cap pulled down over his eyes. "I hafta to hang around for a call," he said through a yawn. "I'll get over there Monday."

"A long-distance call?"

"Just a call." Nate yawned again, and settled himself farther down in the cushions. "Don't bother to ask, because I don't want to discuss it. Or share it, as you'd say. It's personal business." And it would get him out of this godawful town and back into the pool halls of Farberville, where he belonged. Hell, he'd have enough bread to hit all the pool halls in the state, if not the whole damn country. Cold beer and hot women. No more of this aren't-we-centered crap. No more screwing a woman who shrieked about cosmic convergence when she came, or half listening to her discussion afterward about the starlit seeds vibrating in her womb, of all goofy things. No more nonsense—if, of course, his partner was right about being able to predict the moment the policewoman abandoned the stakeout long enough for them to chop the dope and get it out of there.

Too bad his partner was opposed to just going up there and doing whatever was necessary to the woman. They were already facing a murder-two rap at worst, a negligent homicide at best. They were waist deep in shit; one more death wouldn't make a whole hell of a lot of difference.

He realized Rainbow was staring at him. "What's wrong with you?" he said, scowling at her.

"You're not one of us," she said as she crossed her arms and leaned against the doorway. "Your soul is still tortured from bad experiences in the past, isn't it? You're not capable of seeking a higher spiritual plane; you're not even able to explore the present physical reality. You'll never be able to counterbalance those discreative intentions or cleanse your inner channels."

"Blah, blah, blah. You know what—you make me sick. Every time you start gabbling about spiritual planes and cosmic harmony, I want to puke. Hell, maybe I'm pregnant like our fat little friend out behind the counter."

Rainbow's smile tightened until her lips ached. "Then why are you a member of our family, Nate? Why don't you pack your tattered duffel bag and find some new friends more like yourself?"

"When I get the word from my astrologer, maybe I will. Like when Capricorn rises in Gemini, the moon is in the seventh house, Jupiter aligns with Mars, and all that crap, maybe I will." Laughing, he turned his face to the back of the couch.

Rainbow went to the front of the store and dug through a drawer for her astrological miniguide. She was frowning at the squiggles when Poppy waddled over to her. "Capricorn doesn't rise in Gemini," she murmured, puzzled.

"I never said it did," Poppy said. "So what?"

"I was just checking. When's your appointment with the midwife?"

"I was supposed to go this afternoon, but Nate said not to take the truck. My ankles are so swollen I doubt I can walk all the way out there. I guess I'll try to go tomorrow or the next day." Poppy ran her hand over her bulging belly. "If it's not too late."

"You think . . . ? This would be a very auspicious day for a birth, astrologically. Nate's mutters made no sense, but anyone can see that a child born today will have a very solid basis in Scorpio. Oh, Poppy, let's align our vibrations and see if we can induce labor!"

Poppy wasn't all that eager to induce labor, a.k.a. labor pains, but she managed a smile as she closed her eyes and began to hum through her nose. It would be nice to have a Scorpio baby; Scorpios could be very determined and levelheaded.

Mrs. Jim Bob realized things had gotten real quiet. She took the damp washrag off her forehead and sat up, her nose twitching like a rabbit approaching a trap. When she still didn't hear anything (especially along the lines of shrieked profanities or shattering glass), she went to the door and put her ear against it. Nothing.

But it was the kind of quiet that made you shiver if you were watching an old horror movie, because you knew in your heart that the monster was fixing to spring out of the bushes. It was the kind of quiet that comes between the flash of lightning and the boom of thunder, when you nervously count off the seconds under your breath. It was the kind of quiet that blankets a cemetery on a cold, drizzly day.

Mrs. Jim Bob looked outside at the desultory rain coming down. At last, unable to contain her curiosity, she opened the door and peered down the hallway. She took off her bedroom slippers, then crept to the top of the stairs, prepared to flee back to the sanctuary should she hear the slightest noise. No muffled giggles. No sudden gasps or snorts. Nothing. She made it halfway down the stairs without hearing anything but the thudding of her heart. She made it to the bottom.

"Bubba?" she whispered. "Are you nasty little bastards playing hide-and-seek? You're going to be real sorry if I find you."

She did some seeking, and determined that they were gone. Where, she couldn't begin to imagine, but she didn't waste a lot of time on it, either. Mr. Jim Bob had said, albeit with more snarling than anything else, that he'd better not find those bastards in his house if she knew what was good for her. She didn't believe some of his threats, partly because she was a good Christian woman who would never listen to that kind of language, and partly because he was so angry he was incoherent. It was pretty clear, though, that he didn't want to run a makeshift orphanage.

Neither did she. In fact, after giving him a couple of hours to calm down, she'd tried to call him back to tell him she'd think of some way to get rid of the bastards. A snooty desk clerk had informed her that Mr. Buchanon had checked out. No, he hadn't left any messages, and good day, madam. It had turned her blood to chilled tomato aspic.

Now, as she considered it, it came to her that she'd done the kind, generous, pious thing by seeing that the bastards were brought down to town and given food and shelter. That had been her Christian duty. She'd pointed out their sinful ways and instructed them in the path of righteousness. In fact, she'd set them on the path and given them a swift pat on the fanny to start them on their way. She'd done her duty and then some.

There was a dreadful mess on the kitchen floor, but she stepped over it and put on the kettle for a nice cup of tea. More than her duty, she thought as she took out a cup and saucer, a box of tea bags, and her nicest creamer and sugar bowl—the ones with the lavender rosebuds that had belonged to her grandmother.

Arly had taken advantage of her kindhearted soul,

Mrs. Jim Bob told herself. Arly was the one who should have disinfected the bastards and seen to their basic needs. Arly was the chief of police, which meant she was in charge when the mayor and town council were out of pocket. Arly could have put the bastards in a jail cell, where they couldn't destroy someone's lovely home with new beige carpeting.

She poured boiling water into the cup, then took the tray into the dining room and sat down at the table. It was becoming increasingly clear that this whole disaster was Arly's fault. Everybody knew Arly had lived in New York City, which was filled with perverts and muggers and book editors. Not to mention society women, who ran around in skin-tight dresses and miniskirts that were the devil's own designer fashions. They painted their faces and drank martinis all day and slept with each other's husbands all night. Now that she thought about it, Mrs. Jim Bob realized it was no wonder at all that Arly'd been able to trick her like she did. Good Christian women didn't know all the big-city dirty tricks, much less how to avoid being mis-treated and abused by them that did.

"Jim Bob's going to have a word with her," she said aloud, practicing just a tad. "He's going to tell her that she's responsible for all the damage done to our home and carpet. What's more, he's going to make her pay to shampoo the carpet and reuphol-ster the sofa."

There was a navy-blue print fabric over in Far-berville that would look real nice. It had peacocks with their tails all swooped up, and some flecks of beige. The current plaid was dingy, and she'd hap-pened to glance through the fabric samples one day, purely out of idle interest. The peacocks would look fine. And those heathen bastards had probably wiped their filthy hands on the wing chairs, which would look better if they were re-covered in something brighter, maybe rose to counter the navy.

Feeling much better, much better indeed, Mrs. Jim Bob went to the telephone book and looked up a number. When a voice answered, she briskly said, "Perkins, let me speak to your eldest. I'm going to need her to clean today."

She was in the middle of negotiations (Perkins' eldest thought cleaning houses was as delicate a job as brain surgery, and therefore expected to be paid about the same hourly rate) when the doorbell rang.

She told Perkins' eldest to hold her horses, then hurried to the door and threw it open. "I am on the telephone."

David Allen tried a smile meant to reassure her his intentions were good, if not his timing. "I came by to talk to the children. Shall I wait here while you fetch them?" he said, trying to ignore the rain dripping down his collar.

"They're gone. Now, if you'll excuse me, I don't have time to visit with you at the moment." Mrs. Jim Bob started to close the door, her mind toying with the possibility of paying minimum wage just this once. It was something of an emergency, what with Jim Bob most likely roaring up the highway.

"Where'd they go?"

"Now how would I know? I certainly can't read their pornographic little minds, not that I'd want to even if I could. Why don't you ask Madam Celeste?" She again tried to close the door, but someone's foot was in the way.

"When did they leave?" David Allen persisted, despite the pain.

"They left a while back, and they didn't say where they were going. They are not my responsibility, David Allen, and I don't keep track of everybody's comings and goings like I was some spinster at an attic window. Arly's the one who'd better do that, especially if she has a mind to keep her job."

The door closed in the guidance counselor's face. He blinked, then turned and looked as far as he could see in all directions for Buchanon children. When that didn't do any good, he drove over to the Bar and Grill to see if Ruby Bee had any theories. When that didn't do any good because nobody was there, he drove on home and got a beer out of the refrigerator. That did some good.

It may occur to you that a lot of people were lost—and it's undeniably true. For all intents and purposes, Kevin and Dahlia had dropped off the face of the earth. Four Buchanon bastards had taken off for parts unknown. Mr. Jim Bob had checked out of the hotel and was no longer snarling threats from his hotel room. Yes, Baby Buchanon wasn't googooing in the station wagon when Estelle and Ruby Bee came out of Madam Celeste's house, which set off a goodly amount of screechings and wild accusations and indignant rebuttals. Mason Dickerson wasn't available to ask if he'd seen anyone on the road, and his sleek silver car wasn't parked in the driveway. Madam Celeste was in the house, one supposed, but she wouldn't come to the door despite a lot of banging and pleading to do so.

Other people were where they were supposed to be. Nate was still napping on the sofa in the back room of the Emporium, waiting for a call he hoped would liberate him. Poppy and Rainbow were out in the front, sounding off like kazoos. Zachery, the fourth partner, was in the loading area in the back, smoking a joint and enjoying the rain that misted his hair and beard with tiny crystals. David Allen was fiddling with his toys and on his third beer. Perkins' eldest was trudging up the driveway to the mayor's manor, a bottle of ammonia in her purse, while inside same manor Mrs. Jim Bob sat at the dining-room table and sipped tea from a porcelain cup. Brother Verber was scribbling away, his face flushed with inspiration as he thought up increasingly pious expressions that would knock the socks off 'em the following morning at the Voice of the Almighty Lord Assembly Hall.

The minor players were doing minor things of no great import. Kevin Buchanon's mother was hunting for a recipe for sweet potato pie, because her last hadn't been quite spicy enough and she prided herself on the perfect combination of cinnamon and nutmeg. Her husband, Earl, was wondering where the hell Kevin was, but he wasn't worrying all that much since boys will be boys and at least Kevin wasn't in the sweet gum tree peeking at naked hippies. He'd checked first thing, but the tree was uninhabited.

Elsie McMay was hovering near the telephone, just in case the filthy pervert called. Merle Hardcock stood on the north bank of Boone Creek, trying to refigure the angles. Carol Alice and Heather were cross-legged on Carol Alice's bed, thumbing through fashion magazines for ideas for bridesmaids' dresses, Heather being steadfastly opposed to both puffy sleeves and high waistlines, since neither flattered her and she knew it. Carol Alice's fiancé was over in the National Forest with a couple of his buddies, drinking beer, telling risqué stories, and arguing about the best location for a deer stand whenever they chanced to remember the purpose of the jaunt. Gladys Buchanon was squinting at her grocery list, since she couldn't find her glasses again and wasn't about to pay fifteen dollars for psychic revelations. LaBelle was in the little girls' room, cursing that doctor in Farberville who wasn't a day older than her nephew and therefore hardly qualified to prescribe medicine and prod at people's privates. Harve was grumbling over reports that looked like they'd been written by third graders. Decidedly minor things.

* * *

The drizzle was not making me happy. It was making me clammy and cold. It was making my blanket squishy. It was making my coffee watery and my cornflakes droopy. It was making my mood bleaker than that of a bag lady who'd lost her baggage.

No one had approached the pot patch, which meant I hadn't nabbed a single criminal as of yet. I doubted my perps were foolish enough to appear on a miserable, wet, cold day, harvesttime or not. Perps weren't notoriously clever (or they wouldn't be perps—they'd be investment bankers or Mercedes salesmen), but even the dumbest ole boys had enough sense to stay in out of the rain. Squirrels and blue jays and mosquitoes had enough sense to stay in out of the rain. Only chiefs of police were devoid of sense. Not to mention cold and wet and bored and lonesome and apt to come down with pneumonia.

I pulled my jacket more tightly around my shoulders and tried very hard not to succumb to self-pity. I didn't have a whole lot of success. At two o'clock I plodded through the wet leaves to the jeep and called LaBelle. Once we'd gotten through the preliminaries—no, I hadn't seen or heard anything; yes, I was dandy and having a wonderful time; yes, I'd remember rain or sleet to check in—she casually mentioned a telephone call from one Ruby Bee Hanks.

"What'd she say?" I asked without enthusiasm.

"Well, she wanted to know where you were and when you'd be back. I told her in no uncertain terms that the information was as confidential as it'd been the first time she asked, and there wasn't any point in badgering me. Then she asked me something I found right peculiar, if you know what I mean."

"I have no idea what you mean, LaBelle."

"She wanted to know if we'd had anything unusual turn up in the lost-and-found department this morning. I told her about the dentures, the pompom, the three-legged hound, and the pair of spectacles, but she said never mind and hung up afore I could find out what she was looking for." LaBelle moistened her lips, then added, "She sounded kind of worried, although she was trying not to."

A particularly icy drip of rain found its way down my collar. "You don't have any idea what she might have lost?"

"I am not a mind reader, Arly. You ought to ask Madam Celeste about that sort of thing; she's real uncanny."

"Did you check with school about Kevin?" I asked, too discouraged to pursue my mother's latest bit of nonsense.

"He did not come to work yesterday, and Earl and Eilene haven't seen him since the night before that. And don't bother to interrupt, because I asked Ruby Bee if she'd heard from Dahlia and she hadn't. Do you want to file a missing persons report?"

"Not if that means someone might find them." I rogered over and out, then went back to my post, which had a puddle in the middle of it. I dug through the box of cornflakes for a wishbone, aware that it indicated a deterioration of my mental faculties, and came up with a soggy yellow flake. I decided that I would remain on the job until six o'clock, when it would start getting dark. Then, without telling LaBelle or anyone else, I would slither back to Maggody, take a hot shower, and spend the night in my dry, warm bed. I could be back at the patch by seven the next morning. Since the dopers had no idea the patch was under surveillance, they had no reason to risk a broken axle or a broken ankle by harvesting in the dark.

Once I talked myself into that minor dereliction of duty, I felt a little bit better and a good deal saner. I even managed not to snarl at a squirrel too stupid to stay in out of the rain. Almost pegged him with a walnut, but I figured I was merely assisting him in his nut collection. Damn bushy-tailed rat.

"Arly's going to hit the ceiling," Ruby Bee moaned. "She'll never stop talking about how irresponsible we were to lose that precious little baby. The poor little thing's probably been kidnapped by some degenerate pervert who'll demand money for ransom. I'm going to hate to turn over my life savings to a degenerate pervert, but I suppose we'll have to if he calls."

Estelle looked in the opposite direction. "Let's not cross the Brooklyn Bridge until we come to it. Between the two of us we don't have near enough money to resemble a ransom payment, and I for one don't intend to end up in the county old folks' home. Besides, maybe we'll find Baby before Arly comes back from wherever she is and starts getting all haughty about how you lost the baby."

"How I lost the baby? It seems to me that you put the baby out in the car and said he'd be just fine by his little self. You were so all-fired sure there weren't any Gypsies on the road. You were plumb full of confidence that Madam Celeste would identify the father. You were—"

"What do you think she meant?" Estelle interrupted, not enjoying the drift of Ruby Bee's remarks.

Ruby Bee made a rude little noise to let Estelle know just what she thought of the diversionary tactic, then shook her head. "Lordy, I don't know. Celeste claimed she saw a list, but she couldn't come up with any idea where in tarnation there'd be such a thing. We both agree that the hospital's out, and the welfare office hasn't sent anyone to Robin's cabin in a coon's age. So who has a list?"

"It doesn't make any sense," Estelle said. "I was wondering if we ought to go back out there and ask the madam if she has any visions of where to find

Baby, but most likely she still won't answer the door."

They sat in silence for a while, considering options and lists and what to say to Arly when she showed up—which she would, sooner or later. They almost leaped out of their respective skins when the jukebox blared into life and David Allen Wainright joined them at the bar.

"Any word from Arly?" he asked, once he had a beer in front of him and a bowl of popcorn within reach.

"Not recently," Ruby Bee said cagily. "How about you? Did you have any luck interviewing the Buchanon children today?"

He explained how they'd gone off somewhere, and how Mrs. Jim Bob wasn't exactly chewing her fingernails or sweating bullets over their disappearance. He then went on to say that in a way he felt responsible, but he couldn't figure out anything to do about it except have another beer.

Not quite willing to admit the whole truth, Ruby Bee told him how she and Estelle had consulted Madam Celeste concerning the delicate issue of paternity—not that she'd doubted David Allen's professional abilities, mind you, but it never hurt to cover all the bases. Estelle butted in to repeat Celeste's murky pronouncement about a list, and how it didn't make a whit of sense. David Allen was forced to agree.

They had a companionable beer, and then he wandered off. Once the door closed, Estelle jabbed her finger in the air.

"Arly shouldn't have turned over those poor orphans to Mrs. Jim Bob in the first place," she said. "It's no wonder they ran off when they had the opportunity, what with her Bible-thumping and self-righteous sermonettes and all. Not to mention her pie crust, which personally I find soggy."

"Arly's not going to be pleased," Ruby Bee said

with a sigh. "Now all five of the orphans are lost. She'll be fit to be tied when she finds out. She may have my good looks, but she sure does have her daddy's temperament. She'll go on and on about how we wouldn't have lost Baby if we hadn't consulted Madam Celeste, and she'll also claim we were interfering in her investigation by doing so—even though we weren't."

Estelle let out a sigh of her own. "Are you sure LaBelle won't give you any hints about when Arly gets back? I might feel the need to go into Farberville and buy an aqua uniform."

"You're not running out on me, you coward! It was your idea to begin with."

"You're the one who insisted on keeping Baby," Estelle pointed out. "If you'd let him go to Mrs. Jim Bob's house with the others—"

"What'd you say earlier about Mrs. Jim Bob?"

"I said her pie crust was soggy. Now, if you'd let Baby go—"

"Something else," Ruby Bee said excitedly. "You said something about Mrs. Jim Bob thumping her Bible, remember?"

Estelle was tiring of not getting out a single sentence without all the time being cut off. "I may have made such a remark, but I don't see why that gives you the right to blurt out anything that comes into your head."

"What's in a Bible?"

"The Old Testament and the New Testament, Miz Feathers-for-Brains. Chapters and verses like 'Thou shall not interrupt thy friends when thy friends is making a point.' "

"What else is in a Bible?" Ruby Bee continued, her eyes bright enough to compete with the jukebox. "Right in the beginning?"

"I'm not sure I remember my Sunday-school lessons perfectly, but there's Genesis, Exodus, Leviticus, and so forth."

"Before that—right on the first page?"

"I am finding this most tedious," Estelle said. "If you want to see if you qualify for one of those TV game shows where you shout out the answers, that is your business."

"Right on the first page of everybody's family Bible is a record of births, marriages, and deaths. It's a list."

Estelle's jaw dropped so hard it almost hit her chest. "You're right, Ruby Bee. A list of births, marriages, and deaths. We ain't interested in the last two, but we are in the first. Do you think that's what Madam Celeste was referring to?"

"She wasn't referring to a grocery list, for Pete's sake. That's got to be what she was referring to." Ruby Bee's face fell. "Of course, that's assuming Robin Buchanon had a family Bible, which is a stretch of the imagination."

"Or that she bothered to write down the names of the ole boys who fathered her bastards."

"Or that she could write down names or anything else."

"That she had a pencil in the cabin."

"That she knew the names of the fathers."

They both slumped down on the stools and propped their elbows on the bar and engaged in a lot of sighs. At last Ruby Bee pulled herself together, squared her shoulders, and said, "It's the only clue we have, especially since the other Buchanons have run off. We don't have anything else to go on except the possibility that Robin Buchanon kept a list in a family Bible."

"If we find the list, we'll know the identities of the fathers. Maybe Baby was kidnapped by his own father," Estelle added.

"Then we wouldn't have to tell Arly how we lost the little sweetums, or even where we were and what we were doing at the time. Assuming there is a Bible, for one thing, and for another that it has a list." Ruby Bee tried to keep her sense of optimism, but it wasn't easy. "And that we can get our hands on it. Robin didn't live in a condominium on the highway, you know. It's not all that simple to just run up there and pick up this Bible off the coffee table for a look-see."

They finally agreed that there wasn't much choice, and once Ruby Bee'd put up the Closed sign for not the first time, they got into Estelle's station wagon. After all, they told each other several times, they'd been there before on that other distasteful matter. There wasn't any reason why two full-grown intelligent women couldn't remember a few turns here and there. They were still engaged in the pep talk as they turned off the pavement and bounced up a rough trail that led toward Cotter's Ridge.

Hammet made sandwiches and told everybody not to be gettin' crumbs all over everywhere like they was uncivilized animals. They sat in the dim room, watching the soundless antics on the television set. Hammet tried to explain the finer points of the football game, based on observation alone since he'd never seen anything quite so all-fired dumb in his short lifetime, but he could tell not even Sukie believed his theories.

"If they's tryin' to kill each other to win that ball, why don't they have shotguns?" she asked.

"They wants it to last for hours and hours, so all those other people screaming and jumping up and down can watch 'em," he said. "They puts up those numbers to show how many they've kilt."

"Why don't those people jest shoot 'em and put 'em out of their misery?" Sissie asked, equally enthralled by the violence.

"He don' know shit," Bubba inserted.

Hammet settled for an eloquent shrug, since he didn't know shit about it anyway.

* * *

At six o'clock (or maybe a few scant seconds earlier), I stored my blanket and thermos in the tent, then slipped and slid through the sodden leaves to the jeep. The beeper was clipped to my belt, so I would be alerted instantly if LaBelle found some obscure reason to desire communication with me. No one would know I wasn't expiring of pneumonia in a damp sleeping bag on the ridge all night; I would tuck the beeper under my pillow (the soft, warm, dry pillow on my soft, warm, dry bed) and if it beeped, I could go down to the jeep and radio in.

As I drove down the back side of the ridge, I told myself over and over that it wasn't a deadly sin, or even a dereliction of any significance. No, not at all. It was the intelligent thing to do. It was not evidence of weakness or self-indulgence to avoid a slow, miserable death by freezation and ennui. The mythology of superheroes was immature. Television cop shows were aimed at viewers with IQs in the single-digit range. Besides, no one would ever know. So there.

I felt a flicker of guilt as I drove past the abandoned jeep. Maybe Kevin and Dahlia were out there in the woods, as wet and miserable as I'd been for a solid twenty-four hours. They'd taken the jeep late Thursday afternoon; Merle had happened across them toward dark. That worked out without much effort to forty-eight hours. And no one had bothered with a missing persons report, or a search party, or dogs, or helicopters, or anything. No one had informed either set of parents that said twosome were lost somewhere on the ridge.

Then again, there wasn't a bear or a wildcat mean enough to tackle Dahlia O'Neill. With any success, anyway.

I pulled over and cut off the engine. I fiddle with the radio until I got through to LaBelle, who hopped right in with the time. I waited until she ran down, then told her to check with the parents to make sure the prodigal pair hadn't returned. If they hadn't, I instructed her to put out an APB on Kevin and Dahlia.

"You want I should book a posse to comb the ridge?" she asked.

"Not yet. If we bring in a posse, our dope growers won't dare to come back to their pot patch, which means we'll never catch them," I said, sighing. "The dopers committed murder, and I'll be damned if they're going to get away with it because Kevin and Dahlia are snuggled up in a cave somewhere. Maybe Dahlia'll shed a couple of pounds. If they haven't turned up by tomorrow night, we'll do the posse thing."

"Whatever you say, Arly. Have a nice night."

"I fully intend to," I said earnestly. Boy, did I get that wrong.

12

It was dark by the time I hit the highway to Maggody, which was just fine with me since I intended to sneak into town like the cowardly wimp I was. Everything looked dead (normal), but as I braked for a possum in front of the Emporium, the dark-haired distaff hippie came dashing out the door to the side of the road. She gestured for me to pull over, and I obliged, albeit reluctantly.

"Oh, thank God," she gasped, clinging to the jeep. "Poppy's gone into labor, and we have no way to fetch the midwife."

"How far along is she?" I asked, albeit reluctantly.

"According to the manual we ordered from the feminists' commune near Bugscuffle, she could have the baby anytime now. Unless you know how to deliver babies, we've got to get the midwife!"

"We certainly do," I said briskly (and without a trace of reluctance). "Tell me where to find her, and I'll run out there while you—ah—read the manual and time the contractions and boil the water."

"Don't you think you'd better come inside for a minute? Poppy's in the back room on the sofa. She's white and in a lot of pain."

I wasn't going to fall for that one. "I'll go for the midwife. Your friend might be better off at home in bed, you know, or on the way to the hospital."

"Poppy doesn't want to have our baby in a sterile environment with a bunch of strangers poking and prodding her," Rainbow said in a shocked voice.

"Hospital delivery rooms are politically and morally incorrect, and symptomatic of the exploitation of women by male doctors concerned with their own convenience and their ill-disguised need to subjugate women. Natural childbirth is a step in the cyclical cosmic framework that carries us from birth to death and beyond to our next life. Birth should be a joyous family experience in the woman's own bed, where the child was first conceived." When I raised my eyebrows, she added, "Nate left in the truck, and it's too late to move her."

"Where does the midwife live?"

She gave me convoluted directions that began at the edge of town, continued along the county road, and ended on some narrow, unpaved lane that would take me to the top of the hill and the midwife's house. I was informed that I couldn't possibly miss the turnoff, even though it was your basic dark and stormy night. It wasn't the time to suggest a small wager, so I said I'd be back as soon as humanly possible and drove down the county road.

Estelle's house was dark. I'd hoped that I might spot Estelle and Ruby Bee inside, doing something perfectly innocent in the front room. It was not written in the stars (and no doubt they were at the Bar and Grill, since it was Saturday night). The psychic's house was dark, too, but there was a dim glow in what I presumed was the solarium. I idly considered stopping for a bit of astrophysical advice about the turnoff, but drove on like an unenlightened innocent abroad.

For the next two hours I drove up and down every narrow, unpaved lane north of Boone Creek. I knocked on doors and talked to people with more interest in television sitcoms than in the imminent delivery of babies on the sofa of the Emporium office. Nobody had any idea where any midwife lived. It made for some interesting exchanges on rainy porches, but it didn't get me any closer to the midwife.

I finally gave up and drove back toward the Emporium. Once I was on pavement, I realized it was time for a bulletin, so I took one hand off the steering wheel to fiddle with the radio.

"It's a good thing you called when you did," LaBelle chirped. "I was on my way home, and the second shift's not supposed to know what all you're up to. Harvey says not to check in until tomorrow morning."

I noticed that she didn't bother to ask if I'd nabbed the perps as of yet. I agreed not to harass the second-shift dispatcher and was about to ask if she'd heard from Ruby Bee when I almost ran into a pickup truck just before Estelle's house. For a moment it seemed as if we'd end up in our respective ditches, but the other driver squeaked past me. I braked to gulp down a breath and mutter a few caustic comments about fools who drove in the rain without headlights. If I hadn't been in such a hurry to get back to the Emporium, I'd have chased the fool all the way to the far side of hell in order to escort him to the county jail in Farberville (Maggody lacks overnight accommodations).

"Why'd you gasp?" LaBelle demanded. She let her voice drop to a throaty whisper, and I could almost see her licking her lips in anticipation of some wonderfully dramatic spate of gunfire to which she would be an earwitness. "Oh, my Lord, Arly—did you see something suspicious? Are they sneaking up on you? How many are there of them? Are they armed? Are you in some kind of danger?"

In that I was supposed to be on the ridge in a parked jeep, I couldn't explain the traffic situation. "A rabid squirrel," I said, then went on to say I'd report the next morning, and cut her off. Estelle still wasn't home, I noticed as I drove past her house on my way back to the Emporium to report failure.

The front door was unlocked, and light shone

through the curtain that covered the doorway to the office. It blocked the view, but did nothing to muffle the shriek of pain that greeted me. I reverted to reluctant mode as I squared my shoulders and pushed aside the curtain.

Poppy was on the couch, her eyes closed and sweat dotting her face like early morning frost. Every few seconds she moaned and twitched. Rainbow stood over her with a washcloth in her hand. Sitting cross-legged on the desk was a man with a wispy beard, a ponytail, and a broad smile. "Like wow," he murmured, watching Poppy as if waiting for her to levitate or glow. She opted for a more prosaic shriek.

I took a step back. "I couldn't find the midwife. Don't you think we'd better find someone who knows how to do this sort of thing? Anyone who knows how to—"

"No strangers!" Poppy cried. "Please, no strangers."

Rainbow gave her an approving smile. "No strangers; I promise. Arly, Zachery, and I will help you. You just go with the flow, as though you were adrift in a current of love and sharing."

"Where's the manual?" I said grimly.

"I don't think we ought to abandon the station wagon out here," Estelle said. She stood in front of the raised hood, glaring at the steam that curled out of the radiator.

"Nobody's going to steal it," Ruby Bee pointed out as levelly as possible, considering. "We're smack-dab in the middle of nowhere and there's not another living soul within miles of here. Even if someone wanted to steal it, it won't run. Thieves don't drive tow trucks."

"I just don't like to leave it."

"Then get yourself around to the back and start pushing. I am about to freeze to death standing here in the rain while you pretend you know something about station wagon engines. I already told you I am not going to sit in this thing all night long, while bears and wildcats claw at the windows and we turn bluer than a pair of bird-foot violets."

Estelle started to argue, but nothing much came to mind, so she settled for an unenthusiastic nod. "I guess it'll be all right until morning. But are you sure we ought to go up the road? We don't know how far Robin's cabin is, and I'd hate to find out it's ten more miles."

"We know how far it is back to the highway," Ruby Bee said through clenched teeth, having clenched them so they wouldn't chatter—or so she told herself. "We know that a couple of those creek beds behind us are full of water. We know that the longer we stand here arguing, the colder and wetter we're going to get." She came around to the front of the station wagon and shook her finger at Estelle. "If you want to stand here all night and study the spark plugs, you go right ahead. I am seeking shelter, myself. Robin's cabin isn't all that far. It may not be the Flamingo Motel, but it has a roof and some protection from wild animals. She's dead and the children are down in town somewhere, so no one's going to bother us. Now, are you coming or not?"

Estelle had already decided she was, but she felt it wasn't good politics to give in too easily. "There's no cause to get all snippety, Ruby Bee Hanks. I was merely pointing out the possibility of going down instead of up. I always like to explore my options."

"You may explore options all night if you wish. Explore them to your heart's content. I am chilled to the bone, and I am also sick and tired of standing here!" Ruby Bee marched up the road, the sole flashlight held smugly in her hand.

Muttering under her breath, Estelle hurried after her and took the opportunity to bring up (and not for the first time) just whose fool scheme this was and who would have to take responsibility if they were eaten by a bear. Ruby Bee had a few opinions herself. They were still exploring the complex issue of causality and responsibility when they reached the clearing in front of the cabin.

"So there," Ruby Bee said triumphantly. "Didn't I say it wasn't all that far to the cabin? You wanted to walk all the way down to the highway, a good ten miles of creek beds and ruts and wild animals. I told you the cabin wasn't all that far, didn't I?"

Estelle screeched, then caught her companion's arm and jerked her to a halt. "I thought I saw something move."

"Are you going to start worrying about ghosts? Lordy, Estelle, I'd of thought you were a sight too old for that kind of childish squeamishness. We're not over at Madam Celeste's for a seance."

"I thought I saw something move," she repeated in a low voice.

"Really?" Ruby Bee sniffed. "Well, where'd you see this haint? I'll shine the light so we both can see it's a pig or a goat or a dish towel flapping on the clothesline. Will that satisfy you?"

The hand that held the flashlight might have trembled a tad, but it failed to illuminate pig, goat, dish towel, or even the shade of Robin Buchanon flitting about in the weeds. The door to the cabin was slightly ajar. Ruby Bee knocked, just out of habit, then tiptoed in and shone the light all around in case a bear might have chosen the shack for purposes of hibernation. Or at least she told herself as much, in that she wasn't a skittery child who fretted about ghosts and goblins and things that went bump in the night. Not even in a dead woman's cabin on a dark, rainy night.

"You can come inside and close the door," she said to Estelle, who was hovering prudently in the doorway and chewing a fingernail like it was made of milk chocolate. "You know darn well that you were seeing things a minute ago. This is going to be all right. We can light a lantern, and there's a little pile of wood by the stove. We're going to be just as snug as little ole bugs in a rug."

Estelle wasn't all that convinced, but she closed the door anyway since there wasn't any point in getting any wetter than she already was. She figured there were likely to be plenty of bugs in the rug, along with spiders in the corners and snakes under the rickety furniture. However, she and Ruby Bee managed to light the lantern, which helped dispel some of the shadows. Once they had a little fire going in the stove, the room got warm enough for her to stop shivering like a wet dog in a blizzard. But she was real sure she'd seen something flitting around the corner of the shack. Something or someone. She didn't like it one bit. She was trying not to dwell on it too much when Ruby Bee announced she'd found Robin Buchanon's family Bible. In fact, Estelle decided as she went to take a gander at the Good Book, she must have been crazy.

"You are squishing me something dreadful," Dahlia hissed. "You got your heel dug in my leg and your knee's knocking my nose ever' time you move. I don't aim to end up with a bloody nose and blood all over my dress. It makes the worst stain of anything, even grape jelly."

"I'm sorry, my darling." Kevin tried to peer through a knothole, but he still couldn't tell exactly what was going on inside the cabin. Grumbling, he got down and wiggled around until he was facing Dahlia in the darkness of the cramped space. He squatted down so he could whisper right at her face. "We got to stay here until they're gone. I couldn't see who it was, but they might be dangerous or murderers. They might have guns, which would mean I couldn't protect you if they decided to tie us up and then have their way with you—the filthy perverts!"

"Why'd you let them sneak up on you like that?" she persisted, not especially distraught over Kevin's bleak scenario. She couldn't imagine the filthy perverts being able to overpower Kevin, not when he was so brave and cool that he ought to be on Friday-night television.

"What else could I do? I was out on the porch wondering if you were all right—you'd been down here a long time, my precious—when I heard this eerie screech and saw a light bobbling in the night like it was being carried by a ghost. I didn't waste a single second. I rushed down here lickety-split so's I could protect you."

"Did you think to bring toilet paper? There isn't so much as a scrap of newspaper or an old catalogue or anything."

Kevin apologized for the oversight. After a while, his back began to ache something awful from the position, and Dahlia allowed that he could sit on her warm, broad, uncovered thighs. What light there was came through the crescent cutout in a soft path. If it hadn't been for the pervasive redolence, it would have been kind of sweet, like two lovebirds in a cozy wooden cage.

"I'll cast Daffodil Sunshine's natal chart immediately," Rainbow said. She bent down to kiss Poppy's forehead, then trotted into the front room with a lot of chatter about sidereal time and Capricorn ascending.

Zachery lit a joint and offered it to me. "That blew my mind. Wow. I mean, really wow."

I was slumped behind the desk. I waved away the joint (being a police officer requires a degree of self-sacrifice) and looked at my watch. Despite Rainbow's earlier assertion that the baby would be born at any moment, it had taken Daffodil Sunshine five hours to make his entrance. A very long five hours for all concerned. The manual from the feminists' commune, aided by my vague memories of paramedic training at the academy, had seen us through the ordeal. Mother was dozing, exhausted but triumphant. Zachery was more stoned than a quarry. Rainbow was intent on casting the natal chart, which I presumed had to do with astrology. Daffodil Sunshine seemed to have all the pertinent parts. Like one of the good fairies in *Sleeping Beauty,* I wished him Herculean strength; he would need it to deal with future school-yard discussions of his name.

"I'm going home," I said to Zachery. "Pot's illegal, by the way."

He frowned at the joint in his hand. "Still? You'd of thought someone would have legalized it by now."

"Not yet."

"Oh, shit." He took a deep drag on the joint, then squinted at me as the smoke drifted through his wispy mustache. "What about if you grow it yourself? Is that cool?"

I tried to envision him with the energy to garden in the middle of the National Forest. Clearing the patch, planting seeds, lugging water from the spring, bringing in fertilizer—and rigging booby traps. He wasn't my idea of a hirsute Johnny Appleseed, but I had to ask. "It might be, if you're real quiet about it and it's strictly for your own use. All sorts of folks do it in the National Forest, and most of them get away with it. Have you ever tried?" Subtlety was not a requirement; the man was having difficulty understanding the one-syllable words.

"Once," he said, looking sadly at me. "I had this little plant in a flowerpot on my kitchen windowsill back when I was in college. The cat ate it. It must not have been very good shit, because Fritz died that same night."

"You're probably right, then. You do realize that you shouldn't smoke dope in front of me, don't you? I am the chief of police."

"You're the fuzz? I thought you were the midwife, since you delivered the baby. Are you really the fuzz, too?" When I nodded, he slapped his hand on his forehead. "This is a real mind fuck, you know? Some kind of bummer. Wow."

"Wow." I went to the front room, where Rainbow was elbow deep in books, papers, and legal pads. "I'm going home," I said. "Do you want me to transport the four of you to your house?"

"We'll stay here and wait for Nate; he ought to be back soon. Poppy can use the rest, and we need the chart as soon as possible. There are some peculiar connotations of financial activities, since Jupiter's in the eighth house."

I rubbed my eyes, wondering if I was in the madhouse. "Well, I'm off. You ought to have a doctor check the baby, just to make sure he's healthy."

"Oh, that's not necessary; Scorpios are ruled by Pluto, which is very regenerative. Won't you stay for a cup of chamomile tea? I'd like to have a chance to tell you how utterly incredible you were, but I've got to cast the chart. Not only do we need to analyze the Jupiter implication, but we may also have to confront the polarity with Taurus and the fixed quadruplicity. You know what that can mean."

"Doesn't everybody?" I murmured. I caught myself in a yawn and headed for the front door, the jeep, and my bed—if only for a few hours. My grandiose scheme to have a decent night's sleep was not to be, but Maggody had its 756th citizen.

"Thanks again. You must have been a midwife in one of your previous lives. Can I do your chart for you sometime? What's your sign?"

I looked over my shoulder at her. "No trespassing." Once I got to the jeep, I realized there wasn't much point in going to my apartment for such a short time. The departure from it would only depress me. I was reasonably warm and dry after the marathon session in the Emporium office, and the rain had stopped. I could go crawl into my sleeping bag and save myself an hour's drive at the godawful crack of dawn. I could wake up at six and have time for a leisurely cup of coffee before I called in to the sheriff's office with my report that nothing had happened.

"Aw, hell," I said to the empty highway. I then backed up, turned around, and headed for the far side of Cotter's Ridge. Like wow.

"I'm gonna die," Carol Alice said, flat on her back in bed and staring at the ceiling. "I just know it. Something dreadful's fixing to happen. I'm gonna die."

"No, you're not," Heather said firmly.

"I'm gonna die. There's not a doubt in my mind."

Heather put her hands on her hips and tried for a more authoritarian air, like the home ec teacher the day the class had started throwing oatmeal-raisin cookie dough all over the room. "Carol Alice Plummer, you listen and you listen up good. We're all going to die someday, but it ain't going to happen for a real long time. So stop the crazy talk right this minute. Okay?"

"I reckon I should get it over with and save everyone the trouble of waiting around," Carol Alice continued in a hollow voice. "Tell Bo Swiggins I'm sorry that we didn't get married in June, but I don't see how we can if I'm dead. Madam Celeste says that death is hovering nearby, maybe right over my shoulder. I can feel his icy breath on my neck, Heather."

"I thought you promised Bo that you wouldn't go there anymore. He'll be furious if he finds out, you know."

"He can be as furious as he's a mind to be. I intend to be dead, so what do I care?" Sighing, she rolled over and buried her face in the pillow. "Go away, Heather. I got to think about my last will and testimony."

Heather looked down at Carol Alice, wishing with all her heart that Mr. Wainright could whisper some advice in her ear right that minute. She didn't think her best friend in the whole world would actually do something crazy, but she wasn't sure. When Madam Celeste had telephoned Carol Alice out of the blue and told her to come to the house, Carol Alice had been thoroughly spooked; Heather couldn't blame her one teeny-tiny bit for that. Then the madam doing cards and Mesopotamian sand for free—well, that'd been enough to put Carol Alice in a downright hysterical mood. Heather couldn't blame her for that, either.

But you'd have thought Madam Celeste would have said some comforting things instead of throwing the cards on the floor and ordering Carol Alice to get out then and there. And there wasn't any call to go saying that nice Mr. Dickerson couldn't read Mesopotamian sand any more than he could fly round-trip to the moon and back.

Heather patted her friend's shoulder, gathered up her schoolbooks, said good night to Mrs. Plummer, who was in front of the television set in the family room, and then slowly walked home, while she tried to think what to do. She finally decided that she ought to call Mr. Wainright, even if it meant disturbing him right in the middle of the evening when he was—well, sort of off-duty. Then she could call Carol Alice and say all the right words to make her quit talking about suicide and killing herself and wills and testimonies. Her best friend would feel happier, and Mr. Wainright would know that she, Heather Riley, was a mature, concerned, selfless person.

To her regret, Mr. Wainright didn't have the opportunity to discover all her virtues because he wasn't home. To her further regret, she found herself blabbing everything to Mr. Plummer when he called and demanded to know what in tarnation was wrong with Carol Alice, who was moaning and rolling her eyes and refusing to touch her mother's home-made split pea soup.

When David Allen Wainright did get home, he found a bizarre little group huddled on his front porch. Once he got everybody inside and mopped off, he gave Hammet a searching look. "Why were you all waiting on my porch?"

"The door were locked. Bubba said it weren't no trouble to break a window, but I wouldn't let him."

"Thank you." David Allen sat down and took out his handkerchief to wipe the beads of sweat off his forehead. It was the first time he'd seen all of Robin Buchanon's children in one clump, and it was unsettling. To say the least. "I went by Mrs. Jim Bob's this morning to talk to you, but she said you'd left. That right?"

Hammet shrugged. "Iffen we weren't there, we done left. That's right." Several heads nodded in agreement, but it was obvious to David Allen that Hammet was the official spokesman for the group.

"Where'd you go?"

"We jest got wearied of that woman and all the mean things she said about our mam. We decided we wanted to go for a walk without gettin' on the road, so we cut through some folks' yards and a pasture by the creek. We camed out on another road, where we had the good fortune to find Baby in some damn-fool car."

David Allen struggled to understand the intricacies of the narrative. "I thought Baby was with Ruby Bee. In fact, I went by the Bar and Grill and had a word with her, and she didn't mention any of this. When you had this stroke of good fortune, did you see Ruby Bee?"

"The only thing we saw was Baby. He looked mighty lonesome, so we fetched him with us." Hammet glanced at his siblings. "We all got something we wants you to explain. It's about this foster stuff, and gittin' new siblings and a bicycle. Arly's gone, and I figgered you was the next smartest person I knew."

David Allen recounted what he knew of the process, being as truthful and candid as he dared. He admitted a lot of things that didn't sit real well with the Buchanon children, who were squirming and peeking at each other like wallflowers at a cotillion class (although they weren't that, by any stretch of the metaphor).

When he finally stopped, Hammet looked at Bubba and shrugged. "So maybe you don't get a bicycle after all. I still don't think we should tell anybody, though."

"Tell anybody what?" David Allen inserted, rather slyly he thought.

"About our pappies," Sukie said through a finger.

Bubba whacked her on the side of the head hard enough to put her on the floor. "You shut up, you stupid little pig. Me and Hammet is talking together. And shush your howlin' unless you wants another slap."

Sukie didn't shush, which set Baby off to howling, too, and Sissie to scolding both of them. Despite the noise, Hammet and Bubba managed a low conversation while David Allen sat helplessly on the edge of his seat. At last Hammet gestured for David Allen to join him in the kitchen.

"We're gonna tell you about our pappies," he said. "Bubba says that's a darn sight better than going off with some tight-ass social worker lady, and I guess he knows 'cause he's the oldest."

"Great. Let me get a piece of paper and a pencil, and we'll—"

"Oh, we ain't gonna tell you now. We're gonna tell you tomorrow after we goes to church," Hammet said, shaking his head.

"After you go to church? Why would you want to do that?"

Hammet looked at the floor. "Because that holyfied lady said we was going to hell iffen we didn't, and that we'd burn like sticks of kindling. We decided we need to see this church of the almighty place."

"You realize they may not welcome you with open arms?"

"We don' care what all they do. We ain't gonna talk until after we go to this church place."

"But why do you have to wait to tell me about your fathers?" David Allen asked, totally bewildered. "I don't see what that has to do with anything." He went to the refrigerator and took out a much-needed beer, keeping a leery eye on Hammet. "If you want to go to church, I suppose I can take you in the morning, but there's no reason not to—"

"Good," Hammet said. "By the way, we was wondering if we could sleep on your floor the rest of tonight. Baby's got snuffles, and Sukie don't look all that good, neither. If either of them commences to crying, we can stick 'em outside to shush 'em real fast. We won't bother you hardly at all."

David Allen realized his jaw was going up and down but he wasn't making any noise—that he could hear, anyway. Hammet gave him a grin, then went back to the living room and turned on the radio receiver. By the time David Allen numbly followed, Hammet was explaining how Mr. Macaroni had also rigged up this here box where you could find rockets what prematurely crashed in the woods. Course it weren't as good as the ones you used to talk to foreigners in their houses, even if you didn't know what they was saying. For David Allen, the scariest thing was that it almost made sense.

The moon came out about the time I reached my reserved parking space on the back side of the ridge. I took the little package of carob chip cookies that

Rainbow had pressed on me, threw a few branches over the jeep, grabbed my flashlight, and trudged up to my campsite, yawning so hard my eyes watered and my jaw felt like it might pop out of its sockets.

There was no indication I'd been visited by raccoons, bears, skunks, or anything else that might merit concern. Filled with gratitude for that small blessing, I crawled into the tent and secured the flap. My sleeping bag was damp, and my beeper cut into my side as I wiggled around to find a tolerable position, but I was too tired to do more than unclip the damn thing and lob it across the canvas floor.

As I drifted asleep, I did wonder why Ruby Bee and Mrs. Jim Bob had ceased their relentless campaign to speak to me via LaBelle. I must have wasted a good ten seconds on that one.

Madam Celeste stared into the blackness of her bedroom, unable to dismiss the face. The death mask. The wide, unblinking eyes. The flies on the clotted blood. The open mouth. The terror. For the first time in twenty years she longed to be Sarah Lou Dickerson, a gawky, knock-kneed, grimy girl in a faded dress donated by the righteous church do-gooders. Living in a miserable trailer on a rocky patch of mountainside. Being whipped on a regular basis by her pa, when he wasn't doing other nasty things to her. Watching her ma get older and grayer, until she looked worse than the wash on the line.

Grinolli had saved fifteen-year-old Sarah Lou from that, but he'd turned out to be worse than her pa and she'd had enough sense to exit with the first truck driver who'd stopped at the crossroads. Vizzard had been the savior. Although he'd been forty-five years older, he'd been rich and kind—as long as she serviced him (and at his age, it wasn't exactly a daily chore like milking cows; it was more like churning butter once a week). He'd taught her to read and write, and introduced her to a woman who'd understood how Sarah Lou kept seeing things that weren't there and having scary dreams that came true.

She'd been right sad when she'd had the dream about Vizzard choking on the chicken wing, but she knew she couldn't alter the future, so she cooked what she had to cook and served what she had to serve. Despite having the ambulance number handy, she'd found herself a widow with a reasonable inheritance. She'd used it for what she called her junior year abroad, although the studies took place in dim parlors rather than in snooty art museums. Vizzard had been worth the trouble.

But now, haunted by the face that would not go away, she wondered how she would have made out with Grinolli in the dreary apartment above the body shop, or with Vizzard if she'd risked cosmic displeasure and insisted on tuna casserole for dinner. Or if she'd allowed Mason to talk her into trying Atlantic City. Mason did seem to enjoy the bright lights, but they both knew he would go wherever she told him to go. Purse strings were longer than apron strings.

They'd ended up in Maggody, which bore a strong resemblance to Hickory Ridge and all its narrow-minded shabbiness. And as she stared at the ceiling, she figured she knew why. Sarah Lou Dickerson Grinolli Vizzard had no theories, but Madam Celeste ("World-Renowned Psychic as Seen on the Stages of Europe") had a pretty good idea of what was going to happen. The shadow on the ceiling bore a passing resemblance to a chicken wing. There wasn't anyone to consider serving tuna casserole this time.

13

Imagine, if you will, the gossamer rays of pink and orange streaming from the eastern horizon as the sun begins its journey across the sky, lavender now but soon to change to a delicate clear blue. The early birds hop from leaf to leaf, trilling bright little songs of optimism and goodwill, of promised sunlight, of rebirth. Squirrels scamper about on the branches. Raindrops sparkle like rubies and sapphires as the morning light catches them. Idyllic, no?

Now we must mar the bucolic beauty by the addition of one tired, rumpled woman. Her hair has been pinned up without the benefit of a mirror, and her clothes are wrinkled and somewhat dirty. Her face has not enjoyed the improvement of lipstick or mascara. Her shoes are muddy. Yes, it is the upholder of law and order in a small Arkansas hamlet, a police officer dedicated to the apprehension of a vile murderer at any personal sacrifice, the defender of the faith, all that. She is standing by a clearing, her hands curled into fists and her face frozen in a decidedly unattractive expression of disbelief, horror, and outrage (to list only a few). She is so angry that her body quivers like a plucked violin string. Her eyes are dry from the unblinking stare. Her mouth is slightly agape, but her lips do not move despite the little noises that emanate from deep within her. At last we hear two words.

"Holy shit."

This is said not in a loud voice, but in a coarse whisper. The fact that the words are intelligible is to be both noted and commended, because the woman has been incoherent for several minutes. As well we all would be . . .

. . . because they had chopped the marijuana plants. The clearing was nothing but rows of stubble. The sons of bitches had come during the brief time I was gone, and they had stolen their plants. Not exactly from under my nose, since my nose had been occupied with the delivery of a baby. But pretty damn close.

I sank down and leaned against a tree, ignoring the immediate sensation of cold wetness that engulfed my rear end. It could not be. I'd been on the stakeout since Friday night, expecting, or at least hoping for, some activity either Saturday or Sunday. But during daylight, for Pete's sake! They had to be escapees from a loony bin to drive up the trail in the dark. Kevin and Dahlia hadn't made it in full sunlight; I'd survived only because I had a sturdy four-wheel jeep and enough sense to creep so slowly I could have been lapped by a snail.

And then there was the sheer coincidence—which was too much. I'd waited around for twenty-four hours, vigilant and alert and all that professional stuff. Had they so much as driven halfway up the trail, I'd have been ready for them. Had a foot snapped a twig, I'd have had my camera focused. But no one had appeared. I'd waited until dark and gone into town for maybe nine hours total. The sons of bitches had come and gone during those nine hours. Not a minute too early, not a minute too late. Just as though I were an airplane and they were air-traffic controllers watching my blip on a radar screen. And I'd gone blip, blip, blip down the road and all the way home.

I dragged myself to my feet and went over to the trail. I could see the water-filled ruts their vehicle had left. The tracks from my vehicle ran over theirs, however, so it was clear that they'd come while I was gone. There were two sets of footprints, but no one had dropped a calling card. I glared at the trail and ground my teeth for a long while, then went back to the cleared clearing and ground my teeth some more. I said some things that scorched little tufted ears. I went all around the perimeter to search for evidence, then methodically examined every inch of stubbly ground. On my hands and knees.

After I finished not finding so much as a turtle dropping, I thought of some more things to say, some of them about my night visitors and some about my dereliction and its resultant disaster. Some about my avowal to the sheriff that I'd catch the sons of bitches who had murdered Robin Buchanon with their lethal toy. Harve had taken a risk by allowing me to stake out the marijuana patch without any backup. We both knew what the standard procedure was, but I'd been so damned eloquent and sincere and charming that he'd let me do it.

I'd blown it.

I went to my campsite, made another cup of instant coffee, and gulped it down. It was so hot, it scalded my tongue and brought tears to my eyes. That's what I told myself, anyway, as I angrily rubbed my cheeks.

"Hallelujah, it's getting light," Ruby Bee said as she looked through the window. The yard was disgraceful, all scratch dirt and weeds, but the woods beyond looked right pretty in the fresh sunlight.

Estelle twisted in the rocking chair so she could see the window. "Well, it's about time. I don't know when I've spent such a miserable night. I hate to think how many splinters I have in places I don't care to mention. We would have been a sight more comfortable in the station wagon. I could have taken the front seat, and you could have stretched out in the back."

"While freezing to death, I suppose. I told you to go lie down in the bedroom. You're the one who got all nervous and insisted we both sleep in chairs by the stove."

"I didn't think the bed looked hygienic," Estelle countered, "and it was real crude of you to insinuate until all hours of the night that I believe in ghosts. I am not some hysterical widow woman; I merely have standards. The quilt on that bed is dingier than unbleached underwear. You never know what kind of diseases Robin carried, along with bugs and lice. I simply mentioned that the chairs were apt to be cleaner. Of course my station wagon is always clean."

Ruby Bee thought of all kinds of things to say, including references to the undeniable truth that Estelle snored louder than a tractor on an incline, and the likelihood that the station wagon had been destroyed by bears by now. Instead, she went over to the table and tapped the Bible. "Then we wouldn't have found this. It was the reason we came here, wasn't it? How would you have felt if we'd slunk back to town empty-handed, with Arly waiting to ask how Baby's doing?"

"We do have a few interesting tidbits, don't we?"

"As sure as I'm standing here, eyeballs are going to pop out of some people's heads when we announce our news. I can hardly wait to see their faces. I don't imagine Robin has coffee and blueberry muffins anywhere around, so I guess we better start back for town. Do you want to visit the facilities before we leave?"

Estelle shuddered. "I couldn't live with myself if I did. What about you?"

"I think I'll wait for a nice bush along the road," Ruby Bee replied, giving in to a shudder herself.

"At least I'll be able to see the spiders before they crawl on me. Do you have tissues in your purse?"

"I never go anywhere without being prepared for emergencies of this exact kind. Unless you want to leave a note, let's go find ourselves some bushes."

Ruby Bee gathered up the flashlight and the family Bible and stashed both in her purse. Once she was satisfied the fire was out, she and Estelle went out to the porch, closing the door carefully to keep out any varmints, then hurried across the yard and down the trail, where bushes were in abundance. Once they'd each had a few minutes of privacy, they began to trudge down the road, telling each other that it wasn't all that far and they'd probably make it in plenty of time. For what, they weren't real sure. However, haste seemed like it ought to be essential, and so they stepped lively.

"Wake up, my dumpling; I thought I heard voices," Kevin whispered.

Dahlia's head hung forward and she was snoring softly, like an asthmatic old hound dog in front of a campfire. He prodded her shoulder, but it didn't do any good. He wiggled around, relishing his seat in the soft valley of her broad thighs, then let his face fall against a pendulous breast. Nibbling gently so's not to disturb his beloved, he finally dozed off, a contented smile on his face and his Adam's apple rippling in time to the snores.

I packed up the camping gear and took it to the jeep, not worrying that the perps might see me on the trail. It was a little late to lock the barn door. I then went back to the marijuana patch, but no clues had popped up in my absence. There was no point in trying to take plaster casts of the footprints or the ruts in the trail; they were mushy, uneven puddles rimmed with mud. Not exactly prime evidence in a court of law.

When I could think of no further evasive tactics, I fired up the radio and prepared to confess to that father confessor, LaBelle.

Once I'd finished the dismal recitation, she said, "Heavens to Betsy, Arly, do you think they were watching you all that time and just waiting for you to leave? That's enough to make your skin crawl, ain't it?"

"I don't think so," I said slowly. "No one knew that we had discovered the pot patch and Robin's body. There'd be no reason to think the patch would be under surveillance. I didn't mention anything about my trip except that I'd be out of pocket for a couple of days. You, the sheriff, and I are the only people who know anything at all." I heard a sharp intake of breath, and it wasn't mine. "You didn't tell anyone, did you?"

"Merle Hardcock knows about the body. Mebbe he said something."

"He told me he was heading straight for Boone Creek, and would be there all weekend. He also swore on his motorcycle helmet not to say one word about finding the body. Did you tell someone about the murder, LaBelle? That information, coupled with my absence, could have tipped off the perps. Did I spend two miserable nights in a pup tent for nothing?"

"Didn't you tell the Buchanon children that they were orphans?"

"I told one of them, and asked a friend to break the news of her death to the others, but I told them it was an ordinary hunting accident. We get one or two of them a year, so no one's likely to suspect foul play. Did you tell someone there'd been a murder?"

"When are you coming back to town, Arly?"

"Damn it, LaBelle, did you—"

"I got to go, honey. My bladder's about to pop on account of this infection and the medicine that teenaged doctor gave me. I'll tell Harvey the news. Bye-bye."

I let her escape, mostly because I intended to wring it out of her scrawny neck when I got to the sheriff's office. It had not been an amusing weekend, nor had it been worthwhile. Sitting under a bush all day and sleeping on rocks all night would have been justified only by the identification and subsequent arrest of Robin's murderers. Thirty-six hours of futility justified the strangulation of one dispatcher—once I found out to whom she'd blabbed. The Veterans' Auxiliary? The congregation of the Voice of the Almighty Lord Assembly Hall? The Mormon Tabernacle Choir?

As I drove down the road, it occurred to me that I could do something about Kevin and Dahlia now, since it didn't matter if a battalion searched the ridge. Hell, bring in the dogs, helicopters, the Mounties, and the Marines. I wasn't sure what I would do to Kevin when he surfaced, but I was in such a black mood that torture seemed too tame. My mood continued as I bumped down the road, found blessed pavement, and headed for Maggody at a rather brisk pace.

I was still fuming and muttering when I passed the Voice of the Almighty and realized it was Sunday morning. All sorts of folks were on the grass in front of the building, shaking hands and relating the hottest gossip before they went inside for a dose of piety. I was almost past the group when I saw the most peculiar thing I'd ever seen in my life (and remember I strolled the streets of Manhattan in an earlier life).

I slammed on the brakes to stare. David Allen Wainright stood at the edge of the grass. He was tugging at his collar and looking about as cool as a heifer in a slaughterhouse. Next to him were all the Buchanon children. All five of them. Bubba and Sissie were watching the church folks as if they anticipated attack. Sukie morosely sucked on a finger. Baby sat on the grass, chewing on a chunk of sod. My buddy Hammet was the only one in the group who looked pleased with himself; his mouth was stretched in a big grin, and his eyes darted about as if a circus parade could be heard in the distance.

I got out of the jeep and joined them. "Hi, guys," I said cautiously. "What are you doing here, of all places?"

David Allen gave me a bleak smile. "Welcome home. The children opted to sleep at my house last night, and insisted on attending church this morning. Here we are."

"Hi, Arly," Hammet said. "Did you have a nice trip? Where'd you go? I hope you don't mind too awful much, but we all stayed at your house for a whiles yesterday. I made ever'body be real neat and clean, but you may be able to tell we was there."

"Don't worry about it. Why did you insist on church this morning?" I asked, feeling as perceptive as a sump hole in late summer.

"That holyfied woman said we was going to hell like our mama. We thought we'd better see what all there was to the story. She talked a whole bunch about the wages of sin, too. Wages are money, and according to her we all sinned most of every day. Now that Ma's murdered, we got to thinking we'd like to bury her in a pretty box."

David Allen and I studied each other for a long time. When it became clear he wasn't going to field that one, I looked down at Hammet. "That's a real nice idea, Hammet. No matter what happens, we'll make sure your mother is buried in a pretty box."

The good citizens of Maggody had been shooting many a glance in our direction, but no one seemed to have the courage to order us off the lawn. After a few more minutes of milling, they responded to some mysterious signal and started through the door.

Hammet took my hand and tugged it. "Come on, Arly. The show's gonna start without us iffen we don't go inside now."

"I can't go in there," I said. "I'm dressed in dirty clothes and my hair's a disaster. I've got some business to do at the sheriff's office. Besides, this isn't exactly my idea of a good time."

"Aw, please?" he said, his face crumpling.

I was about to reiterate my reasons when a pickup truck stopped at the edge of the highway to discharge passengers. Ruby Bee Hanks and Estelle Oppers thanked Raz for the ride, climbed out of the cab, took a minute to wipe their incredibly muddy shoes on the gravel, then ambled over to our little group. All this time I gaped. And wondered if I'd finally lost my mind. If I was brain dead at last. If I'd been fed marijuana in my sleep.

"Morning, Arly," my mother said briskly. "Why, this is most amazing to see you here, not to mention the children." She jabbed Estelle with a bony elbow. "And Baby, too. Isn't it amazing, Estelle?"

She didn't look all that amazed, and neither did Estelle, who was still wiping her shoes on the grass. I, on the other hand, was merely flabbergasted.

"What are you doing here?" I demanded, perhaps sounding a bit shrill. "Why did you get out of Raz's truck? Why are your shoes and stockings muddier than Boone Creek? Aren't you a member of the Baptist church? And isn't said church down the highway a half mile or so?"

Ruby Bee shot me a smile that she probably thought was sly (I thought it hinted of dementia). "The last time I looked it was there. Now we'd better get ourselves inside. I already hear the opening hymn."

She and Estelle marched toward the church door. After a dazed moment, David Allen, Bubba, and Sissie followed. Sukie scooped up Baby and tucked him under her arm, then trailed after them, her finger still firmly planted in her mouth.

Hammet tugged on my hand. "Please?" he begged in the time-honored tradition of Oliver Twist.

"Why on earth not? After all, we're all crazy and this is some kind of bizarre dream. Why shouldn't we all go to church together like one big happy family?" I realized I was raving, but I didn't care. "Oh, look, there's Hizzoner and Mizzoner pulling up. This is just dandy. It's better than a surprise birthday party."

Hammet dragged me across the lawn and up the stairs. We went across the porch and into a foyer, entertained all the while by the voices of the congregation doing indictable things to a hymn. A few voices faltered as we continued right down the center aisle to the front pew, but no one tried to stop us. Here comes the bride, I hummed with a manic giggle.

Not that we were welcomed with benevolent smiles, mind you. The organist gave us a withering look as she reared back and took off on another stanza. In the pew behind us, Elsie McMay let out a snort of epic proportion. Kevin Buchanon's mother was sniffling into a tissue, but I didn't take that as a personal affront. Looks were dark and smiles frozen.

On one side of me the Buchanons were arranged in a rigid row, their expressions intent and their hands clutched tightly in their respective laps (except for Baby, who was relishing the last blades of grass and Sukie, who would have been lost without a finger in her mouth). I supposed we were in the front pew so we'd have the best odds when the wages were passed out.

On the other side of me Ruby Bee and Estelle stared at the pulpit. I noticed Ruby Bee had a Bible in her lap. At that moment I wouldn't have worried too much if she'd held a pea-green leprechaun instead. Past Estelle was David Allen, who seemed entranced by the dusty floor.

As the hymn died a merciful death, Brother Verber came out through a door beyond the organ. His steps were bouncy at first, but as he neared the pulpit, he caught a glimpse of his visitors and jerked to a halt. His jaw dropped and his face turned white. His sermon notes fluttered to the floor. His eyelids flapped like laundry in a tornado.

I was fully expecting him to clutch his heart and topple right on over. The congregation whispered and stirred behind us, no doubt expecting the same scenario. Just as I decided to offer him my seat, he shook himself into action and stumbled to the pulpit.

"He's not especially thrilled to see us," I whispered to Ruby Bee. I received an elbow in my ribs and an admonishment to hush up.

"Welcome, welcome, welcome this fine Sunday morning," Verber said, although his voice lacked conviction. "I see we have visitors today, and ain't that fine? It's like God is prodding his black sheep back into our flock so we can share our faith with 'em." His voice gained a measure of steadiness as he continued on in that vein. He then announced various prayer meetings and such, led a hymn, and maintained a tight smile while deacons scurried about to collect our "heartfelt generous offerings." I managed to snag Hammet's wrist before he could help himself to the proffered wages, and engaged in a whispered discussion of the intent of the bowls of money going up and down the aisles.

Then came sermon time. Brother Verber was pinked up by now, and sounding normal as he said, "Today I'm going to tell you a story that is frightful, a story of sin and loose behavior, a story with an ending that'll show you what happens when you stray from the path of righteousness. I am referring to the Second Book of the Kings, right there in Chapter nine. I am referring to Jezebel, who everybody knows was a sleazy, filthy whore, and Jehu, who saw to it that she got what she deserved. Jezebel painted her face and tried to seduce Jehu with her female wiles by making eyes at him from the upstairs window, but he was too smart for her. He just looked up at her and said to the eunuchs conveniently hovering beside her, 'Throw her down!' "

By this time Brother Verber was in fine form. Spittle spewed from his mouth, and his fist hit the podium on every third word. "Well, it was a mighty high window, and when they threw the harlot down to the street, she splattered like a ripe tomato. Then the horses trampled on her and stomped on her until there was blood everyplace. If you'd been there, you'd still be scrubbing your clothes to get out the stains." He switched to a melodramatic whisper. "And do you know what all they did next? Do you know? Why, Jehu and his men went inside just as calm as you please and they had their supper. They had their supper the very same way you have your supper in your own home, just swapping jokes and having a fine time while they ate fried chicken and mashed potatoes and corn on the cob. Did they worry about that dead whore's crumpled body out there in the middle of the street?"

He gave his audience a minute to ponder that one, then slammed his fist down. "No!" he cried, now waving the fist in the air. "They didn't worry one whit—because she was a whore! Jehu finally got to feeling sorry about the mess outside and told his men to go bury her, but they came back and said they was right sorry but all they could find was her skull, her feet, and the palms of her hands! That was all that was left of the whore!" Verber stopped to mop his forehead. Several members of the congregation muttered amens, but they didn't sound as if they knew exactly why they were doing it.

Hammet rumbled under his breath. Farther down the row Bubba made the same noise, and Sissie didn't look all that pleased with the sermon thus far. Sukie, on the other hand, looked dumbstruck by the theatrics. Baby was asleep. I crossed my fingers and wished myself to be elsewhere, but it didn't work. It never does.

Verber sucked in a lungful and let it rip. "Now I'm going to tell you what Jehu had to say about that whore, Jezebel. He said that the dogs ate the flesh and that the corpse was dung upon the face of the field. Those were his precise words, because he knew what ought should happen to whores." He sucked in another lungful and gripped the sides of the pulpit as he leaned forward. "And we know it, too. Even in this very day and age, there are whores who are willing to corrupt good Christian soldiers of the Lord. They tempt them something awful. They encourage otherwise moral men to indulge in the sins of the flesh. These whores are about as carnal as you can get! And there is such a whore right here in Maggody. She's smack-dab in the bosom of our little community."

While he stopped once again to mop his forehead, I realized the rumbling along the pew had intensified until I might as well have been sitting beside a hornet's nest. I don't know if Verber heard any of it, but he shot a hooded look at our merry band before continuing.

"But why do we allow it? We're charitable Christians, yes. We're kind and forgiving. We're not the kind of folks to stone a sinner—at least not a penitent sinner who's willing to change her nasty ways. But this whore won't repent! She goes right along tempting men with her big breasts and her curvacious body and her perverted enjoyment of practices way too depraved to describe in the holy house. She encourages those practices—and takes five dollars for doing them!"

He mopped for a minute while the congregation tried to imagine what practices he was referring to, since they sounded interesting. Once he was tidied up, he sternly studied his flock. "What can we do, you ask me? Well, I'm going to tell you what we can do. We can tell this whore we don't want her in our community any longer. We can tell her that we're God-fearing soldiers of the Lord, and we'll no longer tolerate her depravities. We can tell her we're sick of her, that she is an outcast who'd best go somewhere else to engage in her whorin' and moonshinin' and perversions. We can tell her we don't want her kind because we're moral and pure. We are pillars of the Lord!"

I glanced at Hammet, who glanced at Bubba, who sucked in a breath of his own, stood up, and pointed his finger at the figure behind the pulpit. "Pappy!"

And one beat behind him, Sissie leaped up and aimed an equally accusatory finger at the very same person. "Pappy!"

That rather brought the situation to a halt. The silence was such that you could have heard two electrons collide. Maybe a whole sackful of electrons. The proverbial pin would have sounded like a nuclear explosion. Verber recoiled. His face was so frozen in panic that I decided this time we were going to be treated to the spectacle of a public heart attack. Personally, I was enchanted. It made the last three-quarters of an hour worth every tedious second. Ruby Bee and Estelle nodded at each other, leading me to further questions regarding their sanity. David Allen was biting down on his lower lip so hard it was likely to bleed.

Finally there was a noise in the back, followed by footsteps down the aisle. Mrs. Jim Bob stomped right up to Bubba Buchanon and jabbed her finger at him. "You are a filthy little liar! How dare you and this wretched sister of yours make that kind of wild, lying accusation in the house of the Lord?

You ought to be whipped until you can't sit down for a solid week. Maybe a year!"

Hammet now poked Sukie, who picked up Baby and turned around to stare at the back of the room. Every head in the congregation turned too. What we saw was Jim Bob Buchanon, Hizzoner the Moron, sneaking toward the exit. What we heard was Sukie loudly lisp, "Pappy!"

"Liar!" Mrs. Jim Bob howled.

"No, she ain't," Ruby Bee said, rising to the occasion. She held up the Bible so everyone could see it. "What I got in my hand is Robin Buchanon's family Bible. She couldn't read or write real well, but she had enough sense to record the names of her children's fathers. It seems like Brother Verber begat a couple, as did our fine, upstanding mayor. This is proof. The begats are written in the Bible."

And right there in the Voice of the Almighty Lord Assembly Hall, all hell broke loose. It was wonderful. It really was.

14

David Allen, Hammet, and I slipped outside. Even beside the highway we could hear the accusations flying inside the building, with Mrs. Jim Bob the most audible. By a long shot.

"Interesting timing," I said to Hammet.

He gave me a grin of great innocence and shrugged. "We was going to wait until afterward, but he was saying all them low-down things. It jest seemed like the time."

David Allen nodded. "I thought it was well staged, myself. But what about your father, pal? Wasn't he in there cowering behind a pew?"

"No, he used to live over in Emmet, but I think he moved away a few years back. He weren't all that bad. He gived me a dollar once, but of course Her found it and like to slap me silly."

"Do you know his name?" David Allen asked.

"It's in the goddamn Bible." Hammet sighed, then looked up at me with his puppy-dog expression. "Iffen we can't find him, can I live with you? You might get married sometime to a father what wants a sibling for his own little boy—iffen his little boy gets well."

I bent down and hugged him until he squirmed. "Listen," I said gently, "you know you can't live with me. But we'll find your father and let him know about you. You yourself said he wasn't all that bad. And you can come visit me whenever you want—if you don't complain about sleeping on the sofa or being left alone all day while I do police work."

Which I needed to do. I was in the middle of asking David Allen if he'd keep Hammet for an hour when a pickup truck drove past us and stopped in front of the Emporium across the road. My whiskery, dope-smoking friend got out of the truck and waved a half-eaten ice-cream cone at me. I told everybody to sit tight and went across the street.

"How are Poppy and the baby?" I asked.

"They're cool. How about you?"

A dark-haired man with the motions of a panther came out of the store, a gasoline can in one hand and a package of light bulbs in the other. Ignoring me, he glowered at Zachery. "I told you to be back an hour ago. What the hell kept you? Are you trying to fuck with me for some reason?"

"Hey, man, don't come down on me. Rainbow told me to wash the truck. It was so dusty she thought it might contaminate the bottled water or something screwy like that." He grinned at me. "Have you met Nate here?"

"You're the one who wasn't around last night to fetch the midwife," I said pleasantly, considering. "You'd gone off in the truck, so I ended up driving all over the county to find her."

"Yeah, tough luck," he muttered.

I looked at the truck, which was blue and battered —and familiar. "I saw you in the truck last night, by the way. Remember the jeep you almost ran off the road right down there by Estelle's Hair Fantasies?"

"You didn't nosedive into the ditch, lady. You ought to pay more attention when you drive, instead of trying to pin something on me."

"I was talking on the radio, and I might not have been watching too carefully. However, I did have my headlights on. If yours are broken, I doubt those light bulbs will fit. Where were you going? There's nothing down that way until Hasty, which is hardly worth a visit on a bright, clear day. It's unthinkable on a rainy night. It's suicidal on a rainy night without headlights."

"The headlights were on. You've got a loose screw, lady." He put his things under a tarp in the truck bed and started to walk away, but Zachery caught his arm.

"She's a cop," he said in what was supposed to be a whisper.

"Tough shit." Nate shrugged off the hand, then went into the Emporium and slammed the door hard enough to set off the wind chimes that hung in front of the window. Shaking his head, Zachery took out a package of cigarette papers and a Baggie of green leaves. He then remembered who I was, wiggled his eyebrows in apology, and strolled around the corner of the store. A soft "wow" wafted in his wake.

I went back to the lawn of the church. Ruby Bee and Estelle had joined David Allen and Hammet, and the four of them were studying the front page of the Bible.

I tapped Ruby Bee on the shoulder. "Where'd you find that?"

"On the table in the cabin. It was right there in plain sight. I'm astounded you didn't take it when you were there, forcing others of us to run your errands for you."

"Raz Buchanon took you up there in his truck?"

"No, he didn't," Estelle said. "We went most of the way up there in my station wagon, if you must know. Then the engine got all hot and wouldn't go any farther, so we had to hike the rest of the way up the mountain—and all the way down this morning. Once we got to the highway, we stuck out our thumbs and tried to hitchhike a ride for the longest time. Finally Raz happened by and was kind enough to give us a lift for fifty cents."

"And this is how you didn't interfere in my police investigation?" I asked, smiling sweetly.

Estelle warily returned the smile. "For reasons best left unspoken, we decided it was real urgent to learn the names of the Buchanon children's fathers. We went to Madam Celeste, who told us she saw a list of names. Once we thought about it, we realized just where to go. We hadn't counted on my station wagon giving out so that we'd have to spend the night in a haunted cabin."

Hammet glanced up. "It ain't haunted. I done lived there for eleven years and I never seen any ghosts or spooks."

An earlier remark came back to me. I took Hammet's shoulder and propelled him away from the others. Then I bent down so I could watch his eyes as I said, "On Friday I told you that your mother had been killed in a hunting accident. Before the church service started, you said that she'd been murdered. Why'd you say that?"

"That's what the holyfied lady told me and my siblings. They already knew afore David Allen and I got there. She said Her'd been blown to kingdom come by some kind of booby trap."

I had a pretty good idea how Mrs. Jim Bob had learned that tidbit. After all, she'd called LaBelle for two solid days trying to reach me. It was difficult to picture Mrs. Jim Bob growing marijuana in the National Forest, or slithering up in the dark to chop the plants while yours truly was otherwise occupied in town. I concluded (admittedly with a flicker of disappointment) that she was not my air-traffic controller.

"Did you or any of your siblings tell anyone that your mother was murdered?" I asked Hammet.

"No, we din't say nuthin'. After we left the lady's

house, we went to your apartment and watched television 'til it got late and they started showing this picture that stayed the same. That's when we decided to see about this foster crap and decide iffen we wanted to do that or tell about our pappies. We knowed all along; we jest wasn't sure if it were the thing to do."

I, too, would have had reservations about claiming a filial relationship with Verber and/or Jim Bob Buchanon. "So David Allen convinced you to confess?"

"When he got home, he said all kinds of stuff about how we might get sent to other places and not necessarily get a bicycle. It were mighty scary, so I told him we'd tell him after church."

"But instead you prodded Bubba and the others into a public display that caused all sorts of embarrassment for the two fathers," I said, trying not to smile.

"We was gettin' tired of hearing how we was sinners going right to hell on an express train and everybody else was so friggin' perfect they was going to heaven to play harps and dumb shit like that. We decided mebbe some other folks might be on the same train."

Never underestimate the cunning of a Buchanon bush colt.

I returned him to David Allen's custody and went back inside the church. I found Mrs. Jim Bob in the foyer, a tissue clutched in her hand. She gave me a tight frown and said, "What do you want? Did you come to make snide remarks about my husband? Did you come to snicker at me?"

Moi? I shook my head and lectured myself to avoid any temptation to snicker until I was alone, at which time I'd let loose like a gross of candy bars. "No, I came to ask you a question. I know that LaBelle told you about Robin Buchanon's murder up on the ridge. I need to know if you told anyone else, anyone at all."

"LaBelle did mention something about it late Friday afternoon. In that I am not a common gossip, I did not repeat one syllable of it to another living soul."

"You told the Buchanon children."

She turned on her beadiest look. "I had experienced some difficulty in dealing with them. I called several times for you so I could tell you to fetch them, but you didn't have the common courtesy to return my calls. In fact, I called more than a dozen times and LaBelle swore she beeped you without fail." She glanced down at the beeper clipped to my belt. "I guess you're too deaf to hear that thing. Or maybe you think you're too important to answer the mayor's wife's calls. Anyway, I found it necessary to tell those vile bastards about their mother's well-deserved fate. It was the only way I could get them under control."

I realized how much I loathed the woman. However, it was not the time to mention as much, so I settled for a grim stare. "Did you tell anyone else about the murder?"

"Do you think I'd converse with the cleaning girl? Of course I didn't tell anyone else. I was occupied with the mess those bastards left. There are going to have to be some repairs done at my house, and I'm holding you responsible, Arly Hanks. My husband will have a little chat with you later concerning upholstery and paint and carpet cleaners."

"No problem. Let's do the nursery first, shall we? Baby simply adores blue. Sukie, on the other hand, favors brown."

I went back outside, armed with the useless information that neither she nor the Buchanon children had told anyone about the murder. But someone had known that Robin's body had been discovered by the pot patch, and that it was probable that I'd stake out the scene of the crime. Otherwise the gardeners would have wandered up the road to harvest the crop in broad daylight, not the least bit concerned about being caught. The only reason they hadn't—and had managed to track my movements—was because they knew I knew. Only I didn't know what I needed to know. Such as: Who? How? Where was the dope now? Why did I feel as though I was in the land of Oz?

As I stood there waiting for a round-trip ticket for a tornado ride, a high school girl rushed up to David Allen.

"Oh, Mr. Wainright," she gasped, "I'm so grateful to find you. The most terrible thing happened. Carol Alice Plummer went back to Madam Celeste! Now she's all despondent and talking about suicide and killing herself and not marrying Bo Swiggins. She won't even eat. Her pa's madder than a wet hen, both at Carol Alice for being such a silly goose to believe that stuff, and at Madam Celeste for saying it in the first place."

David Allen wrinkled his forehead. "When did she have this session?"

"Yesterday evening. I went over to look through magazines with her, and she was on her bed moaning about suicide. I didn't have any idea how to talk her out of it. I tried to call you, then Carol Alice's pa called me and I told him everything." Snuffles gave way to a flood of tears. "I wish I didn't have anything to do with this!"

He glanced at me as he handed a folded handkerchief to the wailing girl. "This woman causes a lot of problems. Isn't there some way to convince her to conduct her seances elsewhere?"

Ruby Bee bristled. "Carol Alice is too immature, that's all. Madam Celeste has been very helpful to Estelle and me, not to mention to Gladys and Elsie and plenty of other folks. We wouldn't have this Bible if Madam Celeste hadn't told us she saw a list."

"That's right," Estelle added.

The whole thing was driving me crazy, crazy, crazy. I poked a finger at Ruby Bee's chest. "Estelle said earlier that there was some urgent need to learn the identity of the children's fathers. You were so frantic that you consulted Madam Celeste. Why?"

"We were trying to help," she sniffed, retreating under my maniacal glare. Estelle, a loyal sort, retreated along with her.

David Allen stopped patting Heather's shoulder long enough to say, "I bet I know why, Arly. Hammet and his sibs took Baby out of a station wagon and carried him off. I doubt they left a little note."

By this time, most of the congregation not directly involved in the paternity dispute had wandered outside. Everyone seemed to think the second act had started on the gravel stage, and managed to drift a little closer for optimum rubbernecking. Across the street Nate and Zachery came out of the Emporium and stopped to watch us. I was surprised the news vans didn't roll up, or the Goodyear blimp drift across the sky.

"You lost Baby?" I said. "Is that what sent you to Robin Buchanon's cabin yesterday afternoon? You thought that his father might have kidnapped him?"

"We would have gone anyway," Ruby Bee snapped. "The child cries night and day, and I'm too old to be forced to put up with it. If you hadn't dumped him in my lap, I wouldn't have—misplaced the little dumpling."

Estelle nodded. "It was a terrible strain on your mother. Why, she's sprouted dozens of gray hairs since you abandoned Baby on her doorstep."

"I did what?" I howled.

"Dozens of gray hairs?" Ruby Bee howled.

"What about Carol Alice?" Heather howled.

"You'll never touch me again as long as I live," Mrs. Jim Bob howled (from inside the church building, presumably to her husband—but you never know).

"She was a Jezebel," Brother Verber howled (same locale).

Lupine madness provided some degree of catharsis, not to mention a great deal of satisfaction to the audience. Once things quieted down, I told everybody to have a nice day, got in the jeep, and drove sedately down the highway to the PD. For all I knew or cared, they could have formed a pack and loped into the forest to eat bunny rabbits for Sunday dinner.

The office was dusty, which reminded me that I really needed to do something about Kevin and Dahlia—just as soon as I dealt with the dopers. Having resolved that for the moment, I sat back in my comfy old chair and called the sheriff. We had a long talk about the disastrous stakeout, and he was kind enough to say he'd probably have done the same thing. Neither of us believed it, but it was a nice gesture. He then put me on hold and went to talk to the treacherous LaBelle. When he came back, he said he was confident she had not spilled the beans to anyone except Mrs. Jim Bob. He said he'd do something about the missing lovebirds and suggested I take a well-deserved nap. I told him I didn't deserve anything, sympathy included, and hung up.

The dim light and utter quiet were conducive to thought, so I thought for a long while. I thought about who'd planted the dope and subsequently chopped it. You're undoubtedly screeching Nate's name at this page of this book, because that much was pretty obvious: Zachery's steady supply of dope,

Nate's absence at the critical moment, the lightless truck on the road.

That didn't explain how he knew when to return to his patch, however, or who was with him, or where the dope was at the moment. And it didn't prove a damned thing. Obviousness doesn't equate with evidence. And I really did want to nail the sons of bitches for Robin's murder.

I went across the street and up the stairs to my apartment, wondering how much of a mess the Buchanon children had left. As Hammet had promised, it wasn't all that much worse than usual (my feckless Manhattan housekeeper refused to follow me to Maggody, and I never was one for scrubbing toilets; Ruby Bee says I'll get typhoid one of these days). I took a shower, changed into clean clothes, ate a bowl of cornflakes (the only edible item that hadn't been devoured by my guests), and drove back to the Emporium.

The truck was gone. I went inside and found Rainbow in the office. We discussed Poppy's baby and the miracle of birth and the cosmic truth or consequences of Jupiter in the eighth house. I then asked her where I might find Nate.

"I don't know," she said, her smile slipping just a bit. "He's been impossible lately, and if you ask me, his karma has been rotten. He's not the least harmonic. He either lies around the office waiting for mysterious telephone calls, or he vanishes in the truck. He missed Daffodil Sunshine's birth, you know. It was a vital family experience. We were supposed to share!"

"Was he lying around the office yesterday waiting for a call?" I asked.

"Yes, and then about the time it got dark he got his call. He announced he had something to do and drove away. I told him Poppy was having contractions, but he laughed and said it was gas. Now that's rotten karma if there ever was one."

I agreed. After once again declining to have my chart done, I went back to the jeep and myopically gazed at the Voice of the Almighty while I tried to determine my next brilliant move. When nothing struck, I drove down the country road where I'd seen the truck. I doubted Nate could have stashed a hundred pot plants in Estelle's back bedroom without her noticing. I wasn't particularly pleased with Madam Celeste, but I had no reason to think she and Mason were involved in felonious activities. Past their house there was only the rusty car, the dilapidated chicken house, the low-water bridge, and Hasty—ten miles down the road.

Surely he hadn't planned to drive all the way to Hasty without headlights, I told myself as I turned around and drove back toward Maggody. As I approached the psychic's house, I saw Mason pull into the driveway.

"Everybody says ask Madam Celeste," I said aloud, tightening my fingers around the steering wheel until it would have yelped, had it been capable of yelps. "I'll ask Madam Celeste."

I parked by the mailbox and went over to Mason, who was unloading groceries. "Sorry I didn't get back to you on Friday," I said. "Something came up and I had to leave town."

"I shouldn't have knocked on your door at six in the morning. Celeste has been so darn weird about this dead woman's face that I'm scared not to do what she says. She sits in the solarium night and day, laying out tarot cards or shaking the Mesopotamian sand and then reading it. She even canceled all her appointments."

"Except for Carol Alice Plummer. That's the one she should have canceled."

A sack of groceries hit the ground. "Oh, no," he groaned. "Did Celeste get that sweet little girl all upset again? She was sniveling in the solarium the other day, so I made up some silly predictions to cheer her up. Why didn't she just stay away?"

I handed him a can of corn that had rolled between my feet. "The girl's suicidal, which doesn't sit well with her parents or her boyfriend. I guess I'd better have a word with your sister; she really can't upset the local girls like this." And slip in a question about activity on the road the previous night.

Mason said he'd go over to Carol Alice's house and see if he could calm her down with some jovial fortune-telling. The front door was unlocked and there were sodas in the refrigerator, he told me as he drove away.

Madam Celeste was still in the solarium, the cards spread in front of her on the Formica table. When I'd first met her, she'd been sparkling and fizzing like a glass of champagne. Now she looked gray and exhausted. There were black smudges under her eyes, and her hair hung limply on her thin shoulder. I sat down across from her. She regarded me without interest, then moved a picture card a fraction of an inch and let her hand fall away.

"I understand you helped the police in Nevada," I said softly.

"I did, but they resented it."

"I wouldn't resent help. I need all the help I can get. Did Mason tell you that a woman's body was found in the woods south of town?"

"He did."

"I've been investigating the death."

This time her eyes were brighter, although narrowed to slits. "Then you saw this woman's face?" When I nodded, she said, "There had been an explosion, no? Her eyes were opened in shock, her nostrils clotted with blood, her lips cracked and covered with flies?"

"That's a reasonable description," I said cautiously. "Mason said that you'd seen the face before—in a trance."

"I saw a face, but I do not know whose it was. A woman, yes, and dead. The cards insist that there is evil afoot in this town, that there are men who lie and stir up mischief. Not childish mischief, but malicious mischief for their own dark purposes."

"Do you know their names?" Dumb, naive, foolish, but I had to ask. Hell, she might have whipped out a list for me, perps in alphabetical order. Footnoted with addresses and telephone numbers. Not exactly courtroom evidence, but at least a nudge to get me going in the right direction. And it couldn't hurt. So there. Stop smirking.

"Of course not," she said in an irritated voice. "If I knew their names, I would have insisted you come here at once to receive my information and act on it."

"Oh," I said, wondering if I looked all that compliant. "Well, I agree that something's going on in Maggody. Did you happen to see or hear anything last night shortly after nine o'clock?"

"I was here, studying the cards. I saw the King of Wands, the Nine of Swords, and—"

"No, I mean out on the road. A truck. Voices. Lights."

She stood up and went to the window. "I saw no lights in the pasture, but cows do not have flashlights, nor do they converse or drive around. There is nothing out there except the fossils left by the chicken farmer who once worked that land. He is an interesting fellow, by the way."

"Does he live nearby?"

"He lived in this house for forty years, and died in the bedroom where Mason sleeps. He says Mason snores louder than his wife did." She spun around to stare at me. "I cannot help you. You have found the dead woman. Both of us have seen her face—perhaps. I am sure now that it was not that silly high school girl."

Wishing she'd made it plainer to Carol Alice, I went over to the window and studied the pasture, the chicken house, and the distant windbreak of trees. My eyes went back to the chicken house. "Did you hear anything from down that way?" I asked, pointing at the sorry structure. "Maybe a car door slam, or a voice?"

Madam Celeste turned back and followed my finger. "Yes. I heard a thud, but I presumed the rain had loosened a board." Before I could inquire further, she opened the back door and went down the few stairs to the grass. Then, as if pulled by a magnet, she walked toward the chicken house in the far corner of the field.

"Wait a minute," I called as I hurried after her.

She moved ahead purposefully, oblivious to my presence, with all her attention on the building. Although her gaze was directed straight ahead, she did not stumble on the clumps of weeds or snakish vines. I checked once or twice to make sure her feet were making contact with the ground. I couldn't help it.

Once we got there, she stopped several yards from the door. Others of us panted and tried to control our imaginations. I did have enough of my wits intact to see tire tracks in the mud, along with many footprints, as though an army had marched past. Or two men had made numerous trips between the vehicle and the chicken house.

I touched the psychic's arm. "Don't go any farther. I'm fairly sure that there's a half acre of marijuana plants drying in there, and I don't want to screw up the evidence."

She brushed off my hand and walked across the evidence to the door. "Yes, green plants rooted in the sky. I have already seen them. There is malevolence inside this place. I can feel it. It frightens me."

She was not alone. I plowed through the evidence and again tried to pull her back. "I don't think we ought to even open the door, Celeste. Let's go back to the house so I can call the sheriff for a backup. Doesn't that sound like a good idea?"

"I must open the door."

She did. For a minute the two of us gaped at darkness, although I could make out the shadowy forms of inverted plants dangling all the way into the darkness. Celeste felt on the wall just inside the door, saying, "There is light somewhere. Very hot, very bright."

Light bulbs and gasoline. "Don't turn on the light!" I screeched, grabbing at her arm.

"I must." She shoved me so hard, I tumbled backward and sprawled into the mud, breathless. Then she felt the wall again. I heard a click. Beyond her the room lit up, and the marijuana plants were spotlighted. A male voice yelled something in alarm.

And then the building exploded with a blinding flash and a wave of searing heat. Celeste was knocked back on top of me. Flames shot toward the sky. Boards cracked as the heat intensified, then seemed to shatter into red splinters. Brilliant sparks streamed like roman candles. The noise was worse than a train in a tunnel.

I managed to roll Celeste off me, then grabbed her arm and dragged her away from the fire as best I could, in that my body was screaming, my eyes tearing, my legs wobbling so wildly I was surprised they held me. Celeste seemed to weigh several tons, and the mud was treacherously slick. I pulled and slipped and fell and struggled up and pulled again for what felt like hours, all the while cursing at the top of my lungs. To this day I have no idea what I said; I have only a vague memory of the scene, as if it were from a movie watched in childhood.

At last we reached the weedy edge of the pasture. I dropped her arm and collapsed beside her. The chicken house continued to burn; the noise was deafening, the light painfully bright. More explosions sent fireballs rolling upward. The smoke was black. I numbly noticed my hands and arms were black and wondered if the flesh had been burned.

I got to my knees and bent over Celeste's body. Shards of wood protruded from her chest and abdomen. Her eyes were open but unfocused. Blood had already began to clot around her nostrils, perhaps from the furious heat. Her mouth was slightly open, her lips cut and bloodied. As I stared, a fly spiraled down and lit on the lower lip. I shooed it away, then fell back in the weeds, and that was all.

15

Ruby Bee came into my bedroom, a tray in her hands. "I brought you some supper, and I want you to finish every bite of it."

The first two days of being waited on hand and foot had not disturbed me. I'd meekly allowed myself to be bullied, due to lack of any desires more complicated than sleep and liquids to wash down pills. By now it was paling. I felt awful, but not so awful that I wanted this regressive state to become permanent. My burns had been diagnosed as a good assortment of first degree, second degree superficial, and second degree deep. The last would leave scars, mostly on the palms of my hands, since it seems I'd instinctively thrown up my hands to protect my face. For the most part. I wouldn't need mascara or an eyebrow pencil for a long time, nor would I need blusher. A paper bag with eyeholes would suffice.

"What's in the vase?" I said.

"Dried weeds from your little admirer—sorrel and wild marigolds, he said when he brought them." Ruby Bee fluffed my pillows, noted the cover of the book I was reading with a snort of disapproval (escapist stuff, which was exactly what I needed), then put the tray in my lap. "He's been coming over every morning and afternoon to see you, but I told him you were too sick for company. I didn't think you'd want anyone to see you while you look like this. As much as I hate to say it, I've seen stewed tomatoes that looked better than you."

"Thank you for that heartening assessment, Ruby Bee Nightingale. I think I'm up to managing my social calendar from now on. Has the sheriff called?"

"He did earlier this afternoon. I told him you were asleep. The doctor said for you to stay in bed for several days, and I intend to see that you do it. You may have my good looks, but you've always had your father's streak of mulishness. Now are you going to eat your supper or shall I feed you?"

This inspired me to put the tray on the end of the bed, throw back the covers, and struggle to my feet. While Ruby Bee squawked and waggled her finger and predicted all sorts of fatal relapses, I went into the living room and called the sheriff's office.

"Why, Arly," LaBelle said in a noticeably frigid voice. "How are you getting along?"

"Not too badly for a stewed tomato. Is Harve there?"

He came on the line and said he had received the lab reports from the boys in Little Rock at the state crime lab. The explosions had been started by gasoline-filled light bulbs, as I'd guessed. A devilishly clever booby trap designed to destroy the evidence should someone unwittingly flip the light switch. The fact that it destroyed the flippee made it all the more clever. Nate's only mistake was being in the back of the chicken house at an inauspicious moment. I was glad I hadn't been at his autopsy. I get squeamish at wienie roasts.

"So I guess you solved your case," Harve concluded. "The evidence went up in smoke, but your perp did, too. Damn shame about that woman."

"Damn shame," I said dispiritedly. I agreed to come in to write up all the paperwork in a day or two, replaced the receiver, and then gingerly sat down on the sofa and wiggled around until nothing hurt too much. I didn't much feel like crowing over the resolution of the case, however. It didn't feel resolved. It felt frayed, and the little ends were tickling me.

Ruby Bee came into the living room and put the tray in my lap. "You know what the doctor said," she began, her hands on her hips. It is one of her least flattering poses. "You'd better—"

"What police investigation didn't you interfere in?" I asked abruptly.

"Well, yours, of course. I didn't want you to think Estelle and I were involved in Robin Buchanon's murder. We were working on the identities of the fathers. Producing an illegitimate child isn't a crime."

"Did you know where I was most of the weekend?"

"I can't keep track of you when you're all the time running off on these so-called vacations. That darn LaBelle wouldn't tell me, either."

"Did she tell you that Robin had been murdered?"

"She wouldn't give me the time of day," Ruby Bee said with a snort. "All I can say about that is she'd better not enter any counterfeit corn relish in the county fair next year. Not if she values her reputation. Why, do you know she won a blue ribbon this September for—"

"Who told you?" I interrupted.

"One of the judges. He said he recognized the handwriting on the label, even though she'd written over it in ink. He said—"

"Who told you that Robin Buchanon was murdered?"

Don't think for a moment that she didn't know what she was doing. The woman was a pro in the fine art of driving me up the wall, and every once in a while she felt a compulsion to remind me of it. She looked at the tray and said, "Will you eat your supper?"

"Yes, I will eat as much of it as I can. Now will you tell me who told you about the murder?" I shoved a spoonful of chicken soup into my mouth and glared up at her.

"I'll have to think about it, but I'm sure I'll recollect before too long. I don't see what difference it makes. That dark-haired hippie is the one who set the booby traps, isn't he? You practically caught him red-handed in the chicken house. Why does it matter who mentioned the murder to Estelle and me?"

I realized I would have to tell her if I wanted to jar her conveniently muddied memory. "There were two sets of footprints at the pot patch. Nate was psychotic enough to rig the booby traps, but he had a partner. Besides, he was waiting for a telephone call late Saturday afternoon, presumably a tipoff that the patch was no longer under surveillance. When he received the call, he and his partner drove to the ridge, chopped the plants, and were heading for the chicken house by the time I drove back to the Emporium. When I got back to the ridge, I didn't go check to make sure the plants were there; I just crawled into bed and spent a blissful night with the bugs and my beeper for company."

"The sheriff's men found your beeper buried in the mud near the chicken house. A deputy brought it by a day or so ago, and I put it in a drawer somewhere. It was all burned and twisted, and it's not going to beep anymore."

I tried to jiggle the conversation back to the point. "I won't mourn its demise. I would like to discover the identity of Nate's partner, though. Two innocent people died because of someone's greed. Neither Robin nor Celeste had anything to do with it."

"Madam Celeste saw her own face, didn't she? Are you still so sure you know everything, Miss Skeptical?"

"The only thing I'm sure of is that I'm going to start screaming all sorts of terrible things if you continue this petty ploy," I said through a rigid smile. By this time I had a pretty good idea whose name she would finally say. There had been no astonishment from someone when there should have been.

"I don't understand why you're so all fired up, Arly. I was just trying to discuss the case with you in an adult fashion, like they do on television. But if you're determined to be snippety, you might as well know it was only David Allen who told us. He heard it from Mrs. Jim Bob, who said something to Hammet while they were on the porch. So you got all riled up over nothing, didn't you?"

"I guess so," I said, sighing. I couldn't imagine David Allen being involved with Nate, nor could I fathom a way he—or anyone else—could have tracked my movements so perfectly. I tried to lead myself through a scenario that was decidedly mazy. Okay, I told myself, David Allen certainly could use the money, since his child's medical bills were apt to rival the trade deficit. He'd hooked up with Nate, and the two had planted the dope in Robin Buchanon's ginseng patch. One or both had rigged the booby traps as a line of defense.

Then two things happened Friday. David Allen learned that Robin Buchanon had been killed by a booby trap; it wouldn't have required a leap of the imagination to realize where it had happened. And I left on a mysterious trip—mysterious because I should have been in town to deal with Robin's children, reports, and investigative things. But I'd said that I was trotting away for the weekend, see you later. Again, no quantum leap. Surely no one thought I was that irresponsible.

"Where's Hammet?" I said suddenly.

"I believe he said he was going back to David Allen's house. He's been sleeping over in #2 next to me, but he's right enchanted with some macaroni dish David Allen seems to serve him."

I picked up the receiver and slowly dialed the number of the sheriff's department. Harve and I talked for a while, then he transferred me to some young whiz kid who was very patient with my lack of knowledge in his field of expertise. It didn't bruise my ego too badly. The kid probably couldn't handle the subway system in New York, much less the crosstown buses or Pakistani cab drivers.

Hammet answered the telephone at David Allen's house. I thanked him for the dried arrangement and invited him over for cookies and milk. When he asked if David Allen could come along, I said most certainly, then said good-bye before my voice betrayed me. Ruby Bee reminded me that I was wearing an army surplus T-shirt and that my face was shinier than a red billiard ball.

I changed clothes, but I couldn't figure out how to change faces. Ruby Bee left to see how Estelle was doing behind the bar, pausing only to make a comment about the quantity of soup left in the bowl and the way some people went back on their word, even with their own flesh and blood. I shooed her out, then settled on the sofa. When I heard a tap on the door, I yelled for them to come in.

"Hi, Arly," Hammet said. He took a handful of weeds from behind his back and held them out. "More sorrel and some starworts that ain't too buggy."

David Allen came in behind him and offered me a box of candy. "This is from both of us. We figured if you had some aversion to chocolate-covered cherries, we could eat them for you."

"Thank you," I said as I accepted my presents. "You'll have to forgive my appearance. Ruby Bee can't decide if I'm a billiard ball or a stewed tomato. I'm not real thrilled to be either, but only time will help."

"I think you look prettier than a skillet of red-eye gravy," Hammet said, always the gentleman.

I rewarded his effort with the box of candy and told him to sit next to me. As David Allen perched on a nearby chair, I heard a car pull up next to the store. "Hey, Hammet," I said, "let me ask you something. You and your siblings came back here Saturday afternoon, right? You hung around and watched television until it was so late the channels stopped, then you went over to David Allen's and stayed there. All that right?"

He nodded mutely, since his mouth was full of candy.

David Allen gave me a quizzical smile. "I didn't want to call Mrs. Jim Bob so late, and I doubted she'd care where the children were, anyway. She washed her hands of them in the grand style of Pontius Pilate. Should I have bolted my door and left them out in the rain or something?"

"Of course not," I said soothingly. "Once you got home, all you could do was let them in for the night. It was admirable, considering how exhausted you must have been."

"Drinking a beer doesn't require much exertion," he said.

"At Ruby Bee's Bar and Grill?"

"Why're are you asking me all this? I thought we were friends, Arly, so if you've got something to say, just go ahead and say it."

I leaned back and tried to look pained, which wasn't all that hard. "The sheriff ordered me to ask where everybody was that night. It seems there was a holdup in a convenience store just this side of Starley City. Man in his thirties or early forties, blond hair. I know perfectly well it wasn't you, but Harve made me swear I'd get everybody's whereabouts." I was already hating myself before I asked the next question. "Were you at Ruby Bee's having a beer?"

He wasn't convinced by my fanciful story of collecting alibis, but I suppose he thought it was due to my injuries. "That's right, but I don't know if I can prove it. It's always so darn crowded and noisy on Saturday nights that you can't talk to anyone, and the only lights are those dreadful pink things over the dance floor. I don't know that many of the regular customers."

He also didn't know Ruby Bee's had been closed because the proprietress and her sister in crime were climbing the hill to Robin Buchanon's cabin. He'd seen the two earlier in the day, so he had no reason to think they had disappeared shortly thereafter. His lie made me feel a little better.

"I'll assure Harve that you're not a holdup man," I said. "If he insists, we can always dig up some of the regulars; somebody must have seen you. I'm sorry I had to ask."

"No problem," he said, visibly relieved.

I touched Hammet's arm. "So how's it working out with your siblings? Is everybody making friends with his newly found father?"

"That preacher man sent Bubba and Sissie to his cousin's house in the next county, but they were right pleased. The lady has a big house and cooks good. He's just an old fart. Who'd want to live with him?"

"Not I," I said, grinning at him. "How about Sukie and Baby?"

"They're at the holyfied lady's house. Sukie said the lady's been locked in her bedroom since they first got there, and her pa stands at the door and talks to hisself. They got some other woman what cleans and cooks. It din't make a whole hell of a lot of sense to me, but Sukie don't mind, and Baby don't know better."

"And your pa?"

Hammet gave me a long-suffering look. "This social worker woman says she's a-gonna find him if she has to look under every rock between Emmet and the state line. She's likely as not to find him under one."

I glanced at David Allen. "I feel really badly about all this. The worst thing is that we may never learn who Nate's partner was. It had to be someone local, you know. Whoever it was telephoned Nate the minute I was out of the way. They were up and back in less than three hours."

"If we didn't know it was impossible, I'd say they had you under surveillance," he murmured.

Hammet swallowed the gooey mess in his mouth. "How'd they know you was up there to begin with, and how'd they know when you left?"

"A very good question," I said. I limped across the room and poured him a glass of milk. When David Allen declined a beer, I limped back and sat down, hoping I wasn't trembling so hard he could see it. "The first problem, Hammet, is that no one should have known about the murder. But the dispatcher blabbed to Mrs. Jim Bob, who blabbed to you and to David Allen, who blabbed to Ruby Bee and Estelle. I doubt it went any farther than that." I looked across the coffee table. "You didn't tell anyone else, did you?"

"No, I only told those two because of Baby. I didn't realize it was a secret, but I spent the rest of the day fooling around in my garage."

"And then went to the bar?" I said, inviting a repetition of the lie to remind myself not to feel so damn guilty. When he nodded, I continued. "Well, let's presume this partner found out some way and realized that I was staking out the marijuana patch. The next problem is that he seemed to know the minute I started to drive back down the road."

Hammet wrinkled his forehead. "How'd the sumbitch know that?"

"That is the zillion-dollar question. At one point I asked myself if I was an airplane being tracked on a radar screen. But I'm not an airplane, am I?" Hammet shook his head, eyeing me warily in case I really did think I was one. "But," I added, "I did have something sort of like an airplane. Earlier I told my mother I spent the night with bugs and my beeper, but I was wrong. I spent the night with a bugged beeper."

"What's that?" Hammet gasped.

I kept my eyes on him. "Well, a beeper has all these circuits inside it. One of them is called an oscillator circuit, and it can be modified with one little chip. Not a corn chip, mind you. A computer chip."

"Why'd someone be fool enough to modify this oscillator chip?"

"Because then the beeper would emit a special radio frequency that could be tracked just like it was a tiny airplane—or a model rocket. You'd need a radio directional finder, but some people with expensive hobbies have them so they won't lose their toys. Since the beeper was always on my belt, I could be tracked, too."

Hammet's eyes narrowed. "But it weren't always on your belt."

"I know." I forced myself to look at David Allen, who'd turned pale during my electronics lesson. "You took it while we were at the drive-in, and kept it until the next afternoon."

"Yeah," Hammet growled, scooting next to me in a show of strength.

"That doesn't prove anything," David Allen said. "It stayed in the glove compartment right up until I remembered to return it to you."

"That's good to know. That means there's no way your fingerprints might be found inside my beeper, doesn't it? They won't be on the chip or on the inside of the case. It means my theory is the product of shell shock from the explosion."

He looked at his fingertips for a long while. "I didn't even know about the booby traps. The guy was flipped out, a real paranoid."

"You bugged the beeper before Robin's body was discovered."

"I had no idea Robin's disappearance had anything to do with the . . . ah, agricultural venture, but I was worried about you wandering all over the ridge and stumbling onto the marijuana patch by accident."

"I told you that I had given up."

"And then you told me that you were going to ask the sheriff to bring in a posse. I figured you'd dog them every step of the way."

At last someone with a high opinion of my dedication-to-duty level. "I might have tagged along," I admitted.

"After I dropped you two off that night, Nate came by to discuss the details of the sale to a student in Farberville. I told him how worried I was, and he said it was a damn shame we couldn't keep track of your movements on the ridge, since we wouldn't know whether or not it would be safe to go back to the patch to harvest. I said it would be easy if I could convince you to carry one of my model rockets in your pocket. One thing led to another, I suppose. But I didn't put your beeper in the glove compartment with any evil intent; I did that because it was bothering you."

"How'd the dope end up in the chicken house?" I asked.

"Nate spotted it several months ago, when he was driving the pregnant girl to see the midwife. Listen, Arly, he was a classic case of paranoia, right out of a college textbook. I didn't know he was going to pull that stunt with the light bulbs in the chicken house anymore than I knew he had booby-trapped the clearing. You know I would have told you about the booby traps if I'd known about them, don't you?"

I told myself he would have. "If he hadn't put in the booby traps, none of this would have happened. But he did, and two women died because of it. That makes you an accomplice."

"David Allen kilt my ma?" Hammet squeaked.

"No," he answered quickly, looking at us, "I wouldn't have done that. I needed money desperately. My medical insurance covers a lot of the treatments, but my son has a chance for a normal life if he has a transplant, which is considered experimental. I never intended for anyone to get hurt. You've got to believe that, Hammet."

"Yeah, okay," Hammet said graciously. "What the fuck."

I told David Allen that a deputy was waiting downstairs. He gave me a small smile, patted Hammet on the head, and left. Hammet offered me a piece of candy, and the two of us sat there in silence until the box was empty.

"Heather, you'll never believe this!" Carol Ann squealed into the telephone receiver. "It is the most amazing thing. You're going to absolutely pee in your pants when I tell you."

"Go ahead." Heather gazed at the wall, thinking about poor Mr. Wainright and all his troubles. He hadn't even known how mature she, Heather Riley, was, or how concerned and deeply—

"So when I graduate, we're going to get married! Isn't that the most fantastic thing you heard?"

"You and Bo?" Heather hazarded.

"No, silly, me and Mason Dickerson. Didn't you ever hear what I was telling you? He inherited all of Madam Celeste's tarot cards and sand. He says we're going to live in a great big manor house and have servants and six darling children and a shiny red Camaro convertible for me to drive." Carol Alice stopped to take a steadying breath. "Don't you just want to die!"

Heather did not tell her best friend in the whole world that she actually did, sort of. On the other hand, she wondered what it would feel like to kiss a harelip. Or Bo Swiggins.

* * *

Kevin Buchanon grabbed his beloved's hand. "Hurry, my pumpkin, we've got to hide! I hear a car coming up the road. It might be those murderers coming back to get us real good this time."

Dahlia peered out the cabin window. "I don't hear nothing. I don't want to go squish ourselves up again, Kevin. The smell like to kilt me the last time."

He tugged her to the door and pushed her outside. "We have to hide," he said in a wheedling voice. "I can't defend you from murderers if they have guns and chain saws."

"Well, at least let's take some catalogue pages this time."

By the time the deputies arrived at the cabin, the door swung in the breeze but there was no sign of inhabitancy. After a while they closed the door and padlocked it, then drove back down the hill.

Rainbow, Zachery, and Poppy lay naked on the bed, with an equally naked Daffodil Sunshine on a pillow.

"He's definitely got Zachery's eyes and chin," Rainbow said firmly. "That, along with Jupiter and the quadruplicity, convinces me that Zachery has to be the father."

Poppy looked away for a minute, then turned back with a determined smile. "Absolutely. I knew it all along, but I didn't want to hurt Nate's feelings. I could tell the exact moment of conception. It was as if a light began to glow in my womb."

Zachery gazed at said womb as he took a drag off the joint in his hand. "Like—like wow."

Estelle nervously opened her front door and eyed the stranger with the mustache. "Can I help you?"

"*Verissimo*, but you are so breathtaking that I must pause to catch my breath," he said in a thick accent. "That pastel color makes me want to sing an aria. My heart, he is *accelerando.*"

"You are a mite pale. Do you want a glass of water?"

"No, I do not wish to trouble you. Perhaps if I could rest for only a minute. . . ?"

Estelle let him inside, but settled him on the chair by the door in case he had any funny ideas. She insisted on bringing him a glass of water. When she came back from the kitchen, he'd already opened a suitcase and arranged the contents in a semicircle on the floor.

"I knew when first I saw you, my *bellissima*, that you would want only the finest vacuum cleaner with all the attachments, including the carpet shampooer and drapery brush. A lady as beautiful as you would want only the best."

Estelle put her hands on her hips. By the time she finished discussing what all he could do with his vacuum cleaner and all its attachments, his face was about the same shade as her aquamarine uniform.

"Do I really have to go live with that guy in Emmet?" Hammet asked.

"The social worker said he's agreed to take you. We've been over it a hundred times. You can come visit me whenever you want, and I'll come see you, too. It's really better for you to live with a normal family."

"But I like it here. It'll be boring over there. Nothing ever happens in Emmet."

I put my arm around him and gave him a hug. "Don't be silly. Everybody knows that nothing, and I repeat, nothing ever happens in Maggody."